Coming Home
to Maple
Cottage

ALSO BY HOLLY MARTIN

Sandcastle Bay Series
The Holiday Cottage by the Sea
The Cottage on Sunshine Beach

Hope Island Series
Spring at Blueberry Bay
Summer at Buttercup Beach
Christmas at Mistletoe Cove

Juniper Island Series
Christmas Under a Cranberry Sky
A Town Called Christmas

White Cliff Bay Series
Christmas at Lilac Cottage
Snowflakes on Silver Cove
Summer at Rose Island

The Guestbook at Willow Cottage
One Hundred Proposals
One Hundred Christmas Proposals
Fairytale Beginnings
Tied Up with Love
A Home on Bramble Hill

For Young Adults
The Sentinel
The Prophecies
The Revenge
The Reckoning

Coming Home to Maple Cottage

HOLLY MARTIN

Bookouture

Published by Bookouture in 2018

An imprint of StoryFire Ltd.
Carmelite House
50 Victoria Embankment
London EC4Y 0DZ

www.bookouture.com

ISBN: 978-1-78681-603-0
eBook ISBN: 978-1-78681-602-3

This one is for the fabulous Paw & Order, you guys rock

PROLOGUE

Four years ago

Isla stared at the ceiling with a huge smile on her face as she thought back to the moment that had led her here.

The night before had begun innocently enough. After dropping in to see her brother Matthew and his son Elliot as soon as she'd arrived in Sandcastle Bay for her nephew's christening, she had then gone to the pub to meet Leo. And maybe the plan had been to have a few drinks with a good friend and return to her hotel room alone, but that had gone straight out of the window when he'd kissed her on the cheek and whispered, 'God, I've missed you.' Right then she'd been lost to him. They'd spent the whole night wrapped around each other; the sex even more incredible than she'd imagined it would be. They'd dozed occasionally before wandering hands had started them off all over again.

And here she was, lying in his bed in Maple Cottage. The early morning autumn sunshine was dusting his bedroom with gold, showing off the contours of his naked muscled back beautifully. Isla ran a hand down his spine, caressing his warm soft skin, and then slipped it up into his hair, cupping the back of his neck.

There was something wonderfully glorious about being pinned to the mattress by the weight of Leo Jackson, his heart thundering against his chest as he tried to catch his breath from their exertions moments before, his face buried in her neck, his warm breath racing against her skin.

Although she hadn't expected this to happen between them when she had arrived in Sandcastle Bay, it wasn't a total surprise that it had. This thing between her and Leo had been bubbling for a long time. Every time she had come to visit her brother, chemistry had sparked between them. Matthew had often teased them that they should get a room and last night they finally had.

Leo lifted his head and grinned as he stared down at her, looking carefree and happy. She stroked his face and he dipped his head and kissed her briefly on the lips.

'Well, that was undoubtedly the best night of my life,' Leo said, his eyes filled with affection as he gazed down at her warmly. She couldn't help but smile, even though it was quite obviously a line. Leo Jackson was a charmer and his reputation with women definitely preceded him.

'You're so full of it,' Isla laughed.

His caramel brown eyes twinkled. 'What?'

'I bet you say that to all the women.'

'No, of course not.' Leo pretended to be hurt and she arched an eyebrow. 'Not *all* of them.'

She laughed and tried to push him off her to get up but he held her in place, amusement fading from his eyes. 'It was pretty incredible, wasn't it?' he said, softly.

She swallowed down the emotion that was sitting heavy in her chest. Because that had been the surprise. Not that they had ended up in bed together, she'd always known that something would happen between them, but that it had felt like a hell of a lot more than two friends having great sex. Something had passed between them, something so intimate and heartachingly real. The first time they'd had sex, they'd stared into each other's eyes and it was as if she was reconnecting with a part of her that had always been missing. It felt like… coming home.

In the early hours of the morning, when he had dozed as he'd wrapped himself around her, she'd even let herself imagine a wonderful, rose-tinted future with him. Living here in Sandcastle Bay, raising their children together. It was ridiculous. She'd known that Leo Jackson didn't do marriage and happy ever afters, he'd said as much himself, but it didn't hurt to imagine it. Now, in the cold light of day, she felt the need to protect herself from a dream that seemed to be fading away fast.

'It was…' she floundered for the right words to try to play down what she'd shared with him. Nice. Lovely. Those were not words she could use to describe the night before. Her heart was striving to be honest with him, to let him know how special it had been for her, and the word slipped from her lips before she could stop it. 'Magnificent.'

A look of surprise crossed his face. 'Magnificent?'

Isla cursed herself. Way to play it down and be totally cool about what happened between them.

'The sex,' she said. 'You were pretty good.'

'Wow. Pretty good is a bit of a comedown from magnificent,' Leo teased. 'I think I'll go with your first answer. You were pretty bloody spectacular yourself. But I was talking about…' he trailed off and fell into silence.

'Yes?' she prompted when he didn't seem to have anything else to say.

He frowned. 'There was… something else.'

She suppressed a smile. Leo Jackson was not a man who could express his emotions easily. She waited patiently for him to elaborate further but he was evidently hoping she would fill the gaps. She couldn't do that. She'd just told him their night together had been magnificent and that was embarrassing enough.

She ran her thumb over his lips and he kissed it. His eyes were soft as he looked down at her. Was it crazy that she had fallen a little bit in love with him?

They stayed like that for the longest time, just staring at each other. She knew this night had been way more than just sex and, from the look in his eyes, he did too.

A sudden thud at the window broke the spell between them. As she looked over she could see a large seagull on the windowsill outside, peering in at them.

She laughed. 'You have to love life by the sea.'

'It can wear pretty thin after a while,' Leo growled.

She gently pushed him off her and this time he let her. She sat on the edge of the bed. 'We need to get up. We have to be at the christening in a few hours and I need to go back to the hotel to get changed.'

Leo groaned. 'Let's just stay here instead, spend the whole day in bed.'

She turned round to face him in confusion. 'I'm going to assume you said that because you enjoyed being with me so much and not because you don't want to go to the christening.'

He let out a little sigh. 'Let's say it's a bit of both.'

'Leo! You're Matthew's best friend…'

'I know.'

'You're going to be godfather to his son!'

'I know, that's the bit that's bothering me. Why the hell would he choose me to be Elliot's godfather?'

Suddenly his comments the night before about how nervous he was about today made sense. He wasn't nervous about standing up in front of a room full of people, of saying the right words, he was nervous of the responsibility of this new role.

Her heart softened for him even more, this great big, cocky, beautiful man, with a sensitive heart.

'This is very important to Matthew. This isn't just a meaningless day to get gifts and have an excuse to celebrate and drink. After Sadie walked out and he was left to raise Elliot on his own, Matthew wants to make sure that, if anything happens to him, there would be someone there he trusts to look after Elliot. He chose you to be godfather for very good reasons.'

'What reasons? After my dad died when I was a kid, I was a complete flake at school, played up in class, was suspended more times than I could count. Left school with almost zero qualifications. I used to smoke. I'd get into fights. Got caught graffitiing the bus stop and stealing beer from the local supermarket, all before I was eighteen years old. And OK, I've probably calmed down a lot since then, but I probably still drink a bit too much and, erm… enjoy the company of too many women. What kind of role model could I possibly be to Elliot?'

She smiled and rolled over and kissed him. He stroked his hand through her hair, letting out a heavy sigh against her lips.

'You are a wonderful man. Kind, fiercely loyal, generous. I see how you are with Marigold and you have such a lovely way with her,' Isla said, talking about his niece. 'You're patient, protective and fun. She might only be a year old but it's clear she adores you. Matthew sees all these qualities in you. I'm sure he is judging you on the man you are now, not the boy you used to be.'

He smiled slightly. 'I think you see more in me than I do.'

'And Matthew does too or he wouldn't have asked you.'

Leo sighed. 'I can't be a dad to Elliot. I see the way Matthew looks after him and I could never be as good as he is.'

'You don't need to be a dad to him. If, god forbid, anything was to happen to Matthew, I would be Elliot's legal guardian. I will be his mum, dad, aunt and friend. You can be the fun uncle, play with him, take him out now and again, teach him how to play football, explain about shaving and other boy stuff when he gets older, just be there for him in the same way you're there for Marigold. You can do that, can't you?'

Leo clearly thought about that and then nodded.

He suddenly rolled her, pinning her to the mattress again. 'Isla Rosewood, I think I'm a little bit in love with you.'

Her stupid hopeful heart soared at that comment, but she quickly pushed it back down. 'Oh shush, I bet you say that to all the women.'

He kissed her, smiling against her lips. 'Not *all* of them.' He pulled back slightly, looking at her tenderly. 'Stay here tonight.'

'What's this? Leo Jackson wants to spend two nights with the same woman?'

'Well, it was pretty – what was the word you used? Magnificent. I'm not walking away from that any time soon.'

She smiled and nodded. 'OK.'

He kissed her again and she let herself forget the world outside for a few moments. She didn't know what was going to happen between them after this weekend. She was due to go back to London the following day, which was almost six hours away on the train, longer in the car. She had a job there, a life to return to. And Leo had promised her nothing more than a warm bed for the night. But in that moment, wrapped in his arms, him kissing her like his life depended on it, she was more than happy to take it.

CHAPTER 1

Present day

'Marry me?' Leo said, watching her as he took a sip from his mug of tea.

Isla's heart leapt, as it always did when he uttered those words, but then she pushed those silly hopeful emotions away.

'Well, that escalated quickly. I make you a bacon sandwich and a cup of tea and you're proposing to me,' Isla said, picking up her empty plate and taking it over to the dishwasher so she wouldn't have to look at him – this bloody beautiful, incredible, frustrating man.

When her brother, Matthew, had chosen Leo to be Elliot's godfather all those years before, he'd also asked him to take care of her if anything was to happen to him. Had Matthew known that Leo would take that request quite so literally? Did Matthew know that, a few months after his tragic death, Leo would propose to her and keep asking her every week, despite her repeatedly saying no? It had been a year since the first proposal and, no matter how many times she refused him, it didn't seem to put him off.

'You do make an amazing bacon sandwich,' Leo said. He wasn't taking this remotely seriously.

'I'm not marrying you.'

'Why not? We'd be great together.'

And that was true. Over the last year, since Isla had moved to Sandcastle Bay, Leo had become her best friend. He was round her house practically every day, they loved spending time together.

Elliot adored him and the feeling was entirely mutual. She could not think of a better person to raise Elliot with.

She sighed and turned to face him. 'Because we're not actually together. Normally, people date for a while first before they walk up the aisle.'

He waved this fact away like it was an insignificant detail, but it mattered to her. She wasn't going to get married just so she would be financially secure, which was the reason Leo had given when he'd first proposed, and she'd asked why he wanted to marry her. She wasn't going to get married to give Elliot a father figure or because the two of them were great friends. Maybe it was soppy and overly romantic but she wanted love in her marriage, not companionship.

'OK, what would happen if I was to say yes?' Isla asked.

'I'd take you down to the registry office right now and we could be married within the month.'

So no big white wedding for her then. Was it wrong that she wanted that too? She sat down opposite him. 'And then what?'

Had he put any thought into this at all? Where would they live? Would she and Elliot live with him? And if that was his plan, did he really have any idea what it was like to suddenly live with a child full-time?

After Matthew had died in that horrible car accident, it had left a hole in all of their hearts but it had also brought her some joy. Having Elliot in her life made her so happy and she could never regret that. But her life had changed beyond recognition since she had taken custody of her brother's son over a year ago.

Her world was now filled with millions of toys and TV programmes about dinosaurs. She'd get up in the mornings and make a packed lunch for Elliot in a T-Rex lunch box. She'd take him to school where she'd sometimes go in and listen to children read, or she'd go back to their little cottage overlooking the sea and try to find some order in the chaos of toys and books.

She glanced through the window at the little village of Sand-castle Bay as it stretched out in front of her, tumbling down the hill in a haphazard jumble of yellow houses until it reached the great expanse of sea that disappeared into the misty horizon. The sun had come out today, or at least it was trying, leaving whispers of glitter across the waves. Autumn was well and truly here, every tree dressed in cloaks of scarlet, bronze, terracotta or gold. Squirrels were out in force in the garden, busy collecting nuts and seeds for their winter hibernation.

This life was miles away from her busy one in London where she'd been a window dresser for Quentin's, one of the biggest department stores in the world. She used to have meetings with several departments or in a boardroom filled with CEOs and executives, instead of meetings with teachers or social services about Elliot's progress. She would spend her days dressed in a suit, instead of leggings and a long tunic. She would research different cultures, traditions and trends instead of looking through the internet to find autumnal crafty things she could do with an exuberant five-year-old. In her old life, most of her day had been spent creating fabulous colourful window displays which moved or danced, and made people literally stop and stare out on the street. It had made her feel proud and excited to go to work every day. She missed that. Some of her evenings had been spent socialising with clients and sponsors in some of the most exclusive restaurants and bars London had to offer. She would fly across the world several times a year and work in the stores in America, Japan or Dubai. In London, she'd go to theatres and shows with her ex-boyfriend Daniel or spend the night in their very large apartment overlooking the Thames. In the blink of an eye, everything had changed. She had gone from a very successful career in one of the biggest and liveliest cities in the world to being a single mum, unemployed and living in a tiny seaside village in the furthest corner of England.

Although she couldn't be happier with her new life in Sand castle Bay, it was a massive change. Part of her missed who she was before, being a career woman, having a job. Being a mum was one of the most rewarding and wonderful experiences of her life, but it was also the scariest and most exhausting too. There was no switching off at five and going home, and although her old job in London had never really been a nine-to-five occupation, this was twenty-four hours a day. What was the right food to feed Elliot? When was the best time for him to go to bed? What could she do about his nightmares? How did she answer most of his questions in a way that was appropriate for his age? How long was too long to let him watch TV? What was she going to buy him for Christmas? And, probably most importantly, how was she going to keep a roof over their heads and food in their bellies when she had no money coming in?

She didn't think Leo fully appreciated how it would disrupt his life too. Leo was wonderful with Elliot, taking him out, playing with him, explaining things in ways that Isla never could. He seemed to have endless patience, but there was a big difference between being the fun uncle figure and being a permanent live-in dad.

And what of her friendship with Leo? Would that continue just as it was now? Would they be friends who slept in separate bedrooms? Nothing had ever happened between them apart from that one and only incredible night they'd spent together before Elliot's christening. The next day at the christening, she'd heard him talking to some girl he'd slept with the night before he'd been with Isla, and she had realised she was just one of many. She had returned to her life in London and tried to forget how utterly spectacular the evening had been. She had started dating Daniel and that had lasted two and a half years. Leo had probably continued shagging anything that moved. When she had visited Matthew, she'd seen Leo too of course, and they had chatted and been friendly as always, but it had never progressed beyond friendship. Even now, after a year of living in Sandcastle Bay, their relationship remained strictly platonic. It was tactile sometimes, a hug, a kiss on the cheek, and she got the feeling that he wouldn't mind a round two, but they had never talked about it. Would they suddenly go from being just friends to having sex every night purely because they were married?

'You'd sell this place and come and live with me,' Leo said, simply. He was so practical about this, there didn't seem to be the slightest hint of romance about this particular proposal. Nor had there been with any of the others.

'Honeymoon?' Isla teased, but at the same time wanting to test the waters.

For the briefest moment, there was a flash of lust and need in his eyes. He did want her like that.

He cleared his throat. 'If you want.'

God, she wanted to ask him what that honeymoon would be like, whether they'd spend the entire time lying in bed having crazy, wonderful sex.

She dismissed that thought before she could get too carried away with thoughts of what that amazing holiday could be like. Elliot would probably come with them anyway, which would certainly put a stop to the two-week sexathon.

She glanced over into the conservatory where Elliot was occupied with building a castle out of Lego that was almost as big as the room. Another project that Leo had started with him. It was going to be so big that Elliot intended to sleep inside it with their puppy, Luke, who was currently curled up in the corner of the room, like a black furry dragon, one golden eye keeping apprised of what was going on. She smiled at Elliot as he played happily by himself. She couldn't imagine leaving him behind just so she could have hot passionate sex with Leo Jackson for a few weeks. Her heart ached even at the thought of not seeing him every day. If they were to have a honeymoon, it would probably have to be to somewhere like Disneyland.

She turned her attention back to Leo, who was still watching her carefully.

'Why do you want to marry me?' Isla said. She asked him this occasionally, always half hoping that, after months of being very close friends, of seeing each other and spending time together for most of the day, that one day his answer would change.

'You know why.'

'Remind me.'

Leo paused. 'Because…'

For a moment she wondered if he was gearing up to say those three all-important little words.

'Because this situation with Sadie and the house worries me. Because the fact that she still has a parental claim on Elliot, despite abandoning him when he was only one, scares me to death. If she comes back, I can't do anything about Elliot, other than bundle you both in the back of my car and go on the run together for the rest of our lives. But I can do something about the house.'

This was a different answer to the ones he'd given before. Normally he stopped at, 'I want to take care of you and Elliot.' She had no idea he worried about stuff like this.

'Why are you worried about the house?'

He stared at her incredulously. 'Because Sadie still owns half of it. Despite the fact that she walked out on Matthew and Elliot just a few months after they bought the house, and even though he lived in it alone for three years, raising their child by himself, and it was *his* life insurance that helped pay off the mortgage after he died, she still has a claim to it. Thank god that, when they bought it, they weren't joint tenants, otherwise she'd own the house outright after his death. Thankfully Matthew had the good sense to make sure they were named as tenants in common, which means she only has a claim to half the house. But that's still half your home, how can you not be worried about that?'

She shrugged. 'I honestly don't think Sadie is ever coming back. She's in deepest Australia or Thailand somewhere, probably having the time of her life. No one knows where she is, no one can contact her. The courts have tried everything to find her, to try to get her to sign over parental responsibility of Elliot to me, and they have been unable to trace her. She probably doesn't want to be found. Though I'll never understand how a person can just vanish – surely she has friends or family who know where she is.'

Leo shook his head. 'She didn't grow up round here. She turned up here for a seasonal job in the summer and that was when she met Matthew. I don't think she ever had any plans of staying. I do know that she was in foster care when she was growing up, several different foster homes in fact. I don't think she has any knowledge of who her parents were.'

'I didn't know that.'

They hadn't really spoken about Sadie very often; she wasn't someone that Isla wanted to think about much. She'd only met her a few times before she ran away. Isla didn't have a very high opinion of her after she abandoned her own son and Isla's brother, but hearing this information about her made Isla almost feel sorry for her.

'Why would she come back?' Isla said. 'She has no interest in Elliot, she proved that when she walked out on him when he was one year old, and if she had any interest in Sandcastle Bay she would never have left.'

'But if she did come back?' Leo said.

'If she did, then I suppose I would have to sell the house. We'd have to go to court and the judge would decide how much of the house sale she would be entitled to. But solicitors I've spoken to about this are hopeful that she wouldn't get half because of the money that Matthew paid into it over the years. She might get something like twenty or twenty-five percent. But if she did get half that would still leave me with enough to buy a small one-bedroom flat at the very back end of the village. So, whatever happens, we'd cope, we'd be OK,' Isla said, nonchalantly. 'I'm not going to worry about the what-ifs and I'm not going to marry my best friend just so I don't have to worry about money. What will be, will be.'

A smile spread across his face. 'I'm your best friend?'

'You know you are. You're round here every day, playing with Elliot, having meals with us, going out with us. I absolutely adore you.'

'Then what's the problem?'

'Because, Leo Jackson, if one day I do get married, it will be for love. I will be head over heels in love with my husband and he will be crazy in love with me.'

'And I don't fit that bill?' he said, the smile fading away.

She cocked her head and looked at him. 'I suppose that depends. Do you love me?'

He frowned and his eyes cast down to the table. She'd take that as a no.

'I don't deserve to have you,' he said quietly.

She stared at him in shock.

Elliot came running in from the conservatory. 'Leo, I need help with the top of the window. I can't put the bricks on top of nothing.'

'No, we'd need to add some kind of beam over the top to support the weight of the rest of the house,' Leo said, seamlessly. He downed the rest of his tea and stood up. 'Come on then, buddy, let's go and have a look.' He flashed her a small smile. 'Thanks for lunch.'

And then he left her alone, as he talked with Elliot about what they could do about the Lego window.

I don't deserve to have you.

She had no idea what he meant by that and didn't know what to say to it either. He was the most wonderful, generous man she knew, how could he possibly even think otherwise?

She had fallen a little bit in love with him after that wonderful night they'd spent together and, if she was honest with herself, those feelings had never gone away. In fact, they had intensified a lot since she'd moved down here last year. She'd often thought about telling him how she felt but she always held back. Despite her protests, she was finding it increasingly hard to keep saying no to his crazy proposals.

She picked up her mug and nursed it to her chest, watching her two favourite boys play together.

Surely, love shouldn't be this complicated.

CHAPTER 2

Isla pushed open the door of The Cherry on Top, her favourite café in Sandcastle Bay, and saw that her friend Tori and her sister Melody were already waiting for her. Despite it being the end of October, it was still quite busy, the café seemingly doing great business all year round.

She glanced out of the window at the glorious view of Sunshine Beach, the sea today an inky blue under a mackerel sky. The parasols outside on the beach were flapping in a gentle breeze. From here she could see the handful of houses that lined the beach, most of them thatched with brightly coloured front doors and flowers and trees tumbling over the sea wall. Melody's home, Apple Tree Cottage, with its yellow front door, could be seen down the beach. A little way up the beach was Sprinkles, the village ice cream shop that sold the most amazing ice cream in the most incredible flavours. She loved it here in Sandcastle Bay and that view probably had something to do with the café's popularity. That and the amazing food.

She scanned the café tables for Agatha, Leo's crazy, meddlesome aunt, but for once she didn't seem to be here. Isla might actually be able to talk to Melody and Tori without any interference. Although Elsie West from the chemist, one of Agatha's closest friends, was in the corner, so they probably couldn't talk that freely.

Isla moved to the table and greeted them both with a hug and a kiss. At just over four months pregnant, Tori was just starting to show a tiny bump underneath her jumper dress, although it didn't really look like she was pregnant yet.

'How are you both?' Isla asked, as she sat down, although the question seemed somewhat redundant; they both looked like they were glowing with happiness. Melody was completely loved-up with Jamie, Leo's younger brother, and Tori was very happy with her fiancé, Aidan, Leo's older brother. As far as Agatha was concerned, Isla just needed to hurry up and say yes to one of Leo's proposals and then Agatha would have the complete set.

'Good, I have my first baby scan this afternoon. It was put back a few weeks due to one thing or another but it's finally happening today. I can't tell you how excited I am!' Tori said.

'Will you get to know the sex?' Isla asked.

Tori shook her head. 'Probably not. The baby books and online articles say you can usually tell around twelve weeks and we're well past that, but they normally won't confirm it until my twenty-week scan. I'm OK with not knowing. Aidan would really like to know though.'

'I'm so excited that you're going to have a baby,' Melody said. 'Jamie and I have been talking about children recently. I think he'd like a whole football team. He's definitely getting broody watching Aidan getting all excited with your pregnancy and watching Leo with Elliot. Obviously we're not planning on having children any time soon, but it's nice that he's planning for our future.'

Isla watched as Melody touched the blue promise ring that he'd given her, so she would know they were on the same page in their relationship. Isla was pretty sure they would get engaged soon.

'Oh, I saw a job advertised in Meadow Bay this morning while I was over there,' Tori said, rooting around in her bag as she looked for the details. 'They want someone to do tours of the caves down there, Clark's Cavern, you know, that big tourist attraction.'

Isla had been there with Elliot and he loved looking through all the nooks and crannies and hearing about the bears and other animals that used to live there thousands of years before.

'Don't you need some knowledge of history or geology or something like that?' Isla said, doubtfully.

She hated this lack of confidence in herself but she had been trying to find a job for the last twelve months with no success and she had started to doubt her abilities. Initially, when she had moved to Sandcastle Bay, she had wanted to be there for Elliot. They had both been dealing with their grief and she'd wanted to be around for him as much as possible. She knew it had made a big difference to him to be there when he came out of school and to put him to bed every night.

She'd had money saved up from her wages in London and, when she sold the flat she'd shared with her ex, she got some money from that. Matthew's life insurance had helped too, so she hadn't been too worried at first. But after the first few months she had started looking for a job.

She had spent her life studying and learning the craft of being a visual merchandiser, taking every course she could, and had even got a master's in it a few years before. She was an expert in her field but that meant nothing when faced with a tiny seaside town with only a handful of shops and cafés. To be honest, it was a little humiliating and more than a little worrying.

There was no work down here unless she wanted to retrain as a bricklayer or JCB driver, something she had been seriously considering. Villages like Sandcastle Bay relied on tourists and when the season came to an end so did the money. But even the seasonal jobs were very few and far between. Of course, there would be jobs in some of the bigger towns but that meant quite a bit of travelling and she still wanted to take Elliot to school every morning and pick him up at the end of the day. Melody, Tori, Leo or her mum would obviously be happy to help out now and again but she couldn't ask them to commit to doing it on a regular basis. It wasn't fair and he was her responsibility. Jobs that ran inside school hours were almost impossible to find and she had applied for anything that did over the last year, but she was always turned down for either being overqualified or not having enough experience. This one would probably be no different. Money was now getting increasingly tight and, by the end of the year, it would all be gone. Her friends and family knew that the search was getting a bit desperate and had taken it upon themselves to tell her of any jobs they had seen or heard about. Her next-door neighbour, Annie, came round most days brandishing an advert for some job or other, most of them wildly unsuitable.

Tori found her phone. 'Here, I took a photo of the advert. It doesn't mention anything about historical knowledge, just says you need to have good interpersonal skills, be confident and be able to deliver engaging presentations to visitors.'

She could definitely do that.

'I'll send it to you,' Tori said.

'Thanks, I'll take a look,' Isla said.

Emily, the owner of the café and Leo's sister, came over then to take their order. At eight months pregnant with her second child, she looked ready to pop at any moment. She didn't look tired though, in fact she was radiant. Isla guessed she would probably keep working there until her water broke, that was the sort of determined person Emily was.

Isla quickly grabbed a menu as Tori and Melody rattled off their orders before Emily turned to her. 'I'll have the pancakes with bacon and sausages please.'

Emily wrote it down. 'So, you guys ready for the Halloween parade?'

Isla smiled. The café was already decorated in little bats, skulls and spiders and she could see lots of pumpkin-topped cupcakes in the cake cabinet. As it was half term there were going to be lots of Halloween-themed and autumnal activities for the kids to do, culminating in a big fancy dress parade through the village and a bonfire party with a huge firework display at the weekend. As

Leo owned his own firework display company, this time of year was always his busiest, but he made sure that he always had time for the fireworks in Sandcastle Bay.

'It's all Elliot's been talking about for weeks,' Isla said.

'Marigold too. She still can't decide what she wants to dress up as. She's cutting it a bit fine for me to get something ready,' Emily said.

'The theme is Heroes and Villains, right?' Melody asked.

'Yes. I think she wants to go as Spiderwoman, which will be a pink and blue costume instead of red and blue, apparently.'

'Is there a Spiderwoman character?' Tori asked.

'Marigold thinks there should be.'

They all smiled. Marigold was Elliot's best friend and she certainly had a mind of her own.

'What are you all going as?' Isla asked quickly, to try to avoid the question of what Elliot wanted to dress up as. They would make such a big deal out of it if they knew.

'Hermione Granger,' Emily said.

'Princess Merida,' Tori said. 'I'm a bit short of red-haired heroines.'

'No idea,' Melody said. 'I think me and Jamie might do something matching, like some kind of duo.'

'What about Elliot?' Emily asked.

'Well,' Isla said, slowly, as she faced the inevitable overreaction. 'He has two ideas. He either wants to go as Batman and Leo will be Robin.'

'Oh that's so cute, would Leo be up for that?' Melody said.

Isla nodded. 'You know he would do anything for Elliot, including being Robin to his Batman.'

'What was the second idea?' Tori asked.

'You can't tell Leo, Elliot wants to keep it a surprise.'

They all nodded.

Isla checked that Elsie West wasn't listening, but she was clearly distracted by Seth McCluskey, the surf instructor, jogging past the window with no top on. Isla took a deep breath because she knew they were going to go nuts over her answer.

'I explained to Elliot what a hero was and he wants to go dressed as Leo.'

'Oh my god,' Emily said, holding her heart.

'That's so sweet,' Tori said, and Isla could see she was on the verge of tears, her baby hormones making her extremely emotional.

'Oh god, could you guys be any cuter?' Melody said.

'What's going on?' came a voice from behind them and they all whirled round to see Leo's aunt Agatha had just walked into the café. Her newly dyed hair was bright green today, no doubt as part of the Halloween festivities. She was wearing a bright purple dress with large orange pumpkins. She clashed horribly but she neither knew nor cared. Isla liked Agatha but now that Leo's brothers, Aidan and Jamie were completely loved-up, the pressure on Isla and Leo had intensified even more.

'Nothing,' Isla said, hurriedly. If Agatha got even the slightest sniff of any gossip, it would be round the whole of the village before the end of the day, whether it was true or not. And Agatha certainly didn't need any encouragement when it came to Isla and Leo's relationship, or the lack of one.

'Well, obviously it's something. Tori is in tears over there,' Agatha protested.

'Oh, I have something in my eye,' Tori said, dabbing at it with a tissue.

'Both eyes?' Agatha asked as she settled herself at their table. She turned round and called across to the other corner. 'Elsie, what did I miss?'

Elsie turned round.

'Tori's going for her first baby scan this afternoon, Melody and Jamie have been talking about having children, Isla might apply for a job at Clark's Cavern,' Elsie started, and Isla stared at her in shock. She really had been listening to every single detail. 'And then they talked about Halloween costumes for the parade and I'm sorry to say I got distracted by young Seth McCluskey running past with no top on.'

Agatha scowled at her.

Elsie shrugged, unapologetically. 'That boy is cute. If I was twenty years younger…'

'You'd still be way too old for him,' Agatha scolded. She turned back to the table. 'Well?'

'It's just Elliot's costume for the parade,' Isla said, frantically trying to think of something that wouldn't implicate Leo. Agatha was desperate to see them married off and Isla didn't want to add any fuel to that fire. 'He's thinking about going as Luke Skywalker because Luke was Matthew's favourite character.'

Isla winced at that lie, feeling immediately guilty. Especially as Elliot had chosen Leo as his hero, not his dad. But he saw Leo every day, whereas he hadn't seen his dad for nearly eighteen months. Though she knew that Elliot still missed Matthew terribly, children seemed to be made of hardier stuff than adults when it came to grief.

'Oh. That is very sweet,' Agatha said, then turned to Emily. 'I'll have the mushroom soup please.'

'We have pumpkin soup too,' Emily offered.

'Oooh, that does sound nice, I'll have that,' Agatha said.

Emily hurried off back behind the counter and Agatha turned back to Isla. 'Where is your young man this afternoon?'

For a moment Isla wondered if she meant Leo, before she realised she was talking about Elliot.

'Leo's looking after him,' Isla said. 'They're making the "World's Greatest Most Spectacular Lego House". Elliot wants to sell tickets for people to come and see it.'

'I'd buy tickets,' Melody offered. 'If Leo has anything to do with it, I'm sure it's going to be amazing.'

'Oh, it will be,' Isla said.

'Leo sure is spending a lot of time round your house lately,' Agatha mused as if it was a mild observation and not the prelude to some interfering.

Isla sighed. 'He wants to be there for Elliot.'

'He wants to get into your knickers, you mean,' Agatha said, pulling no punches.

'He wants to marry her,' Melody said, dreamily, and then immediately closed her mouth at a glare from Isla.

Agatha shrugged. 'Same thing.'

'He does not want to marry me just so he can get into my knickers,' Isla protested.

'So why does he keep asking?' Agatha said.

'Because he loves her,' Melody said, unable to keep her rose-tinted opinions to herself.

'He simply wants to take care of me and Elliot. He's worried that Sadie still owns half the house and what I'll do when all the money runs out. That's as far as it goes. It's just a great friend looking out for me, nothing more.'

'I think you should sleep with him, see if you have any spark there at all,' Agatha said.

Isla had no doubt they would have spark. The memory of that wonderful night they'd shared was seared on her brain forever. The sex had been incredible.

'You don't want to marry him and then find out you have zero chemistry,' Agatha went on.

Melody hid her smile behind her drink. Only she knew about the night Isla had slept with Leo four years before. Isla hadn't told anyone else.

'I don't think that would be an issue. Whenever they're together the chemistry sizzles between them,' Tori said and Isla passed her an incredulous look. Why was she joining in too? Tori gave a smirk and a little shrug. Were they all in on this together?

'Are you not tempted at all to... hide the sausage?' Agatha asked, making a circle with one hand and poking her finger through it.

'Not one bit,' Isla said.

Three disbelieving faces stared back at her.

'OK, sure, of course I've thought about it—'

'I knew it!' Agatha cried. 'Don't think about it, just do it. Next time he comes over, just push him down on the sofa, straddle him and do the no pants dance.'

Isla snorted. 'And should I do this with Elliot in the next room?'

'I'm very happy to babysit for such a good cause,' Agatha said.

'Me too,' Melody giggled.

Tori laughed and gave Isla the thumbs up. 'We'd be happy to have him.'

Emily came over with their order then, carefully placing the food on the table. 'What are you all laughing about?'

'Leo and Isla bumping uglies,' Tori helpfully supplied, between her laughter.

'Are you?' Emily looked shocked and delighted by this wonderful news.

'No, of course not,' Isla said.

'Are you planning to?' Emily asked.

'No,' Isla said at the same time that Agatha, Tori and Melody all answered, 'Yes.'

Isla sighed. 'Ignore them. I am not planning on sleeping with your brother.'

She picked up her knife and fork and started eating, hoping the conversation would be halted by the food.

'Why the hell not?' Agatha said, tucking into her pumpkin soup and then waving her spoon around to make her point. 'It's clear to anyone watching that you're completely in love with him.'

'Because he's not in love with me,' Isla said, exasperated.

'Oh, rubbish. Of course he is in love with you. No man is going to give up dating just so he can be a good role model for a child who isn't even his. He is round your house every day and most nights. Don't tell me all that is out of loyalty to Matthew.'

'It is,' Isla insisted.

'Oh, leave her alone,' Emily said. 'If they're going to get together, they need to be left to do it on their own.'

Agatha opened her mouth to protest but Emily cut her off.

'If I come over here and you're still talking about this with Isla, I won't give you one of my cupcakes. They're made with caramel and apple, which I know is your favourite, decorated with a cute pumpkin on the top.'

Agatha closed her mouth with a snap. After a moment she spoke; evidently being quiet was not one of her strong points. 'You'd really deprive your poor old aunt of her favourite cake, the one and only treat that I have in my life.'

'Don't pull that old lady card with me. Change the subject or no cake for you,' Emily said and moved off back behind the counter.

Agatha waited until Emily was busy serving someone else and then leaned into the table.

'My spies tell me he's bought you a ring,' Agatha whispered. Clearly the threat of no cake was not enough to stop her meddling.

Isla put down her knife and fork and immediately looked at Melody, who owned the one and only jewellery shop in Sandcastle Bay.

Melody shrugged behind a mouthful of sandwich. She quickly swallowed. 'Don't look at me. He certainly didn't buy it from my shop.'

'Where did he get it from?' Isla asked.

'The jewellery shop in Meadow Bay,' Agatha said, knowledgeably.

Tori shook her head incredulously. 'You really do have spies everywhere.'

'That ring could have been for anyone,' Isla tried.

'It's an engagement ring.'

Isla stared at her in shock, her food forgotten. Leo had bought her a ring. She'd always thought his proposals weren't remotely serious, but a ring was a big statement.

'If he proposes with that ring, would you say yes then?' Agatha pushed.

Isla hesitated long enough for Agatha to smile triumphantly, as if she had won.

'No, I wouldn't,' Isla said, firmly, picking her knife and fork back up.

'You hesitated,' Agatha said.

'I was just thinking what I would do if he proposed with a ring.'

'You'd say yes, of course,' Agatha said.

'Not unless it comes with a declaration of love. I'm not walking up the aisle with anyone without that. And unless you want me to tell Emily that you're still hassling me about this then I suggest you change the subject,' Isla said. So much for a peaceful lunch.

'Me and Jamie have been looking at rings,' Melody blurted out, desperately trying to save Isla from any more torture.

It worked. Agatha's gaze immediately turned to Melody instead. 'He's going to propose?'

Isla sighed with relief that she would get a reprieve, at least for now.

'Things are going so well between us,' Melody said, taking another bite and chewing it slowly, obviously playing for time. Isla used the pause to continue eating her lunch. 'We spend every night together either at my house or his. Even his animals have completely accepted me. Do you know, I got a hug from Dobby the turkey last week? Have you ever had a hug from a turkey before? It's the sweetest thing.'

'The proposal,' Agatha urged, impatiently, clearly seeing this change of subject for what it was.

'Well, I think he'd like to keep the moment a surprise, but we were talking about engagement rings the other day. Of course, owning my own jewellery shop, there's a lot of pressure to pick the right ring and he can't really buy it from me if it's going to be a surprise. But he was in the shop the other day when a man came in to buy an engagement ring for his girlfriend. He spent ages choosing and looking until he found one he liked. After he'd left, Jamie said that choosing an engagement ring was a tricky business and then we got on to the subject of which ring in the shop I would want to be proposed to with.'

'Did you tell him?' Agatha said eagerly.

'Well, I have no idea what my ideal ring would be. I've helped hundreds or thousands of couples to choose the perfect ring over the years but I don't know what I would choose for me. To be honest, Jamie could propose with a plastic ring from a bubble-gum machine and I'd still say yes.'

Tori nodded as she touched the blue moonstone ring on her left hand. 'I barely saw the ring Aidan proposed to me with before I burst into tears. I love this ring, it's so pretty and unique, but I would have said yes to any ring.'

'I think if any man goes to the trouble of buying a ring, you should say yes,' Agatha said, giving Isla the side eye.

'Emily!' Isla called, waving her hand to get her attention.

'OK, OK, I'll shut up,' Agatha muttered. Obviously the cake *was* a good incentive.

Emily wandered over and glared at Agatha. 'Is she still giving you a hard time?' she asked Isla.

Agatha did a zipping gesture over her mouth, either to indicate that she wouldn't say anything more or that Isla shouldn't say anything.

'Can I just get a glass of water please,' Isla said, smiling sweetly. Emily clearly wasn't convinced that was the reason that Isla had called her over in the first place. She gave Agatha a stony glare and walked off.

Agatha mumbled something under her breath about only trying to help, which Isla decided to ignore, going back to her lunch.

'You could always propose to Jamie,' Agatha suggested, turning her attention back to Melody.

Melody laughed. 'Yes I could.'

'Sometimes I think women hold off from telling the man how they feel for fear of getting hurt. But I think sometimes it's worth the risk. Sometimes you have to know, sometimes you have to take your life into your own hands,' Agatha said, with the subtlest of glances at Isla. Obviously that was directed at her, not at Melody, who was probably very confident about how Jamie felt for her.

'I'm very happy to wait for Jamie to ask this time. I did ask him out, after all, and we've only been going out with each other for three months. I'm not in any rush,' Melody said.

Agatha looked like she was going to press Melody further so Isla decided to step in.

'And how is your romance with Stefano going?' Isla said, pointedly. The poor man who owned the Italian restaurant in the village had been the object of Agatha's affections for a very long time and there was nothing subtle about her attempts to convince him they would be great together. As far as Isla was aware, he was still fending off her advances.

'Ah, the man is just too shy. But sometimes men need a little persuasion, a little nudge in the right direction,' Agatha said, obviously turning the conversation back on her.

'How are the wedding plans going?' Isla asked Tori before the conversation could be diverted back to Leo again.

'Really good. I keep thinking I should be more stressed than this with only a month to go. I wonder if I've forgotten something major, but everything seems to be going smoothly. It's only going to be a small affair anyway. We're having a big buffet, not a big fancy sit-down meal, and really it's only family and close friends. So if something goes wrong, we'll get by on the day. Honestly, as long as Aidan is there, I'll be happy. The rest of it will work out,' Tori said, serenely.

Isla smiled. How wonderful to be so completely secure in her relationship that she didn't really care whether the party was a big success or not. The day was about Tori marrying Aidan and that was the only thing that she cared about. Other brides went completely bridezilla about it all, but Tori seemed beyond calm.

Isla experienced a sudden pang of jealousy. Would she ever have that? A man who loved her completely, through the good times and the bad. Someone who would love Elliot like he was his own. Her thoughts turned to Leo. God, she so wanted that man to be him. But her battered heart was wary of being broken again. She had been with Daniel for two and a half years, they had talked often about a future together, but just a few days after Matthew had died and she had told Daniel she would be taking custody of Elliot, he dumped her. He certainly hadn't seen a future that was for better or worse. Isla knew that whoever she ended up with had to love her and Elliot unconditionally. Leo, as far as she knew, had never had a serious relationship with anyone and she wasn't sure, despite his proposals, whether he really wanted one.

The door to the café was suddenly pushed open and the light was blocked out temporarily by Aidan Jackson, the oldest of the three brothers. He shared the same good looks as Leo, but Aidan looked carefree and happy, something she hadn't seen in Leo for a very long time.

She watched Tori's face light up at the arrival of her fiancé and she stood to greet him, giving him a brief kiss on the lips, not caring who saw.

'Hello beautiful,' Aidan said, smiling against her lips. He moved his hand to her belly. 'Are you ready to go and see our little Pip?'

'I can't wait.' She grabbed the remains of her sandwich and wrapped them in a napkin. She quickly kissed everyone at the table goodbye and, with a little wave from Aidan, they left the café hand in hand.

Isla stared after them wistfully. She looked back at Agatha, who gave her a meaningful look.

Maybe Agatha was right. Maybe she should take control of her own life. If she wanted something badly enough, then maybe she should go after it.

Though how she was going to do that, she didn't know.

CHAPTER 3

Isla dusted the frost and specks of dirt from Matthew's gravestone, placed a towel on the floor and sat down, curling her knees up to her chest. Here, tucked in the corner of the graveyard, the trees had shed their loads, leaving a jewelled carpet of leaves in cranberry, plum, tangerine and lemon, all sparkling with the light frost that seemed to be clinging onto the day.

She sighed as she stared at the name on the stone, written in gold. It didn't feel right talking to this headstone as if it was Matthew. This lifeless, black stone was not a fair representation of the man who lived his life with so much laughter and adventure. But she didn't have any other place to go.

When he was alive, they'd called each other at two o'clock every Saturday for a chat and a catch-up. Occasionally she'd have a little chat with Elliot too, but mostly with Matthew. There were other times in the week they might phone each other, but Saturday was almost an unwritten rule. For some reason she had decided to continue that tradition, even if it was one-sided.

'How are you?' Isla asked. 'Still dead, I see. Personally I think you're just attention-seeking.'

They'd always had a relationship based on banter, sarcasm and generally taking the mick out of each other in that affectionate way that brothers and sisters have. It didn't seem fair to do it now when he couldn't defend himself, but she'd always greeted him with some sarcastic remark and she didn't want to change that.

'So, Elliot says hi,' Isla said.

She'd brought Elliot to Matthew's grave a few times after his death but he clearly didn't get that this stone was supposed to be somewhere to visit and talk to his dad. And she didn't want Elliot to remember his dad like this. She preferred to talk to him about the good times, and to share photos and videos. Elliot knew she came here to talk to him and, most Saturdays, he would give her a picture he had drawn for his dad.

'He drew you this.' She pulled today's offering out of her bag and smoothed it out before turning it round to show Matthew. 'This is a picture of me, Elliot and Leo, and Luke of course.'

She paused long enough for Matthew to look at the picture. She had long ago stopped being embarrassed about talking to a headstone like this, showing it pictures or videos of Elliot from her phone. She had no idea whether Matthew was here or not – she didn't know what happened to someone's soul or spirit when they died, whether they stayed with their loved ones or moved on in some way – but this chat helped her to feel close to him and she wasn't ready to say goodbye yet. Judging by the fresh flowers on his grave, Melody and her mum probably weren't ready to say goodbye either.

She turned the paper to look at the picture, wondering what Matthew would make of this. In the early days after Matthew's death, Elliot's pictures were of him and his dad. That had soon changed to Isla, Elliot and his dad, until eventually Matthew had been replaced by Leo.

'Elliot loves Leo and I think the feeling is entirely mutual. Leo is wonderful with him. You definitely chose the best person to be his godfather. Elliot still misses you, of course. We all do.' Isla felt a pressing need to convince Matthew that he hadn't been forgotten, despite what the picture showed. She closed her eyes for a moment, remembering his face, his wicked laugh. 'I miss you so much.'

She opened her eyes again. Some days she could come down here and chat endlessly. Other days her heart hurt too much for polite chitchat with a black stone.

'Elliot is teaching Luke a new trick. He can now give his paw in return for a treat. He follows Elliot around everywhere, he's a right character. I think you would have loved him. Mum and Trevor seem to be getting serious – he's clearly smitten with her and I think he might propose soon. Can you imagine Mum getting married again? But he makes her happy so that's all we can ask for, isn't it? Dad broke her heart when he left and I never thought she would be happy again, she was so angry with the world. Well, you were there, you had to put up with it the same as the rest of us.'

Isla looked up at the peach and turquoise sky. Life with her mum, Carolyn, had been difficult for many years. After her husband had walked out on her and their children, her mother had withdrawn from the world, her friends and even her family. She had been so angry, mostly with Isla's dad. Isla had been angry at her dad too for many years, and though they did speak on the phone now from time to time, they had never been close again. He had let all of them down the day he had abandoned them to be with the woman he was having an affair with. It was obvious that he had different ideas of what family meant. Marriage and kids – that kind of commitment was for life.

Isla looked back at the headstone and realised that Matthew, if indeed he was there, was probably waiting for her to continue. She smiled at the thought of some sarcastic remark he'd pass her way.

'But she's mellowing now, spending time with Elliot makes her happy and Trevor is nice. A little serious sometimes, but she's… lighter somehow. He makes her laugh. I'm not sure we will ever have that close bond that other daughters and mums have, but she's making a real effort now, you can see that. And, talking of proposals, I think Jamie might propose to Melody soon as well. You should see them together, they are so in love it's ridiculous.'

She paused in her monologue and closed her eyes again, remembering the good times, the fun they had, the jokes she and Matthew

used to play on each other. The pain grew in her chest but she loved
these memories too much to never take them out and look at them.

She heard a noise by her side and she looked up to see Leo
standing over her. She quickly wiped her eyes so that Elliot didn't
see her crying as she looked around for him.

'Your mum has him,' Leo said. 'She popped by and they've
gone to the Golden Bridge.'

Isla smiled. Elliot loved that place. It was a very posh restaurant
on the cliff tops and they treated Elliot like a king every time
he went there with his nan. He always had a hot chocolate with
whipped cream drizzled with maple syrup, and the staff would
sneak a little cake onto his plate too.

'How did you know I was here?'

'I was driving past, saw you sitting here. I thought you might
like some company.'

Isla hesitated for a moment as she shut her memories away.

'Or I can leave you alone, if you'd prefer.'

Isla shuffled over on the towel and patted the ground next
to her. Leo smiled and sat down, looping an arm around her
shoulders and kissing her forehead. She leaned her head against
his shoulder.

They sat there for the longest time in silence, listening to the
birds sing in the autumn sunshine, the distant sound of the waves
on the beach. She appreciated that Leo didn't push her or try to
talk to her. Just being here was enough.

After a while she looked up at him. 'Do you ever come here?'

He sighed. 'I used to. But there's only so many times you can
say you're sorry.'

She frowned in confusion. 'Why are you sorry?'

He didn't answer as he stared out over the sea. Eventually he
spoke. 'I just miss him too.'

She didn't really understand what he meant but decided to let
it go. People dealt with grief in very different ways.

She stood up and held out a hand for him to help him up. 'Come on, let's go home.'

He stood up and looked at the grave. 'Give me a second.'

She nodded and walked a little distance away. She watched him for a moment as he placed his hand on top of the headstone. He whispered something she couldn't hear but his eyes locked with hers as he spoke and she guessed it was about her. Probably renewing his promise to look after her.

Leo walked over to her and looped his arm around her shoulders again. 'Come on, I think you need a hot chocolate too.'

'With whipped cream?' she teased.

'Of course and I'll even throw in the maple syrup.'

She grinned and leaned into him on the way back to his car.

Leo did look after her, every day. Not with the promise of a home and with his empty proposals, but with his friendship. Matthew had given her a wonderful gift with Leo and she knew her brother had planned it that way.

⟡

Leo stared at the bubbles rising in his pint, his thoughts a million miles away. Well, not millions of miles away. More specifically, half a mile up the road at Hot Chocolate Cottage. He had to smile at that. When Matthew and Sadie had bought the house, Sadie had insisted on calling the place Champagne Cottage and it had stuck even after Sadie had left; Matthew had been far too concerned with raising a baby all by himself to worry about the name of the house. When he had died and Isla had moved into his home to raise Elliot, she had thought the name was pretentious. She had asked Elliot what his favourite drink was instead and the name Hot Chocolate Cottage had been decided upon. Leo thought that theirs was probably the only house in the whole of the UK with such a unique and interesting name.

But that was Isla all over, unique, interesting, special. He loved that she considered him to be her best friend.

His thoughts turned to the cemetery that afternoon. It had been a long time since he had been to Matthew's grave. He felt too guilty. If there was a god or higher being that decided who lived and who died, why take someone who was good and decent and kind instead of a self-absorbed asshole like him? And through his selfish actions, Matthew was dead and Leo got to have Isla back in his life again. That felt all kinds of wrong. He'd seen her in the graveyard as he'd driven past and stopped the car, deliberating for the longest time whether he should join her. But that was one thing he was surprisingly good at: being a friend, being there for her when she needed a shoulder to cry on. Although his motives were far from altruistic, her company did help to ease the guilt ever so slightly.

Leo's younger brother, Jamie, came and sat down opposite him.

'What's with the face?' Jamie said, slipping out of his jacket and throwing it over the back of the chair.

'There's no face,' Leo muttered, finishing off the remains of his pint. He didn't normally drink alone but Jamie was late. He was always late actually, always busy with some sculpture or work of art. Lately he had been busy with his new girlfriend, Melody, too.

'Sure there is. You're sitting there looking like someone stole your favourite toy.'

He scowled at Jamie in the hope his little brother would let it go, but Jamie clearly couldn't care less and decided to push it even more.

'Let me guess, you and Isla have had a row?'

'No, we never argue.'

'But this is to do with her.'

Leo sighed.

'How about I get the drinks in and then you can tell me all about it?' Jamie said, standing up. 'Another pint?'

Leo shook his head. 'Just an orange juice for me.'

Jamie smiled affectionately and went off to the bar. Leo never had more than one or two beers whenever he went down the pub, not any more. The frequency of his visits to the pub had changed too. He'd go once or twice a week to catch up with his brothers, instead of going every night. A lot had changed since his best friend, Matthew, had died.

Jamie returned with the drinks just as there was a ringing in Leo's pocket. Leo fished out the walkie-talkie, the smile filling his face before he'd even responded.

Elliot's little voice came through the speaker. 'This is Batman to Robin, come in Robin.'

'This is Robin, what do you need, Batman?' Leo said.

Jamie snorted as he sat down and handed his brother his drink. Leo didn't even care that any remains of his cool guy image was disappearing faster than a new ice cream flavour at Sprinkles. He looked around the pub and a few men were grinning at him.

'I just wanted to say goodnight,' Elliot said.

'Goodnight buddy, I love you.'

'I love you too,' Elliot said. 'Will I see you tomorrow?'

'You can count on it.'

'Goodnight Leo. This is Batman, over and out.'

Leo waited to see if there was any more from him – over and out didn't always mean the conversation was finished – but the airwaves stayed silent this time. He pocketed the walkie-talkie and took a sip of his orange juice, steadfastly ignoring the look from Jamie.

'Leo Jackson!' Jamie teased, shaking his head. 'Never in my wildest dreams did I ever think I would see the day when I heard you tell someone you love them.'

'Piss off.'

Jamie was undeterred. That was the good and bad thing about brothers. They never took offence, which also meant that Jamie wasn't going to let this go any time soon.

'Though I would think a certain someone else would appreciate hearing those words from you even more,' Jamie said, waggling his eyebrows mischievously.

Jamie never normally stuck his nose too much into his business, but since he had been loved-up with Melody Rosewood, Isla's sister, Leo felt like both of them had made it their mission to interfere as much as possible. Melody, especially, had set her heart on Isla getting her happy ever after with Leo, and now it looked like she had roped Jamie into the hopeless cause too.

'Isla has turned down my proposal of marriage probably about a hundred times, I don't think she's hoping I'll tell her I love her at all.'

'Why do you think that is?' Jamie said, all humour gone now. Leo looked up at him and saw the concern in his eyes. Were they really going to have a serious conversation about this? Normally they stuck to much more lighter topics.

'Because she doesn't think I'm good enough,' Leo said.

'No, you don't think you're good enough. Don't put that on her.'

He hated how insightful his brother was sometimes.

'Come on, think about all the women I've slept with. She doesn't want a man like that.'

'I think there was an element of that when she first moved to Sandcastle Bay,' Jamie said, honestly. 'After Daniel dumped her when she told him she was taking custody of Elliot, she was bound to be feeling a bit fragile. They were together for… what was it, two, three years? I think she saw a future with him. There's been no one for her since and I imagine whoever she goes out with next will have to be someone she trusts completely, not just for her sake, but for Elliot's too. I guess, knowing your reputation with women, she would have thought initially that you wouldn't be a contender, or that you wouldn't want something long-term, but she has seen how you have changed over the past year. We all have.'

'I proposed to her this morning. She still said no.'

'What are you offering with that proposal?' Jamie asked.

'I would take care of her and Elliot. She would never need to worry about money again, she wouldn't need to worry about her home being taken from her.'

'She wants more than that?'

'What else can I give her?'

'Your heart?' Jamie said, exasperated.

Leo grunted. 'She said as much this morning, that she would only marry out of love, but I can't give her that.'

'Why the hell not? It's clear to anyone in the village that you two are crazy in love with each other.'

'She doesn't love me. She can't… And if she does, she would fall out of love with me pretty quick once she knew the truth about Matthew's death.' He closed his eyes, briefly. She would hate him and deservedly so.

Jamie's face fell. 'You're still carrying that guilt with you? You were like this after Dad died, carrying that weight around with you for years and that wasn't your fault either.'

Leo sighed. He had been just a kid when his dad had died from a heart attack after a day out cycling with Leo. Of course, at that age, he'd taken that on himself. In his mind, if he hadn't persuaded his dad to go out on the bike with him, he'd still be there. It was only many years later when he had done some research into his dad's condition that he realised that what the doctors had said at the time was true: it could have struck at any time, even when his dad was watching the TV. He had let go of the guilt he'd been carrying for all those years, though the pain and regret of how he'd acted in the years after his dad's death still stayed with him. His mum, brothers and sister had been grieving too, but on top of that they'd also had to deal with his bad behaviour and crappy attitude for the next few years. They didn't deserve that and he was surprised they had stuck with him. But this was different.

'I might not have been responsible for Dad's death but I am responsible for Matthew's,' Leo said, quietly.

'Matthew's death was not your fault.'

'You know as well as I do that if I'd said something, if I'd done something, Matthew would still be alive today. Elliot would still have a father, Isla would still be living in London, probably getting married to that idiot Daniel. She's here in Sandcastle Bay because, the night Matthew died, I did nothing to stop it happening. She lost her job, her boyfriend, her brother because of me. I shouldn't get to benefit from Matthew's death. Being with Isla would be like winning the lottery and I don't deserve that.'

'It wasn't your fault. We can all drive ourselves insane with the what-ifs and the if-onlys. What if Alan had not lost his job, what if he hadn't gone home and had a row about it with his wife, what if he hadn't come here to drown his sorrows and gone for a walk along the coast instead, what if the old landlord here had more concern for why Alan was drinking so much and refused to serve him after a few drinks. What if any one of the thirty-odd other people who were in the bar that night as well as you, including Trevor Harris, the local policeman, and Alan's brother, stopped for a second to see how Alan was getting home. What if Matthew had not been running late, what if the babysitter for Elliot had turned up on time. Accidents happen, and it was tragic and heartbreaking, but it most definitely wasn't your fault.'

Leo shook his head. He had been torturing himself with this for over a year. He had seen how drunk Alan was, which had been unusual for him. He'd watched him stagger out of the pub and thought nothing more than that he'd have a hangover the next morning. He'd had no idea he'd get in his car and attempt to drive home, or that a minute after leaving the pub Alan's car would slam into Matthew's so hard that Matthew was killed instantly. Every day since, Leo had thought about how different life would be if he had just stopped to help Alan out of the pub, made sure he had got in a taxi safely. If he had, his best friend would still be alive. He had to live with that guilt every day. None of it was fair. As he watched Elliot grow into this brilliant little boy, it hit him hard that Matthew would never be around to see it, and that he got to benefit from it instead.

'Have you spoken to Isla about this?' Jamie asked.

'No. I meant to. After Matthew's death I was going to tell her it was all my fault but—'

'It was not your fault.'

'But it never felt like the right time. She needed me when she came here to look after Elliot, she needed a shoulder to cry on, someone to hold her hand in the role of being a new parent. If I'd told her, she wouldn't have let me anywhere near her. I didn't want to take that away from her too.'

'God, you're a tortured soul,' Jamie said with frustration. 'How can you let this ruin your life? So many lives have been affected by this, don't let it destroy yours. Although Matthew's death ripped a hole in Melody and Isla's hearts, they are happy here now, there was some good that came from it. Isla loves being a mum to Elliot. Matthew would have been delighted if you and Isla got together, you know that, and he clearly would be happy with the way you are raising Elliot. You're amazing with him. Don't you think you're due some happiness as well?'

Leo thought about what his brother said. Could he really let go of this guilt and move on with his life? If he really wanted Isla to marry him, he was going to have to.

CHAPTER 4

'OK, all we have to do is thread the string through the holes in the acorns,' Isla said. She smiled with love for Elliot as he stuck his tongue out of the corner of his mouth and carefully poked the red string through the tiny hole she had drilled in the acorn.

They had spent a fun afternoon the day before with Leo and her mum, walking through the woods and collecting as many acorns as their pockets and bags could hold. When Leo had left to meet Jamie down the pub, Isla and Elliot had painted them all a range of different colours so they looked like beads of different shapes and sizes. They had painted the acorn caps too as they were also going to be beads for their necklaces.

'Hello!' Leo called as he let himself into her house, the way he always did. He was round her house almost every day, sometimes during the day, sometimes in the evening for dinner, some days even both. She wondered how he managed to run a successful firework display business when he spent so much time with her and Elliot. Not that she was complaining, she loved these times they spent together. It was almost as if they were a proper family.

'We're in the dining room,' Isla called and a few moments later Leo appeared. Luke, their puppy, ran around him excitedly as if it hadn't only been a day since the last time he had seen Leo. Leo threw his jacket over one of the chairs, gave her a kiss on the cheek and followed up by squeezing Elliot in a big hug and kissing the top of his head. She watched Elliot smile at the affection Leo showed him. God, she loved this man. Would it really be the worst thing in the world if she married him? If she lived the rest of her life like this? Being married to her best friend actually sounded pretty great.

'What are we doing?' Leo said, picking up one of the acorns and looking at it as he sat down on the other side of Elliot.

'Making acorn necklaces,' Elliot answered.

'Oh cool,' Leo said. Following Elliot's lead, he picked up a blue piece of string and threaded it into the acorn as if this was the most normal thing in the world. Maybe it was, now both their lives circulated around Elliot. 'Now what do we do?'

Elliot laughed. 'You need more than one acorn on your necklace. We are making a beaded necklace.'

'Oh right, of course,' Leo said, a smirk pulling on his lips as he picked up another acorn.

'No, you need an acorn cap next, so they go al-ter-nat-ively,' he said slowly, to get the word right.

'Alternately,' Isla corrected. 'One acorn, one acorn cap.'

'Got it,' Leo said, a big smile on his face. He was obviously enjoying himself as much as Elliot was.

Elliot deliberately waited to see which colour cap Leo chose and then chose the same colour for his own necklace. Isla suppressed a smile. Elliot plainly adored him.

They worked in companionable silence for a while, concentrating on the job in hand until they all had a string of brightly coloured acorn beads and caps.

'These are such a cool idea,' Leo said, holding his up for a second and then putting it over his head.

Elliot immediately put his on too.

'It was Elliot's idea,' Isla said.

'Ah, good job, buddy,' Leo said.

Isla smiled. He was so good with Elliot.

'I'm going to ask Melody if she wants to sell them in her jewellery shop,' Elliot said as he helped Isla to put her necklace on.

'I bet she will love these,' Isla said.

'I'd definitely buy them,' Leo said.

'You would?' Elliot's little face lit up.

'Of course.'

'How much would you pay?'

'One million pounds,' Leo said, which made Elliot giggle.

'We're going to do some painting next,' Elliot said. 'Are you going to paint with us?'

'I love painting,' Leo said, rolling up the sleeves of his shirt.

Isla giggled. 'You might not like this kind of painting.'

Leo paused halfway through rolling up one of his sleeves, revealing strong tanned forearms. She had a sudden memory of being held in those arms, with his naked body on top of hers. Christ! She shook her head slightly to clear it of those wonderful images. It felt somehow wrong to be thinking of that when Elliot was sitting next to her.

'What kind of painting are we doing?' Leo asked.

'Why don't we go outside into the garden and you can see for yourself,' Isla said.

Elliot hopped down from his seat and ran out through the back door.

Leo smiled at her. 'What do you have planned for me now?'

'Don't worry, you can just watch,' Isla said, feeling a little sorry for him. His life had changed beyond recognition since Matthew's death too and she felt bad sometimes that Leo had never really signed up for any of this. She never wanted to assume that Leo would want to be a part of any of the activities she did with Elliot – she didn't want to push any of that responsibility onto him – but he'd taken to the role of honorary dad like a duck to water.

She walked outside, Leo following her and Luke trailing behind him. The sun glinting over the sea made her stop and shield her eyes for a moment. The view from Hot Chocolate Cottage was magnificent. The golden yellow houses of Sandcastle Bay tumbling down the hill, the sea stretching out for miles in front of them, the little boats bobbing out on the water. Matthew really had chosen well when he'd bought this house. The garden was long enough for Elliot and Luke to play in and Marshmallow Cottage, Elliot's treehouse, was another great addition to the house that Matthew had added.

The days were getting decidedly nippy now. There had even been frost on the windows and on her car this morning, although the sky was a gorgeous periwinkle blue right now, as if still trying to clutch onto the last edges of summer. The trees, however, had already packed up their bags: most of them were semi naked, with remnants of gold, copper and scarlet clinging onto the brittle branches with no more than a whisper. Most of the leaves were on the floor like a beautiful jewelled patchwork carpet.

She turned her attention to Elliot, who was already dancing across the large sheets of paper taped to the patio. They had an area about five metres squared to work on and she had already laid out trays of paint in brown, red, gold, and orange.

'We're going to paint an autumn tree… with our feet,' Isla said.

Elliot giggled. 'But our feet will get dirty.'

'That's the idea, buddy,' Leo said. To her surprise, he was already undoing the laces on his boots and stepping out of them. Elliot duly did the same.

'We'll do the trunk and branches first, so we're going to step into the brown paint,' Isla said. In reality, she knew the finished thing was probably not going to look anything like a tree, despite her instructions, but at least they would have fun doing it.

She watched as Leo gingerly stepped onto the tray, the paint oozing between his toes. 'Weirdest feeling ever,' he said.

He stepped onto the bottom of the page somewhere in the middle and proceeded to walk open-legged up the paper to create two parallel lines for the outline of the trunk of the tree. Elliot stepped into the paint next, squealing with laughter as the cold paint squidged over his tiny feet.

'Step between my footprints buddy, you can do the bark pattern of the tree,' Leo said.

Elliot did exactly as he was told, slowly at first and then gaining speed. Leo caught him by the waist as he got around halfway up the sheet.

'We need to do the branches carefully. Do a line here to there,' Leo pointed. Elliot followed the instructions, putting one foot directly in front of the other as Isla stepped into the brown paint and joined them on the paper. She went up and down the trunk a few times, filling in some of the gaps that Elliot had left behind. The basic tree shape didn't look half bad with Leo helping to point Elliot in the right directions for the branches.

She stepped off the paper onto a wet towel, which she wiped her feet clean on, and then Leo and Elliot did the same.

'Now the leaves are a bit more… free,' Isla said, gesturing to the coloured trays at the top of the paper. Elliot ran round and hopped into the red paint. 'Just go wherever you want to go.'

Elliot jumped onto the paper and started running around, leaving little red footprints in his wake. Leo chose the orange paint and Isla stepped into the gold and they all started moving around each other, going back now and again to top up on the paint on their feet. Elliot couldn't stop laughing the whole time, clearly having a whale of a time.

Isla span round, her hands in the air, and slammed straight into Leo, his hands going instinctively to her waist to steady her.

She looked up into his caramel brown eyes, alight with amusement, and she had an overwhelming urge to reach up and kiss him. For the briefest of seconds, his eyes glanced down at her lips. God, was he thinking about kissing her as well?

She realised Elliot was watching them and she slipped out of his arms and took the little boy's hands, dancing around with him until the top half of the paper was completely filled with different-coloured footprints.

Isla stepped off and wiped her feet on the towel and Leo and Elliot did the same, Leo bending down to make sure Elliot's feet were completely clean.

Elliot turned round to admire their work. 'Look at our brilliant family tree!'

Isla smiled. He had got it in his head lately that they were a family, especially after learning about families and family trees at school. Lately, several of the drawings had been of the three of them. He'd recently brought a painting home titled *My Family* with a picture of Leo, Isla, Elliot and the puppy Luke, although Leo hadn't seen it. Isla didn't know what to do with Elliot's misplaced ideas. She didn't want to say that Leo wasn't part of their family because he was, in every way that mattered, even if technically and biologically he wasn't. But she also didn't want to encourage those ideas and lump Leo with that responsibility if he didn't actually want it.

Leo bent and picked Elliot up, sitting him on his hip. 'That's right buddy, our family tree.' He kissed Elliot on the head and the little boy hugged him tight.

Isla stared at them, her heart filling with so much love for Leo. When he looped an arm around her shoulders and brought her into the group hug too, she thought her heart might just explode out of her chest.

God, if he asked her to marry him right then, she knew she would say yes.

Movement at the back gate caught her eye and Isla looked over to see Karie Matthews, her social worker, standing there smiling at them.

Isla quickly disentangled herself from Leo's arms and went over to greet her with a hug.

Karie had been in their life ever since Matthew had died. She had been round almost every day at the very beginning, helping Isla with the sudden transition to being a new parent.

Isla had been terrified that Karie would think she wasn't doing a good enough job and take Elliot away from her. But all Karie had wanted to make sure was that Elliot was healthy and happy with Isla, and once she saw that he was, the visits had become less and less frequent.

'Hey, this looks like fun,' Karie said.

'How long have you been standing there?' Isla said.

'Long enough,' Karie grinned.

Isla blushed, wandering if Karie had seen her and Leo practically on the verge of kissing.

'Hi Karie!' Elliot called over. 'Do you like our family tree?'

'Very much,' Karie said. 'It's beautiful.'

Isla noticed all humour had gone from Leo's face. He always worried when Karie came over.

'You got time for a cup of tea?' Karie asked and Isla nodded. She checked back with Leo, who reassured her, 'We'll be fine.'

Isla smiled, knowing they would be, and followed Karie inside. Karie sat down at the kitchen table, slipping her coat over the back of the chair.

Isla set about making two cups of tea, wondering what it was that had caused Karie to visit on a Sunday. It had been nearly two months since the last time she had seen her, though she knew the paperwork for making Isla a legal guardian of Elliot was still ongoing.

Taking parental rights from his mother was an almost impossible thing to do. Despite the fact that Sadie had walked out on Elliot when he was only one, and not bothered to make any contact since, apparently she still had rights. It was a complete legal minefield, with seemingly hundreds of hoops to jump through. Isla and Karie had been pushing to make Isla's guardianship a legal adoption but the courts were keen to keep things as they were, which technically meant that Sadie could come back any time and gain custody of Elliot. Karie insisted if that happened they would have a strong case to contest it as it would not be in the best interest of the child. Isla just had to hope and pray Sadie wouldn't turn up. While she thought it unlikely, the threat seemed to be permanently hanging over their heads.

Isla brought two mugs to the table and sat down opposite Karie, holding her mug to her chest.

Karie took a sip of her tea.

'I haven't got a lot of time as I have another visit in half an hour over in Meadow Bay. I know I could have emailed you for the sake of speed, but I wanted to tell you face to face. I have some news.'

'Good news?' Isla said, realising she was holding the handle of her mug that little bit too tight.

'I think so. A date has been set for your adoption court hearing.'

Her heart leapt in her chest. 'What does that mean?'

'It means, that after over a year of trying to locate Sadie, of doing everything possible to try to find her, they've agreed to let the adoption go ahead, which will sever any rights she has as a parent. The court hearing is set for November fifteenth but I think really at this stage it's just a formality. We go there, the judge will listen to all the evidence, we cross the T's, dot the I's and Elliot will be legally yours.'

'Oh my god, that's it. Then it'll all be over?' Isla said, her heart thundering through her chest.

'That's it, once that's over, there'll be no more paperwork, no more court visits. You'll be a family.'

Isla let out a rush of breath she had no idea she had been holding.

'Oh, thank god. I have never wanted anything as much as I wanted this and I never thought it would happen. You have no idea how relieved I am.'

'Congratulations, I'm happy for you. Elliot couldn't be in better hands.' Karie took another mouthful of her tea. 'I'll be here a few days before the hearing to go through everything. There will be a few more bits to sign but you don't need to worry about any of that for now. I'll drop you an email, explaining it all.'

Isla nodded, numbly. She couldn't believe this was finally happening.

Karie finished her tea and glanced out the window at Leo and Elliot playing in the garden together.

'He's so good with him,' Karie said.

'I know, I'd be lost without him,' Isla said. She watched Leo show Elliot how to do a handstand and his shirt fell down round his chest, revealing a toned, muscular stomach and a thin smattering of hair that travelled from his belly button and disappeared into his jeans. She had stroked her hand down that hair. Once. Many years before.

She caught Karie watching her and she quickly focussed her attention on a few crumbs on the table.

'Have you accepted any of his proposals yet?' Karie said.

Over the last year, Karie Matthews had become a good friend. They had chatted over many cups of tea about Elliot, his occasional nightmares, his grief for Matthew, how he was getting on at school. And with Leo's constant presence it was only natural that he would crop up in their conversations too.

'No, and you know why.'

Karie grinned. 'I know why you think you shouldn't get married, but I saw the two of you out there and let me tell you, in all my years of working with families and couples, I don't think I have ever seen two people so in love with each other as you two clearly are.'

Isla smiled. 'We're friends, he cares about me. That's as far as it goes.'

Karie gathered her bag together and slipped her coat back on. 'Why don't you ask him?'

Isla laughed. 'Because my fragile heart couldn't take it if he said no.'

'Then tell him how you feel and see if he says it back,' Karie said as if it really was that simple. 'Look, things are finally coming together for you now. I'd love it if you could become a proper family. I'm sure Elliot would love it too.'

'Oh, going for the guilt trip now, are we?' Isla teased.

Karie laughed. 'Just think about it. I'll be in touch.'

Isla stood up to hug her and Karie let herself out through the back door, waving goodbye to Elliot and Leo as she left.

Isla sat back down at the table feeling shaky with relief; she couldn't help the tears that filled her eyes. Although she had thought that Sadie was never likely to come back, she hated this cloud that had hung over them, this threat, no matter how small, that one day she could lose Elliot to a woman who couldn't care less about him. And now, in just a few short weeks, Elliot would be legally hers.

She looked up as Leo let himself into the kitchen. Elliot was still playing in the garden with Luke.

'What's happened, what did she say?' Leo looked panicked, clearly mistaking her tears for those of sadness rather than happy relief. She quickly wiped her face. He took her hands and pulled her to her feet. He glanced outside at Elliot. 'There's no way I'm letting them take him from you. My cousin has a place in Canada, it's a little lodge in the middle of the woods. We could take Elliot tonight, they'd never find us.'

Christ, he really was serious about going on the run with them.

She reached up and stroked his face, placing her fingers on his lips before he came up with any more crazy plans to escape from the law.

'You are an amazing, wonderful man, and I don't know how I got so lucky to have you in my life, but there'll be no running from the authorities tonight. Karie came to tell us we finally have a date for the adoption hearing. She thinks it will just be a formality now and that the judge will give me full parental responsibility. The adoption will be final.'

He stared at her and then he broke into a huge smile. He grabbed her into a huge hug and then swung her round laughing.

'Oh god, I'm so relieved. He's really going to be ours?'

Ours.

Her heart leapt at that word.

He must have seen her face because he quickly backtracked. 'I mean yours, obviously.'

She placed a hand on his heart. 'He'll be ours. I don't need a ring on my finger or a big declaration of love to see what's right in front of me. You love that boy and he loves you. You're as much part of his family now as I am.'

He smiled and kissed her head. 'And I'm going to take really good care of him, of both of you.'

'You already do.'

She looked up at him.

God I love you.

Maybe Karie was right. Maybe it was time she told him how she felt.

Elliot burst into the kitchen. 'Luke has paint all over his paws.'

Leo laughed and broke away from her. 'That's because he wants to be part of our family tree too.'

He followed Elliot back outside. Evidently, her declarations of love would have to wait.

CHAPTER 5

'Hey Annie,' Leo said to his assistant as he threw his keys down on his office desk the next day, his mind still filled with Isla.

'Morning, Leo dear. I have some news,' Annie said.

Leo flopped down in his chair and stared at his blank computer screen for a moment. It took a few seconds for him to realise that Annie was packing her things from her desk into a box; her photos, her plants, even her beloved George Clooney calendar he had given her last Christmas disappeared inside the box.

He stared at her for a few moments in confusion. Annie had worked for him at The Big Bang from as far back as he could remember, back when it had just been the two of them organising local firework displays and not the large team of pyrotechnic experts organising huge professional corporate displays that he had now. She was efficient, friendly, the clients loved her, and quite honestly she ran the company single-handed. She was probably in her fifties, extremely glamorous in that effortless way some people managed, and tried to mother him more often than he liked.

'Please tell me your news isn't that you're breaking up with me,' Leo said. 'I don't think my fragile heart could take it.'

He watched her put her stapler into the box. This looked like serious business. They had talked about redecorating the office a few weeks before. Had Annie perhaps organised for it to be done without telling him, and she was simply packing everything away so it wouldn't get damaged in the decorating process?

'I'm breaking up with you,' Annie said simply.

He watched her for another moment and his heart sank into his stomach. It was quite obvious she was serious.

'Wait, you're leaving?'

'I am,' Annie smiled, serenely. 'We won the lottery.'

'Is this one of those times when I get all excited and you tell me you won ten pounds?'

'Five numbers and the bonus ball. One hundred and forty-one thousand, two hundred and fifty-six pounds and thirty-three pence.'

Leo whistled appreciatively. 'Wow, really?'

Annie nodded, the biggest smile on her face.

'Congratulations, that's amazing. When did this happen?' Annie lived next door to Isla and he was surprised he hadn't heard the whoops of delight.

'Last week, but we didn't want to tell anyone until the money was actually in our account. It cleared this morning.' Annie put a small pink teddy that said 'Grandma' across the belly into the box too. 'Me and Bill are going on a world cruise. We leave on Friday, we'll be gone for six months initially but we might extend it. And when we come back, I think it's high time I retire.'

'Retire? But you're what, fifty-one, fifty-two?'

'I'm sixty-eight, dear. I should have retired years ago but I enjoyed working here at The Big Bang, planning the perfect display for our customers' needs. I also enjoyed fending off the calls from the thousands of women that used to ring up on a daily basis to ask you out or to thank you for the wonderful time they'd spent with you the night before. But mostly, dear, I loved working with you. However, now it's time to spend my retirement with my husband. The mortgage is paid off, the children are all grown up and scattered around the world, so we're going to do something for ourselves for a change.'

Leo smiled, despite his heart sinking, and he stood up to hug her. 'Oh Annie, I'm happy for you. I'm going to miss you like crazy, but hell, I can't think of a better thing to do with the money. Go and enjoy yourself.'

'We intend to.'

He gave her a squeeze. They both knew she should have given him some kind of notice period and that leaving at one of the busiest periods of the year was going to leave him in the shit, but he didn't care about that right now. She deserved this.

'Well, my resignation is effective immediately. I have a ton of stuff to sort out before we fly out on Friday, but I haven't left you completely in the lurch. I've organised a temporary replacement for you.'

'You have?' Leo looked at his watch. It was ten minutes past nine. How had she managed that already?

Annie nodded as she pulled back and continued packing. 'She can come and work for you for the next few weeks until you can find someone else. Or you know, keep her on if she meets your needs. You choose.'

Who had Annie found so last-minute? Leo didn't hold out any hope that it would be someone good.

'Does she have any experience in displays?' Leo asked.

Annie paused. 'She has vast experience in displays.'

The way Annie said it suggested that it wasn't entirely true. She must have seen his face because she smiled. 'She'll be here in ten minutes and you can interview her yourself. If she's not suitable, show her the door.'

Annie put the lid on the box and she leaned up and kissed him on the cheek.

'Thanks for being an amazing boss.'

'Thank you for being a phenomenal assistant,' Leo said, lifting the box. It didn't weigh much but within a few minutes Annie's very existence from the office had been wiped clean. 'Let me help you out to the car.'

'You're a good lad, Leo Jackson. I only hope your new assistant can look after you in ways that I never could.'

'No one could replace you, Annie Brooke,' Leo said, following her out to her car. He frowned as he considered what she'd just said. What did she mean by that? He cringed. 'How old is my new assistant?'

Annie shrugged. 'Probably around your age.'

Leo only hoped it wasn't someone he'd slept with once, many moons ago. That would be beyond awkward: to be faced with an ex who possibly still had feelings for him. If she was willing to work for him at such short notice, it was a distinct possibility.

'This is probably her now.' Annie indicated the red car coming up the gravel driveway in a cloud of dust that billowed around it. 'Be nice.'

'I'm always nice,' Leo said.

Annie rolled her eyes and got in the car. 'I'll send you a postcard.'

With that she drove off and Leo was left alone, waiting for the arrival of the car that was bringing him his new assistant.

As the car drew closer and the dust began to settle, unease spread into his stomach. He recognised the vehicle.

The car stopped and the most beautiful blonde woman in the world got out, her hair blowing around her like some kind of banner.

She smiled when she saw him and, despite the fact that his brain was shouting that this was a terrible idea and that you should never mix business with pleasure, he knew for a fact that he would be hiring her on the spot.

CHAPTER 6

'Hey!' Isla said, closing the car door and walking over to Leo. 'Is Annie around?'

'She just left.'

Isla frowned in confusion. 'She just phoned me and asked if I'd give her a hand for a few hours.'

Leo couldn't help smiling. Isla had no clue why she was here. Of course Annie would have asked Isla; living next door, Annie would have known that Isla was struggling to find a job. Though the very fact she hadn't mentioned who was coming in for the job and hadn't even told Isla she was here to interview for the job, suggested that Annie probably had some ulterior motive.

'Why don't you come inside for a moment?' Leo said, greeting her with a kiss on the cheek. When had that long since become the norm? He didn't have that tactility with any other woman outside of his family and there was nothing sisterly about his feelings for Isla.

'OK,' Isla said uncertainly and followed him inside.

He gestured for her to sit down and set about making two cups of tea. How should he play this? She had no idea she was here to interview for a job. He could give her a drink, make up some excuse and then let her leave. Having her work here could be all kinds of awkward, not least because he was hardly able to contain his feelings for her when he was around her house, let alone if he had to see her all day at work too.

He turned round with the two mugs and sat down at the desk.

'I've never been here before, it's quite nice,' Isla said, looking around. 'Where are all the fireworks kept?'

'We have a storage place out the back.'

'Are you getting ready for the firework display here at the weekend?'

'It's all in hand. We'll probably set it up on Saturday morning.'

'Elliot thinks you have the coolest job in the world,' Isla said, sipping from her tea. 'I have to agree with him.'

'Really?'

'Yeah, you create... magic. Though to be honest I have no idea how any of it works. How do you do all those firework displays to music?'

'Oh, it's all computer-programmed now. I can show you if you're interested?'

'I'm very interested,' Isla said, keenly. 'I think it's fascinating.'

He smiled. Someone with enthusiasm for the job was exactly what he needed.

'Elliot pretty much wants to have his own firework display company when he's older.'

'He will always have a job here,' Leo said and then cleared his throat. 'As do you, if you want one?'

She frowned in confusion. 'You're offering me a job?'

'Annie quit. She won the lottery. Her and Bill are going on a world cruise.'

'Oh my god, really?'

He nodded.

'That's amazing. I'm so happy for her,' Isla said.

'I know, it's great.'

'But she just quit?'

'Yes, about fifteen minutes ago. She leaves on Friday. She said she had organised a replacement and here you are.'

'Wait, what? That's not what she said to me. She asked if I could come up and give her a hand.'

'Yes, with being my assistant.'

She stared at him for a few moments, a frown creasing her beautiful face. 'Have you engineered this?'

'Engineered Annie winning the lottery? I'm good but not that good.'

'No, giving me a job because you know I need one. You don't have to save me, Leo Jackson.'

'I know. This isn't that. To be honest, I had no idea she had asked you until you got out of your car. This was not my doing, this was all Annie. But I do need an assistant. I haven't got time to go through the process of advertising and interviewing, at least not until Christmas and New Year is out of the way, so if you can help till then that would be great. If you would prefer not to because you think it would be awkward working with your *best friend* then that's fine too. I completely understand.'

The frown was still there, her arms still folded across her chest, like she didn't trust him.

'I don't know the first thing about fireworks.'

'Annie tells me you have vast experience when it comes to displays,' Leo grinned, knowing now what Annie had meant.

'Window displays, yes.'

'Ah, it's the same thing,' Leo lied. 'It's about interpreting the clients' needs and putting on a show for the customer.'

Isla smiled slightly. 'I do know how to do that.'

'Well, there you go.'

'I have Elliot to think of,' Isla said, her defences going back up.

'I'm sure we can be flexible about your working hours, make sure it fits around his school day. I can always pick him up from school as well. All the setting up of fireworks are normally done in the mornings anyway, so I could be free to look after him while you're finishing off at work.'

'He's off school this week for half term. I promised to do a load of stuff with him. There's the great acorn hunt and the pumpkin-

carving competition and we're going to roast marshmallows on
the beach and—'

'And you can still do all those things. My working day is really
flexible and I have several pyro teams who do a lot of the setting
up for me,' Leo said. His working day *had* become a lot more
flexible over the last year as he had taken a huge step back from
a lot of the displays and setting-up side of things so he could be
there for Isla and Elliot more often. 'I can do some of those things
with Elliot while you're here, or maybe your mum and Melody
can look after him for a few hours here and there. I really just
need someone to answer the phone and deal with enquiries over
email. You could answer a lot of the emails from home.'

'OK,' Isla said, cautiously.

'OK you want the job?'

'I'm thinking about it.'

Leo took that as a yes. He could see she was wavering.

'So, let me show you Annie's system.' He stood up and faltered
for a moment. He had no idea how Annie ran The Big Bang.
Events appeared in his diary as if by magic and he wasn't sure if
she kept printed records of the clients' details or if everything was
on the computer. Isla would need to know the right questions to
ask a potential client and the prices for various different options
and he wasn't sure where Annie kept all that stuff. Whenever his
assistant had gone on holiday before, her daughter Ruby always
used to help out and Annie had handled making sure Ruby knew
what she was doing. But Ruby had moved from Sandcastle Bay a
few months before so he couldn't even call on her to help Isla settle
in. Maybe Annie would agree to come back for a brief handover.

His eyes fell on a bright red A4 ring binder with Isla's name
written across the front. He frowned in confusion. He had seen
Annie busily putting stuff in this folder all last week, but he hadn't
thought anything of it and it certainly hadn't had Isla's name
on it then. He picked it up, thumbing through all the clearly

labelled segments, and he couldn't help but smile. Annie really was efficient. This was everything Isla would need to start the job and more – from a basic enquiry form that she could fill out with each phone call and the questions she would need to ask, to a list of different fireworks and their effects, and instructions on how to add the details to the electronic diary. The folder was so detailed, Elliot could probably come in here and run the office for him.

'Well, this looks like a good place to start.' Leo handed her the folder. 'Why not look through this and if you have any questions you can ask me.'

Isla flipped through it. 'Annie really did plan for this, didn't she?'

'It looks that way.'

'Is she trying to set the two of us up?' Isla asked.

'I think the whole village would like to see us get together,' Leo said. 'Shame they'll be disappointed.'

'Not necessarily,' Isla said, standing up, and his heart leapt at that sudden glimmer of hope. 'One day you might fall in love with me.'

He watched her as she kicked off her shoes and curled up on the sofa to read through the folder. His heart was striving to tell her that that day had happened a long time ago.

'So I tell you I love you and you'll say yes to one of my proposals?'

'If you genuinely mean it,' Isla replied, without looking up from the folder.

'I would never say those words unless I meant them.'

'Then yes, I would marry you.'

'But you said you would never get married unless you were in crazy in love with the man,' Leo said.

There was silence from Isla for a moment then she looked up and gave him a level gaze. 'Yes, that's right. I would never walk down the aisle unless I was completely in love with the man.'

He stared at her, his heart thundering in his chest.

Was she in love with him? Was that what she was saying?

It was.

Christ, she was in love with him.

He had no idea what to do with that. He wanted to walk over there, gather her in his arms and kiss her. He wanted to tell her he loved her too and he had for a very long time. But he couldn't do that.

He cleared his throat awkwardly. 'I need to sort out some fireworks ready for a display tomorrow. I'll be in the warehouse if you need me.'

He walked out the door and, as it closed behind him, he heard Isla sigh softly. 'Well, that went well,' she said.

CHAPTER 7

Leo started taking down fireworks from the shelves and loading them into boxes ready for his pyro team to take them to a display tomorrow morning.

His heart was roaring, his stomach was churning.

Isla was in love with him.

How the hell had that happened? More to the point, when did it happen?

Although he supposed the how and when didn't matter, just what he was going to do about it.

They couldn't be together like that, he didn't deserve that. And she deserved far better than him.

But then he had been proposing to her for the last year – how had he imagined it would turn out if she said yes? Would it really be a marriage of convenience, just two friends living together in the same house? Would that mean that neither of them would be in a romantic relationship with anyone else for the rest of their lives as well or would they continue to date other people?

Or… would they be husband and wife in every sense of the word?

A kick of desire shot through his stomach, followed by those wonderful memories of that amazing night they'd spent together four years before. Would their marriage be like that? Best friends during the day and lovers at night? He definitely didn't deserve that.

Being with Isla definitely felt like he was benefitting from Matthew's death in some way. She wouldn't be here if Matthew hadn't died and he was responsible for Matthew's death, at least partly. It just didn't seem right. Plus, how would she feel when she found out? Despite what Jamie had said about it not being Leo's fault, he knew Isla would hate him for it. But even if she didn't, and if somehow he could get past the guilt of having her in his life, she deserved better than him.

He grabbed a box of silver dragons and sighed.

Almost his whole life he had been told he was worthless, useless, would never amount to anything. After his dad died when he was a kid, he couldn't have cared less about school and would often bunk off lessons or skip school altogether. His dad would have been ashamed of him for how he had behaved. His teachers and head teachers had been less than kind about his abilities, his attitude or his hope for any kind of decent future.

And even though he'd grown up a lot since then and now ran his own successful business, there were some villagers who still thought he was trouble. He supposed his reputation with women didn't help

He picked up a box of falling leaves and put that on the crate.

He'd never really had any serious girlfriends; his longest relationship had lasted only about five weeks. But the women he had been with knew that it was never going to be anything long-term. One of them, Emma, had even told him that no girl would ever want to marry him, that he was the type of guy you had fun with but wouldn't spend forever with. Another girl he'd been seeing, Rachel, hadn't been blunt enough to tell him to his face, but he'd overheard her laughing about him with her friends in the pub when one of them had teased her about whether she loved Leo or not.

'*Oh hell no, it's nothing serious. I can do a hell of a lot better than that, he barely has enough qualifications to rub together,*' Rachel said.

'*Can you imagine bringing him home to your parents as the man you were going to marry?*' said one friend. '*They would die.*'

They all laughed.

'*My dad thinks he'll be in prison before he's twenty-five,*' said another.

'*That would not surprise me.*'

'*He is good in bed though,*' Rachel laughed.

'*Well, at least he's good at something,*' her friend said.

And while Rachel had not been anyone he was particularly attached to, he had been hurt that his reputation in the village was such a poor one. No one expected him to amount to anything. What they'd said, what all his teachers had said, had stuck with him. He was no good for anything.

Every woman he'd been with since then had lasted no more than two or three dates. There was no point in getting serious with anyone as he clearly wasn't long-term relationship material. And he hadn't cared what anyone thought of him, hadn't cared that the women were just seeing him for the sex. He'd never grown attached to any of them.

Until Isla.

He paused as he grabbed a box of comets.

That night had been something different. When he'd kissed her all those years ago, when he'd slept with her, it had been something so much more than just sex. Maybe it was because she was his friend, not just some woman he was sleeping with, that made it more special. It had been the only time that he'd actually considered forever with someone. But Isla obviously hadn't thought that way. Despite his invite to stay with him a second night, she'd made some excuse about being tired and went back to her hotel alone the evening after the christening. Then she'd disappeared back to London, and though he had seen her occasionally whenever she visited Matthew, there had been no mention of that wonderful night ever since. She'd seen him just like the other women saw him, just as someone good for sex and a fun time.

When she'd come to live in Sandcastle Bay after Matthew's death, all those old feelings for her came flooding back, though

he'd never told her how he felt. There'd been a million reasons
why he hadn't. She had been distraught for the first few months.
It hadn't been the right time. He had been caught up in his guilt
over Matthew's death. She needed a friend more than she needed
sex. But he supposed, ultimately, he hadn't wanted to be rejected
by the one person who mattered.

And now she had fallen in love with him.

He wanted to march back into his office and tell her he loved
her too. And then celebrate that love on the sofa she was currently
sitting on.

She must see some redeeming features in him if she had fallen
in love with him, if she thought he was good enough to be in
Elliot's life and help her raise him.

Could he be that man she saw? Could he really be the man
she deserved?

God, he didn't want to do anything to hurt her, and if he
pursued this it would no doubt end in disaster, just like everything
else in his life.

He was a better friend than he was boyfriend or husband material. Maybe it'd be better for both of them if they stayed that way.

※

Leo didn't come back.

Isla spent an hour looking through everything in the folder
and then decided to attempt to reply to some emails. There were
quite a few, mainly enquiring about small local displays over
Christmas and New Year. She did her best to answer their questions, referring to the red bible of fireworks whenever she didn't
know the answer. She wasn't sure if she was doing the right thing
but, as Leo had completely abandoned her after her half-arsed
attempt at confessing her feelings for him, she decided she had
to do the best she could do with the job.

It got to twelve o'clock and there was still no sign of Leo. As she had told Melody she would only be a few hours and had promised Elliot she would take him to the dinosaur museum in the next town that afternoon, she knew she had to go. She wasn't quite sure what Leo meant by flexible working hours to suit her, but this week was a bit of an exception to the norm. He would just have to cope without her this afternoon.

She wandered out of the office and headed for a large, barn-like building that was probably where Leo was sorting out the fireworks. Or studiously avoiding her.

Isla pushed the door open and there was Leo sitting on an old sofa, bouncing a tennis ball at the exact angle where it would hit the floor, then the wall, and bounce back into his hand again with very minimal effort.

'So this is what you do with your working day?' Isla said, attempting to sound light and cheery while, inside, her heart was hurting.

Leo let the ball fall to the floor.

He stood up, pushing his black curly hair off his face, which was what he usually did when he was uncomfortable about something. 'I don't think this will work, you being here.'

Isla's heart sank. She hadn't expected to have a job when she woke up that morning, but now she had been at it for a few hours she quite liked it. It was good to feel useful again, to have something fill her mind other than kids' stories and TV programmes. The morning had been quite easy and, though she knew she had only scratched the surface of everything that Annie did for the company, she thought she was going to enjoy working there. And now it was over before it had even started.

'Well, it won't if you're going to be an ass about it,' Isla said.

Leo's eyebrows shot up. 'I'm not being an ass. I just... don't want you to get hurt.'

'Why would I get hurt?' Isla asked in surprise.

'Well...' Leo fumbled for an explanation and settled for pointing his finger between him and her.

'OK, yes, I have feelings for you and you don't return those feelings. It's no big deal,' Isla shrugged, trying to carry off the lie. 'It's not exactly big news. Leo Jackson is the sort of man that goes after the women he wants like a lion would hunt a deer. If you had any feelings for me, you would have pursued me a long time ago.'

He stared at her. 'That's not... I didn't—'

'And it's for the best really, that we don't get together. Because what would happen when it ends, when you get bored of me? What would that mean for Elliot? He needs you more than I do so we're better off staying as friends,' Isla said.

'I would never do anything to hurt Elliot,' Leo said, finding his voice at last.

'I know you wouldn't, not intentionally. But if we were to start something and it came to an end, you wouldn't want to keep coming round to see Elliot, because you wouldn't want me to get hurt. That would destroy him.'

'I wouldn't do that.'

'Really? You've been in here avoiding me all morning because I told you I had feelings for you, and you just tried to sack me from the job you gave me a few hours ago because of it too. Your solution to me telling you I have feelings for you was to run away, so don't tell me you wouldn't react badly to us ending.'

Leo clearly had no words.

'Now, I'm going to go and pick up Elliot and spend the afternoon with him. Tonight you're going to come round for dinner as normal, and tomorrow I'll be here to work and we'll just pretend this whole debacle never happened. I'm not going to lose my best friend over this, am I?'

He paused then shook his head. 'Definitely not.'

'Good.'

She turned and walked out and he didn't call her back, which she was glad for. Her chest hurt, the burning ball of emotion at the back of her throat hurt and she'd quite like to have a little cry in the car before she picked up Elliot.

He didn't love her. And though she had guessed as much for the last year, there had always been that glimmer of hope. Now there was none.

CHAPTER 8

Isla pushed open the door of The Cherry on Top and spotted Melody and Tori sitting near the windows at the back, overlooking the beautiful Sunshine Beach. Luke and his brother Rocky, Melody's puppy, were asleep under the table looking like they'd both spent the morning playing on the beach. Tori's puppy, also from the same litter, wasn't there but Spike tended to follow Aidan around on the farm. There was no sign of Elliot, which caused her a moment of alarm, until she heard his unmistakable giggle coming from the kitchen. No doubt he and Marigold were 'helping' Frankie, who had been hired recently to help Emily with the cooking. There was no sign of Agatha either.

Isla greeted Melody and Tori with a hug and a kiss and then flopped down on the chair.

'You OK?' Melody asked.

She let out a big sigh. She'd had a little cry on the drive back into Sandcastle Bay but she would be damned if Leo Jackson would get any more of her tears.

'Well, I have a date for the adoption hearing for Elliot, after which he will formally become mine. I now have a job which I think I might enjoy and I made a complete idiot of myself this morning in front of Leo. So, you know, peaks and troughs,' Isla summarised.

She helped herself to a bit of the chocolate cake that Tori was eating to commiserate herself. There were two pieces of great news there, so why did her heart feel so heavy?

'The adoption is going to be final?' Melody said and Isla nodded. 'That's fantastic news.'

'I know. It's taken so long, I never thought it would happen.'

'I'm so happy for you. Does that mean he'll be your son?' Tori asked.

'Yes, technically, though I can't see that he'll suddenly start calling me Mum any time soon. I think it'd be weird if he did. I'm still his aunt. I think asking him to call me Mum would confuse him.'

'Ah, this is amazing news. You and Leo and Elliot will be a proper family,' Melody said, always seeing the fairy tale.

'No we won't,' Isla said firmly. 'Leo will always be there for Elliot, and I appreciate that more than you know, but we'll never be a proper family.'

Tori and Melody stared at her, obviously a bit stunned by her firm tone.

'I'm sensing this is to do with you making a fool of yourself in front of Leo this morning,' Tori said. 'What happened?'

Isla sighed. She told them all about the lovely day they'd had the day before, the family tree they'd painted, the moment they had shared, and how Leo had accidentally said that Elliot would be theirs after the adoption as if he already considered them to be a proper family. She told them how she'd thought about telling him how she felt, to see if he would say he felt the same. She told them about the job that had fallen into her lap and how everything in her life seemed to be falling into place.

'So this morning I told him,' Isla said.

'You just came right out and said you loved him?' Melody asked.

'Well, I didn't say the words, but I made it very clear. I don't see how there could be any misunderstanding.'

'And?' Tori said, leaning forward eagerly.

'He stood up and walked out the office and then I didn't see him for nearly three hours.'

Their faces fell. She knew how they felt.

'You told him you loved him and he walked away?' Melody said, incredulously.

'Yes. I felt such an idiot. I don't know what I was thinking.'

'You were thinking that he's round your house every day, that he hugs and kisses you every time he arrives or leaves, you're thinking that he looks at you like you're a goddess, and that every single person that sees you together assumes you must be a couple or can't understand why you're not. None of this was in your imagination,' Tori said. 'Even Aidan thinks Leo is in love with you and he's his brother.'

'Jamie and I were talking about you two the other day, he's convinced Leo loves you too,' Melody said. 'What about the statue he made for the Sculptures in the Sand Festival in the summer?'

Isla remembered it all too well. Everyone had been tasked with making sculptures of the thing they loved the most in Sandcastle Bay. Although Leo had made a horse with a storm and waves crashing inside to represent the sea when it was at its most tempestuous and wild, he had also made parts of it mirrored. When he revealed the statue to her, he had made sure she and Elliot stood in the exact place that they could see their reflections clearly in the horse's neck. Tori and Melody were convinced he had been trying to send her a message, that he really did love her too.

'He made a horse,' Isla said. 'Maybe we saw what we wanted to see.'

'He gave you a slice of the famous heartberry cake at the heartberry love festival in the spring,' Tori said. 'Men only give their cakes to the women they love.'

'He was just sharing it with Elliot and he offered me some too. I don't think there was any symbolism in it,' Isla said sadly.

'You said you didn't actually say the words this morning, maybe he misunderstood,' Melody tried. 'Maybe he just left you in the office because he had work to do.'

'I went and found him and he tried to give me the sack.'

Melody had her face in her hands, making her look like *The Scream* by Edvard Munch.

'He said he didn't want me to get hurt,' Isla said, feeling bad that she was now painting Leo in such a bad light. He was her best friend and he had been there for her so much over the last year. He was wonderful with Elliot. It wasn't his fault if he didn't return her feelings. 'I told him that just because I have feelings for him and he didn't return those feelings, it didn't have to get all weird between us. So I know there was no misunderstanding.'

Melody suddenly looked thoughtful. 'There's something else going on here.'

Isla sighed and took the menu. 'I don't think so. I think we all just hoped that he shared those feelings and projected what we wanted to see onto him. We found meanings in words and gestures that were never there.'

'Jamie said he thinks he doesn't deserve you,' Melody said.

Isla looked up from her menu. 'He said something like that to me the other day. Why would he think that?'

Melody and Tori shrugged.

Emily appeared at their table to take their order.

'Is my little man behaving himself back there?' Isla asked.

'He is in charge of sprinkle distribution on the cupcakes Frankie is making. It's safe to say this batch of cupcakes will have a lot of sprinkles,' Emily said.

Isla laughed. 'If he's being a pain, just send him out to me.'

'Elliot couldn't possibly be a pain. Besides, Marigold is keeping him in check and Frankie adores him.'

Isla returned her attention to the menu for a second.

'Emily, why would Leo think that he doesn't deserve Isla?' Tori asked.

Isla blushed. She really liked Emily but she wasn't sure if she wanted to discuss her sort-of relationship with her brother with her.

'Oh god, he's such an idiot,' Emily said, sitting down at her table and looking like she was getting herself comfortable. Although Isla wondered if it wasn't just an excuse to take the weight off her feet for a few minutes, almost impossibly, her baby bump looked bigger than the last time she had seen her. 'When our dad died when we were kids, Leo reacted really badly to it. I think he blamed himself. Leo had persuaded him to go on a bike ride that day and when he came home, Dad had a heart attack. The doctors said that he'd had issues with his heart for a long time, that it was only a matter of time before it gave in, but of course Leo thought it was his fault.'

'Oh god, that's awful for him. To live with that guilt must have been horrible.' Isla's heart broke imagining Leo as a little boy taking all that on his shoulders.

'I think he accepted later that he wasn't to blame but for several years after Dad died that guilt manifested itself as anger. He acted out for the next few years, messed around at school or missed school altogether, got into trouble with police, got drunk too often… He was a bit of a mess.'

'He's told me this before,' Isla said. 'I don't care about any of that. Why would stuff he did fifteen, twenty years ago make a difference to the man he is now?'

'Because everyone thought he was worthless, that he would never amount to anything. Many of his teachers even told him that. His girlfriends laughed at the possibility that he could ever be anything serious for anyone. There were even bets that he would end up in prison. At the end of school the class did one of those silly polls: which kid will most likely be famous, which kid will get married first, which kid will be a millionaire. There was one – which kid will most likely end up in jail – and all his classmates said it would be Leo. He tried to pretend he didn't care, even lived up to his reputation for a few years, drove around on a dirt bike, wore the leather jacket, even took up smoking for a while to cement his hard-guy image. But he did care. The fact that everyone thought he was worthless did affect him and I think it's kind of stuck with him ever since. He has never had any kind of serious relationship because I don't think he saw that he would have any kind of future with anyone. You're the longest relationship he's ever had.'

'We're not—' Isla started.

'But you are. You're closer than most couples. And it's not just friendship, you can see that. You might not have the intimacy but you're definitely in a relationship. He loves you.'

Isla shook her head. 'I told him how I felt and he basically bolted out the door.'

Emily's eyes softened. 'I just want to hug him and shake him sometimes. I guarantee that this is everything to do with how he sees himself and nothing to do with you. You spend almost your entire life thinking you're worthless, it's hard to break that mentality. I think you just need to talk to him. Tell him why you fell in love with him, the qualities you see in him. Maybe then he might start seeing himself like that too.'

Isla stared at the menu. Could Emily be right? The thought of having that conversation with Leo made her cringe. She had already embarrassed herself in front of him by telling him her feelings but now his sister wanted her to persuade him that he was wrong and they did deserve a chance.

'I know it seems like hard work, but I promise you he's worth the risk.'

Isla smiled, knowing Emily was right about that at least. Maybe it would be worth one more go.

CHAPTER 9

'What are we having for dinner?' Elliot said as he sat on the unit top, swinging his feet.

'Meatball bolognese,' Isla said, taking the dish out of the oven.

'Is Leo coming?' Elliot said, insightfully. He knew her bolognese was Leo's favourite.

'I think so. He's busy with work so he might not be able to,' Isla said, not wanting to tell Elliot that she had left things rather awkwardly with Leo earlier and he might make some excuse and not come rather than have to face her again.

'I like meatball bolognese, it's my favourite,' Elliot said. Anything Leo liked was Elliot's favourite. 'When we move into Leo's house will we still have meatball bolognese?'

Isla paused in stirring the sauce over the meatballs. 'When are we moving into Leo's house?'

'When you get married.'

Dear God, was everyone out to try to get them together?

'Marigold said you would get married soon,' Elliot said, simply, as if it wasn't the biggest life-changing decision of her life.

'Did she?'

'Leo asks you all the time, doesn't he?'

She turned her attention back to the meatballs. She had thought she and Leo had been a bit more subtle about the proposals than to let Elliot overhear. Apparently not.

'I think…' Isla said carefully. 'That when Leo asks me to marry him, he's only joking.'

'But Marigold says you love each other and when two people love each other they get married.'

'There are different types of love,' Isla said, putting the lid back on the pot and returning it to the oven. 'There are friends who love each other, like I love Tori, and there are brothers and sisters who love each other, like I love Melody and loved your dad, but I wouldn't get married to them.'

'But Tori and Melody are girls,' Elliot said.

'Girls can marry girls and boys can marry boys. Eva and Rosie are married,' Isla said, referring to the two women who ran the tattoo shop in the village.

'I didn't know they were married,' Elliot said.

'Yes, they got married because they love each other very much.'

'Like you and Leo?'

Isla cleared her throat as she measured out the pasta twirls into the saucepan.

'You love chocolate, right?' Isla said. 'It's your favourite thing in the whole world to eat. You'd eat it all day every day if I let you.'

'Yes! Chocolate is the best.'

'Leo loves me like you love chocolate. He likes spending time with me every day and I'm probably one of his favourite people, but he's not going to marry me, just like you wouldn't marry chocolate,' Isla said. This analogy was getting confusing for her; she wasn't sure what Elliot would make of it.

'Yes I would,' Elliot said.

'I don't blame you buddy, chocolate is the best thing in the world ever,' Leo said.

Isla swung around and saw him standing in the doorway.

Shit.

How long had he been standing there listening to her attempts to explain love to Elliot?

'Leo!' Elliot said, his whole face lighting up as he launched himself off the unit top and into Leo's arms. 'Would you marry chocolate?'

'Yes I would,' Leo said, tipping Elliot upside down and holding him by his feet.

Elliot squealed with laughter.

'And will you marry Isla?'

Leo looked up and fixed Isla with a meaningful glare which Isla found impossible to read.

'Maybe one day.'

'Yay!' Elliot cheered.

Isla flashed Leo an angry look. She had deliberately made him his favourite meal for dinner with the hope that they could talk about them and how he really felt for her, but now she was mad.

'Elliot, can you go and wash your hands before dinner please?' Isla said and from the way his smile fell from his face she knew she hadn't been able to keep the anger from her voice.

'They're clean,' Elliot said.

'They are not, you've just been playing in the garden with Luke for the last hour. I saw you digging for worms,' she said, trying to force her voice to sound more normal.

Elliot giggled. 'I found a really big one.'

'Go on buddy, go and wash your hands,' Leo said. 'If we're quick we can go out in the garden to see if we can spot him again before dinner. But no digging this time, just looking.'

Elliot raced off and a few seconds later she heard the thunder of feet as he ran up the stairs.

Leo moved to give her a kiss on the cheek, but she stopped him.

'Don't do that.'

His face fell. 'Don't do what? Kiss you?'

'Make empty promises to Elliot. I'm a big girl, I can handle disappointment just fine, but he's five. Don't promise him we're going to get married when we're not.'

'I didn't promise him. I said, maybe one day.'

'And all he heard was one day and in his mind, he thinks that's one day really soon. He's already talking about coming to live with you, because Marigold has told him we love each other and we're going to get married. I was just trying to explain to him that's not going to happen.'

'Maybe it will,' Leo said, moving closer.

Isla stopped herself from groaning in frustration.

'Had a change of heart, have we? Suddenly decided I'm the love of your life?'

He stepped even closer, so she could feel his warmth, his sexy tangy scent enveloping her. Despite the fact that she was mad at him, she suddenly wanted him to do all manner of wonderful and dirty things to her.

She looked up at him, wanting to push him away and haul him close at the same time.

'Maybe I have,' Leo said.

'My hands are clean!' Elliot yelled, running back into the kitchen. 'Let's go and find that worm.'

Leo smirked as Elliot pulled his shoes on and Luke ran around him in excited circles. He placed a kiss on her cheek, just like he always did, but somehow this felt different – as if it was laced with intent.

'*Maybe…* We can talk later when little ears can't hear us.'

Isla nodded numbly and Leo stepped back and followed Elliot outside.

'No touching anything with your nice clean hands,' Leo said as the door closed behind them. 'If you see the worm you can only point at it with your elbow.'

Elliot burst out laughing and took Leo's hand, running off with him down the end of the garden.

That was a conversation she was suddenly very much looking forward to.

Isla closed the book they had been reading. Elliot had chosen *Rumble in the Jungle* as his bedtime story, which was apparently his all-time favourite, but Isla suspected it was because it was one that she and Leo always read together, and any time together as a family was always a good thing in Elliot's book. Leo would do the deep voices of the bigger creatures and she would do the more high-pitched voices of the more delicate creatures. Leo would always throw in a lot of actions, too, which Elliot loved.

'Goodnight little man,' Isla said and kissed him on the cheek.

'Goodnight buddy,' Leo said, kissing him on the head.

'Love you,' Elliot said sleepily, closing his eyes with a big smile on his face.

'Love you too,' Isla said.

God, her chest hurt just looking at him. It was funny. She'd always loved Elliot, he was her nephew and she adored him, but somehow In the last year that love had intensified.

She gave Luke, who was snoring softly on the end of the bed, a pat on the head and left the room.

Leo was waiting for her at the doorway as she turned on the nightlight and closed the door so it was ajar.

She looked up at him. 'He adores you.'

'The feeling is very mutual.'

She smiled and reached up and stroked his face. He turned his head and kissed the palm of her hand. Her heart leapt and his eyes darkened.

'Shall we go downstairs? I feel like I need a glass of wine,' Isla said, her breath unsteady.

Leo nodded.

She followed him downstairs, admiring the broadness of his shoulders, his strong arms, remembering what it was like to be held in those arms.

She walked into the kitchen and went to the fridge as Leo settled himself at the table.

'Want a drink?' Isla said, pouring herself a glass of white.

'No thanks, I think I'd rather keep a clear head.'

Isla let out a heavy breath. What did he want to keep a clear head for?

She sat down opposite him and he smiled at her.

He took her hand and her heart went into overdrive. Maybe this conversation could wait. Maybe all they needed was to reconnect again, as they had that wonderful night four years before.

He stroked his thumb over the back of her hand. 'I hurt you before and that's the very last thing I'd want.'

'It's OK—'

'It's not. Especially as I've left you thinking that I don't have feelings for you when I do.'

Her mouth was dry, goosebumps erupting over her body.

'Feelings that go way beyond just friendship and way more than what I feel for chocolate,' Leo went on.

She laughed slightly, suddenly afraid, nervous and excited all at once.

'I panicked because… I wasn't sure what I had to offer you—' Leo started.

'Someone who is wonderful, kind, generous, funny. I wish you could see what an incredible man you are.'

'I don't feel I deserve you.'

'Don't put me on a pedestal. I'm not a goddess.'

'It's not that. I mean, you are a goddess obviously,' he grinned. 'It's just…' A darkness passed over his face. 'Being with you feels like I'm benefitting from Matthew's death. If he hadn't died, you wouldn't be here. You'd probably still be with Daniel.'

'And what a lucky escape that was. That man was never going to be my forever. I should have seen it sooner.'

'Do you never think about that kind of thing?' Leo asked. 'You have Elliot now and he is the love of your life.'

'Without wanting to sound too deep, I'm sure there's some famous quote that says something like, *In darkness there is always light.* Matthew's death was heartbreaking but it gave me the greatest gift of all. Of course I'm not happy that Matthew died, but I'm not going to feel guilty for finding happiness from his death. Lots of good things have happened in the last year. I now live in one of the most beautiful places in the world and... his death brought me to you.'

He winced a little and she wasn't sure if she'd said the wrong thing.

'Regardless of what happens between us, I will always be grateful to have you in my life,' she explained.

'You had me in your life long before he died. I'm not just here because of that.'

It was true, they had a connection many years before his death.

'I often think about the night we spent together,' Leo said and her breath caught in her throat. 'Do you?'

'All the time,' Isla said, without thinking. 'You never talk about that night, I thought that you had forgotten.'

He looked surprised. 'I remember every glorious detail. Why would you think I could forget that so easily?'

'Because you've been with hundreds of women.'

'There's not been hundreds,' Leo said.

'OK, maybe hundreds is a slight exaggeration, but I was just one of many.'

He frowned. 'You were different. You knew that.'

She sighed because when he had been holding her in bed, kissing her, staring at her with adoration, she had thought that maybe they had something, and then any glimmer of hope was dashed on the rocks just a few hours later.

'The day of the christening, I heard you talking to that woman. The woman you slept with the night before I came down. Just twenty-four hours before you were telling me you'd had the best night of your life, you had someone else in your bed. We weren't together, you didn't owe me anything, you were free to sleep with as many women as you want, but I did realise then that I was just a face in the crowd. I didn't feel like I was any different from the rest of them.'

He didn't say anything for a while.

'I didn't have her in my bed.'

'I don't see the difference.'

'The difference is I've never taken a woman back to my house before. You are the only woman I've ever made love to in my bed.'

She stared at him, biting her lip. She guessed that was pretty significant. 'So are you saying you want to recreate that night?'

'Oh hell yes.'

She couldn't deny that she wanted that too. But was that all he was offering?

'But I don't just—' Leo was interrupted by a heavy knock on the door.

Isla debated whether or not to ignore it but, whoever it was – probably Melody or Tori – would know she was in.

'Hold that thought,' Isla said, getting up and heading to the front door.

She opened it to find a woman standing on the doorstep. In the darkness Isla couldn't really see who it was. But then the woman stepped forward into the light.

'Hello Isla.'

Isla felt her stomach lurch, the bottom dropping out of her world. Because, standing on her doorstep, was the one person she hoped she'd never see again: Sadie Norton, Elliot's mum.

CHAPTER 10

Isla had no words. Nothing. What the hell was Sadie doing here after all this time? The courts had used every tool at their disposal to look for Sadie since Matthew's death nearly a year and a half before. They had searched every country Sadie had been in or had any connection to, they had looked under every stone, but she was nowhere to be found. The snake had finally slithered out of its hidey hole now though, and by the look in her eyes, she was hungry.

Luke growled next to her. It was the first time she had ever heard that noise come from his puppy mouth. He had obviously come downstairs from Elliot's room to investigate when he'd heard the knock at the door.

Oh God, Elliot. Panic rose up in her so fast she thought she was going to be sick. She couldn't lose him. There was no way she was letting Sadie have him. Giving birth to him did not make her his mum. Sadie had abandoned him years ago, severed all contact, she didn't care about him or love him. But what if the courts didn't see it that way? Karie had already explained that removing parental rights from a mother was so much harder than removing them from a father, that's why the adoption process had taken so long. But surely the courts would rule in Isla's favour. Elliot was happy with her, he was loved and taken care of. But what if they gave custody to Sadie?

She wanted to slam the door in her face and then take Elliot and run. What had Leo said, his cousin had a lodge in Canada? Suddenly that was looking more and more attractive.

'Oh yes, you have every right to look guilty,' Sadie said.

'What do you want?' Isla asked, her heart pounding in her ears.

'You're living in my house. And I want it back.'

The house? Sadie was here for the house? Isla nearly sagged with relief. She would gladly hand over the keys right now as long as Sadie signed over parental responsibility for Elliot to her. Maybe she should suggest that, a house in return for her son. But she didn't even want to mention Elliot – what if Sadie wanted to see him?

'Is that all you're here for?' Isla asked, then cursed herself. She didn't want to remind Sadie that there could possibly be any other reason.

Sadie blinked as if she didn't understand the question. Had Elliot really not crossed her mind at all?

She heard movement behind her and then Leo swore loudly.

'Nice to see you too, Leo,' Sadie said. 'Are you living here as well? Wow, it's a big old party at my house.'

'It's not your house,' Leo snapped.

'I think you'll find my name is on the deeds, which makes this house mine.'

'Half yours,' Leo said. Isla couldn't find any words. She was still in flight mode, so she was glad Leo seemed to be handling it for now.

'What do you mean, half mine? My name was on the deeds with Matthew. Now he's dead, the house is mine,' Sadie said, coldly.

No sympathy, no sensitivity. This was Isla's brother they were talking about. And, what was even worse, Sadie had shared a bed with him, a home, they'd had a child together. How could she be so lacking in any sadness or grief?

'You weren't joint tenants, you were tenants in common,' Leo said. 'Believe me, I've had the best solicitors I could find look at this in the hope I could get your name taken off the deeds, which I couldn't. But they assured me tenants in common means you only own half the house. Matthew left his half of the house to Isla. She has as much right to live here as you do.'

Sadie's smug smile slipped. 'I don't understand.'

'No, I don't suppose you do,' Leo said, tartly. 'If this goes to court, I suspect we would get a lot more than half the value of this house, as it was Matthew's life insurance that paid off the entirety of the mortgage. The judge would look at that and how much you put into the house initially. You might only get a few thousand out of this and the court fees alone would take most of that.'

'But—'

'What did you think would happen here? You decide to come back and try to claim a house you haven't lived in for four years as your own, and you think we're just going to hand over the keys? I suggest you go and get yourself a solicitor and it better be a good one. Once you've had some advice, then we can discuss terms and how you wish to proceed, but for now you're trespassing on private property and we're asking you to leave.'

Sadie stared at Leo in shock. He put his arm around Isla to guide her out of the way and closed the door firmly in Sadie's face.

Isla watched as Leo paced across the hall angrily, his fists clenched at his sides. He moved back to the window by the side of the door and peered out.

'She's gone,' Leo said. He turned back to her. 'Are you OK?'

Her body was shaking, her heart was racing, she felt sick. Tears welled in her eyes. She was the very definition of not being OK.

'Hey, don't cry,' Leo said, his hands on her shoulders. 'It's going to be fine, we're going to fix this.' He pulled her into a hug and, with her face against his shirt, his arms around her back, stroking her soothingly, she cried against his chest.

'She's not taking Elliot, there's no way in the world I'm letting that happen,' he said, instinctively knowing what she was most upset about.

'Why did she have to turn up now?' Isla said, finding her voice. 'Two weeks' time and he would have been mine.'

'I know, but the courts are not just going to hand him over to her. They will consider what is best for him and being with a woman he doesn't know who completely abandoned him to travel around Australia and Thailand is not the best thing for him. We will fight this every step of the way and, if we lose, I'm dead serious about running away to Canada. I know someone who can do fake IDs, they would never find us. I will take care of you both.'

Isla pressed herself against his warmth, trying to shut out the pain in her heart.

'I don't want her anywhere near him.'

'Then let's go to mine tonight, pack up a few things, camp out there for a few days or until this whole thing blows over, then if she comes back she won't see him. She's here for the house, that's all she wants. She didn't even mention Elliot.'

Isla sniffed and looked up at him. 'She didn't, did she? God, that makes my heart ache a little. How can she just not care about him?'

'Because she's a cold-hearted bitch. She's here for the money, that's it.'

'I haven't got any of that either. I have around three thousand in my account and with careful planning I can make that last until the new year. I have nothing to give her.'

'I know, it's OK, we'll sort this. We can speak to a solicitor tomorrow, get some advice. Don't worry.'

Isla couldn't stop the tears from falling. What a complete mess. But Leo was right, if Sadie was here for Elliot, she would have mentioned him, asked about him, asked to see him. The only thing she cared about was the house and that made Isla feel a tiny bit better.

'Please don't cry.' Leo cupped her face, wiping the tears from her cheeks with his thumbs. 'I'm going to take care of this.' He kissed each eye, capturing the tears on his lips. He kissed her cheeks where the tears had run down her face and then he gave her a brief kiss on the lips. Her breath caught at the sweet, tender intimacy and she looked up into his eyes. He pulled back slightly, his eyes searching her face, and then he kissed her again and this time he didn't stop.

※※※

Oh god, the taste of her was complete heaven. This was everything that had been missing in his life for the last four years.

He hadn't meant for this to happen now. He had just been trying to comfort her. One little kiss of friendship to say that it would be OK. But now he was kissing her, he just couldn't stop. The timing couldn't be worse, she was upset, this was not how he imagined them reconnecting again after all this time. But Isla seemed to be as into this kiss as he was, wrapping her arms round his neck, sliding her tongue inside his mouth, pressing her warm body against his.

He pinned her against the wall, but the movement of it caused her to catch her breath, letting out a little gasp against his lips.

'Leo,' she whispered.

God, his name on her lips was like a song calling him home. He moved to kiss her again but she pressed her hand gently against his chest, stopping him.

Crap. This was all wrong. He couldn't have picked a worse moment to kiss her.

'Sorry, I didn't mean to—'

She stroked his face. 'Don't be sorry. I just can't right now, my head is a complete mess and I don't know what I'm going to do about this whole Sadie situation. Just… hold that thought for a few days.'

'I will, I promise. Come and stay with me at Maple Cottage for a few days, then we don't have this worry of Sadie turning up and seeing Elliot. If she wants to pursue this, she needs to go through the courts, get a solicitor, do it properly, not turn up on your doorstep and be all aggressive. You don't need to put up with that crap. Stay at mine until we can sort it out.'

Isla nodded. 'Let me go and grab a few things.'

Leo stepped back and watched her go upstairs. He moved into the kitchen and tidied everything away and loaded the dishwasher. Heading up to the first floor, he saw Isla was finishing off packing some clothes into a bag so he crept into Elliot's room. He was fast asleep, starfishing across the bed. Once Elliot was asleep you could pretty much do anything with him and he wouldn't notice. It was cold outside so Leo wrapped Elliot up in his duvet and then scooped him up in his arms. Elliot stirred slightly, his eyes fluttering open for a second before he drifted back off again. Leo looked around. It seemed like Isla had already been in here to grab some of his clothes as the drawers were open but he spotted Elliot's favourite cuddly rabbit so he picked that up too and then carried him down to the car. He plopped him in his booster seat and somehow managed to get the seatbelt around him without unwrapping him from the duvet.

He stood back up just as Isla was coming out of the house with two bags and a rucksack of Elliot's toys, followed by Luke. He moved to take them off her and she went back to lock up the house. He stowed the bags in the boot and they both got in the car, Luke curling up on the back seat next to a sleeping Elliot.

It was only a short distance to Maple Cottage and soon they were doing the whole thing again in reverse, Leo carrying Elliot to the room he always slept in whenever he stayed there, which Leo had painted with spaceships and planets. He tucked Elliot into the bed and Luke dutifully curled up right by his feet again.

When Leo walked back into the hall, Isla was waiting for him. 'Is he OK?'

'He's fast asleep and none the wiser. It'll be a nice surprise for him when he wakes up tomorrow.'

Isla smiled. 'Thanks for having us over.'

'You're very welcome, any time.'

'I feel wrecked, like I've just run a marathon. Think I'll just go to bed and then hopefully tomorrow, once I have a clearer head, we can decide on what we're going to do. Thank you for being there tonight.'

'I'm always here for you,' Leo said.

She stepped forward and wrapped her arms around him, resting her head on his chest. He held her there for the longest time. At least she wasn't crying now – being here obviously made her feel calmer – but he was happy to hold her as long as she needed.

Eventually, after they'd stood there for a few minutes, it was quite obvious she wasn't letting him go any time soon.

He decided to throw caution to the wind. 'Let's go to bed.'

She didn't even hesitate, she just nodded against him.

He took her hand and led her down the hall into his bedroom.

Christ. His heart was already in his mouth, remembering the last time she had been in his bedroom. He knew nothing was going to happen tonight, she wasn't in the right frame of mind for that, but he was very happy to just hold her.

She stared at the bed for a moment. Was she remembering that wonderful night as vividly as he was?

'My pyjamas are in the bag downstairs,' Isla said. 'I'll just go and grab them.'

'Borrow one of my t-shirts,' Leo said, not wanting her to leave and then change her mind.

'OK.'

He grabbed a t-shirt and passed it to her. He expected her to go into the en-suite to get changed but she started getting undressed right in front of him.

He tried to look away.

'Why are you embarrassed?' Isla laughed. 'You've seen me naked before.'

'Yes, I have,' his eyes flitted back to her of their own accord. 'And I've forgotten how glorious it was.'

She smiled and pulled the t-shirt over her, hiding her wonderful body from view, before climbing into bed.

He quickly got undressed too.

'Do you want me to shield my eyes as well?' Isla said.

He was glad to see she was still smiling after tonight's events. 'No, feast away,' Leo said, striking a pose.

She laughed.

He pulled on pyjama bottoms, switched off the light and climbed into bed next to her, immediately pulling her into his arms. She snuggled against him.

It was weird that they were able to do this with such ease. They'd never done this before. One incredible night that neither of them had mentioned again, three years during which they saw each other occasionally, but as soon as she had moved to Sandcastle Bay they had been almost inseparable. Maybe it was that they both needed each other after Matthew's death. Or maybe, if they'd given each other a chance all those years before, they would always have been this close. He wasn't sure what was going to happen between them now. He was pretty sure she loved him, and he damned well loved her, though neither of them had said those words. He still felt it was wrong somehow that he should benefit like this from Matthew's death, especially as he was at least partly to blame. But maybe he had paid his dues. He had looked after Isla and Elliot as if they were his own family. Surely Matthew would be happy to see that. Maybe it was time to find happiness again, to follow the light out of the darkness.

Isla sighed in his arms. 'Tomorrow I need to speak to a solicitor and I need to talk to Karie about all this and I'd be lying if I said I wasn't scared. But right now this is exactly what I need.'

He stroked his hand down her hair and she looked up at him. The moonlight was streaming through the window and she looked magical. God, he wanted her here in his bed every night, this was where she belonged.

She leaned up and kissed him briefly on the lips. 'And this, I really need this.' She kissed him again and he damned well kissed her back. He tightened his arms around her, pulling her on top of him, feeling her warmth in every fibre of his body, filling him with a happiness he hadn't felt in a long time. He stroked his hands down her back, desperate to touch her but not wanting to take this too far. This was heaven, it was everything he ever wanted.

The kiss continued and this time she showed no sign of wanting him to stop. He rolled her, pinning her to the mattress as she held him close with her arms and legs wrapped round him. Right then, he didn't care if he went to hell for this kiss, he wanted her, and for once he was going to follow his heart.

CHAPTER 11

Isla woke the next day wrapped tightly in Leo's arms as she lay on his bare chest. She kept her eyes closed, enjoying the moment of bliss for a few minutes, not ready to face the world yet. Because right here in Leo's arms, she could pretend everything was perfect in the world. This was where she was supposed to be. If she kept her eyes closed she could stay in this heaven forever and not have to face the stress of talking to solicitors and social services about Sadie's return.

She heard a noise next to her, a shuffling, and her eyes flew open. There was Elliot, standing next to the bed, his eyes wide as he contemplated the scene before him. Her heart leapt in panic as she tried to see it through his eyes. Isla and Leo, lying half naked in bed together, wrapped in each other's arms as if they had spent the night in the throes of passion, even though nothing had happened other than a kiss, one incredible kiss. How could she even begin to explain this to him?

She just had to act normal.

'Morning, beautiful boy,' Isla said, her usual greeting for him, though her voice had taken on an edge of panic.

'Why are we at Leo's house?' Elliot said.

'I thought we could have a sleepover. You like sleeping over at Leo's house,' Isla said. She was glad he had led with that question; it showed he wasn't that bothered about finding them in bed together. It was going to be OK.

'Why are you in bed with Leo?'

Crap.

She felt Leo stir and stretch beneath her as he woke.

'Oh hey buddy, how you doing?' Leo said, his voice sounding a lot calmer than hers at Elliot finding them together.

'Elliot was just wondering why we are in bed together,' Isla said.

'Because Isla was a bit sad last night and needed a cuddle,' Leo said, without any hesitation.

She smiled. It was the truth and it was very simple.

Elliot nodded, then frowned. 'Why were you sad?'

'It's OK, I'm not sad any more,' Isla lied. 'Why don't you brush your teeth and then we can have pancakes for breakfast.'

'Yes! I love pancakes!' Elliot ran from the room.

Isla looked up at Leo and cringed. 'I can't believe he caught us in bed together.'

Leo shrugged. 'We weren't doing anything, just hugging, he's seen us hug plenty of times before. Besides, he's probably going to have to get used to us sleeping in the same bed together.'

Her heart leapt. 'Are we going to do this again?'

His eyes searched her face as he stroked his hands down her back. 'Well, when we get married we will.'

She laughed. 'And we should probably practise for that.'

'I think that's a good idea,' he said. 'We need to know who lies where and other such important details.'

'Yes, those are things we need to sort out before we walk down the aisle.'

'And as you're staying here for the next few days I think it makes sense to practise tonight as well.'

'I agree.'

He smiled. 'Well, as much as I'd like to stay here all day, we have pancakes to make.'

'Urgh, can we just stay here? I don't want to face everything I have to do today to sort out the mess Sadie has created.'

'We're going to do this together, you're not in this alone,' Leo said.

'You have to work.'

'I have people who work for the company who can take care of stuff for me. You're more important.'

'You don't even have an assistant. Maybe I can do a few hours this afternoon—'

'*This* is more important, you don't need to worry. Emails can wait, phone calls can go to answerphone. A few days isn't going to make any difference to my company. Besides, I have more business than I can handle, I don't think a few missed calls is going to hurt me. Sort this out, take the time you need.'

She sighed and nodded.

'I need to talk to Karie. I guess this means my adoption hearing will be postponed.' Her voice caught. This was spectacularly unfair. All she wanted was to give a loving home to her nephew, to give him stability. She had been fighting for the last year to give him that and, just when it finally looked they were going to get it, Sadie had to return like the Wicked Witch of the West.

'We are going to fix this, I promise. She's not interested in Elliot, and the stuff with the house is a pain, but we'll sort it.'

'I know.'

'Do you think we should tell Elliot about Sadie?' Leo asked.

'I don't know. Part of me thinks we shouldn't say anything. I want to keep everything normal for him. I don't want to worry or confuse him. He has no memory of her, he was only one when she left. If all this blows over then he doesn't even need to meet her, but my heart says this is not going to be as simple as we would like. Maybe I should prepare him rather than suddenly landing it on him.'

'Why don't we see what Karie says about it? I'm sure she's seen this kind of thing before,' Leo said.

'Really? Our situation is a little more complex than most.'

'It's not straightforward, no, but I'm sure Karie will know what to do for the best.'

'I hope so,' she sighed and kissed his chest. 'Come on, we have pancakes to make.'

She got out of bed and threw some clothes on, deciding she'd have a shower after breakfast.

Isla padded downstairs, followed by Leo, and she saw that Elliot was busy drawing a picture at the table, his wax crayons moving furiously over the page.

She poured three glasses of juice and took one over to Elliot.

'What are you drawing a picture of, honey?' Isla asked, leaning over him and kissing him on the forehead. She took a sip of her orange juice.

Elliot leaned back so she could see and she nearly choked on her juice. There was a picture of two stickpeople in bed together, the blonde one lying on top of the man. But the pink he had used for the bodies made it look like both of them were naked.

'It's for Agatha,' Elliot said, simply.

'You know, that's such a beautiful picture, I'd love to have it on our wall at home,' Isla tried.

Leo leaned over to look at the picture too, his eyes widening and a huge grin spreading on his face.

'Good job, buddy. Why don't we stick that up on my fridge for now, then you can take it with you when you go home.'

Elliot handed it over to Leo and watched as he pinned it up on his fridge. 'Are we going home today?'

'We're going to be staying with Leo for a few days,' Isla said, hoping that Elliot wouldn't ask why.

His face lit up with excitement. 'Are we moving in with him? Marigold said we would.'

'Um, no, just staying for a little while,' Isla said as Leo started getting the pancakes ready.

'Oh.' His little face fell slightly. And then it fell even more. 'Are we going to be here for Halloween?'

'Maybe. We have a few… problems with the house. So we might be here for a few days.'

'But you promised we would decorate the house for Halloween,' Elliot said.

'I know I did, honey, but maybe we can decorate your room here instead. We can make the whole room Halloween-themed with spiders and bats and pumpkins and whatever you like. Would that be OK? I even saw some spooky-looking duvet covers in town, we could go and buy them for the bed too.'

'The ones with the ghosts that glow in the dark?' Elliot said, excitedly, his mood changing again.

'Yes, those.'

'Yay! Those are super cool.'

Crisis averted.

'We have the golden acorn hunt this morning. I'm so excited. If we find all the acorns we win some chocolate,' Elliot said.

Ah crap. She had promised she'd take him to that. Before she got a job and before Sadie turned up wreaking havoc over their lives. Now she felt like she had a ton of stuff to sort out this morning.

'I'm not sure—' Isla started.

'You should go,' Leo said. 'Keep everything normal, remember.'

'But—'

'I will sort out the house stuff,' Leo said, his reply hopefully vague enough for Elliot not to understand. 'Why not give Karie a call and see if she can come round here this afternoon?'

Leo was being remarkably calm about this.

Isla looked at Elliot and he looked back at her with wide hopeful eyes. She didn't want to let him down but sorting out this mess with Karie had to take priority.

'Elliot, I really need to see Karie today. I'll call her and see when she can meet me. If she can do this afternoon then I'll definitely take you to the acorn hunt this morning, but if she can only do this morning, would you mind going with Melody or Nanny instead?'

He looked a little disappointed by that but nodded anyway.

She hated Sadie a little bit more right then.

The sooner they could get this sorted and get her out of their lives the better.

As it happened, Karie wasn't able to meet Isla until that afternoon. Leo had heard Isla briefly explaining over the phone that Sadie had come back. The swearing that Leo could hear from the other end was neither professional nor ladylike, but it had made him smile to hear that kind of passion for their case. Karie wanted Elliot to stay with Isla as much as they did. It had been Karie who had been pushing the judge towards an adoption rather than a guardianship, which was what Isla currently had. She would fight for them, he knew that.

Leo had packed Isla and Elliot off on the golden acorn hunt and then sat down to make some phone calls.

Kim Nash was one of the best solicitors around. She had looked over the deeds to Isla's house when Matthew had first died, in the hope that Isla would inherit the house fully. Although there was nothing Kim could do to remove Sadie's name from the deeds, she was confident that, if it went to court, the judge would not give Sadie half the value of the house. Leo knew he had to call her now to get some advice on how to proceed and get her to take their case should it get that far.

He picked up his phone to call her but it rang before he could dial out. It was Thomas, his godfather.

That was odd. Thomas never called him. He would be at work right now too. He ran his own law firm on the far side of the village, which sounded a lot grander than it was, the firm being just Thomas and his wife, who was his secretary. But as far as Leo knew he was always very busy. Leo quickly answered the phone.

'Thomas, are you OK?'

'I'm fine, son. Listen, do you have half an hour to come in and see me?'

'I, um… not really. I—'

'You're busy, I know. Sadie Norton has just been in to see me.'

His heart missed a beat. 'I'm on my way.'

Leo strode into the office a few minutes later and Jeannie, his godmother, came round to greet him, hugging him and giving him a kiss on the cheek.

'Go on in dear, he's waiting for you.'

He walked into the little office where Thomas was sitting at his desk. His godfather gestured for him to sit down. Leo watched him carefully. He looked… tired. Christ, he hoped he wasn't ill. Or maybe it was just so many years in the job wearing him down. He was always busy with clients from the village. He had a kind, grandfatherly approach which many of the villagers liked. Although back in the day, Leo knew he'd had a bit of a reputation for being a bit of a dragon. He had clearly mellowed with age. There was no dragon in him now, more of a… newt than anything else.

'Sadie Norton came in to see me about an hour ago,' Thomas said, not bothering with any preliminaries. 'Asked if I would take her case and help her to get her house back.'

'I hope you told her where to go,' Leo said.

'I did nothing of the sort,' Thomas said.

Leo stared at him in shock. 'You took her case?'

'I did.'

'But why?'

'Because someone has to.'

'It doesn't have to be you,' Leo protested. He couldn't believe this. He'd always liked Thomas, he had many qualities, and loyalty had always been one of them.

'If it wasn't me she would have gone to someone else,' Thomas said.

'So?'

'It could be someone far savvier and gung-ho than I am.'

Leo's anger faded away slightly.

'I'm sixty-four, Leo. I've been doing this job since I was a lot younger than you. When I first became a solicitor I was passionate, I cared, I wanted to fight the good fight. I read every article, every paper, every book that I could get my hands on.'

'You had an excellent reputation in the village and beyond,' Leo said and then inwardly winced that he'd used the word *had*.

'I suppose if you do any job long enough you become jaded and tired. I've fought on the wrong side too many times. I've fought for cases where I didn't think what I was fighting for was right. I've helped wives screw over their husbands and husbands screw over their wives. I can't say I'm particularly proud of my life as a solicitor. I probably should have given it up a long time ago.'

'I think a lot of people in the village would have missed you if you had,' Leo said.

'I've been spending more time down the allotment lately than I have here. I'm supposed to retire in six months but Jeannie and I have been talking over the weekend. I'm sure you've heard about Annie and Bill going off on this world cruise? Well, we've decided to shut up shop, close the business and start enjoying our retirement now too. We've even talked about going to Florida for Christmas. Anyway, we were coming in for the next few weeks to tie up all loose ends, let all of our clients know, sort out any paperwork. I had no intention of taking on any new clients. But when Sadie walked in here this morning, I felt sure taking her case was absolutely the right thing.'

Leo still wasn't entirely sure he followed.

'I'm not a good solicitor, Leo. I was, but I'm not any more, because I simply don't care enough. Taking her case means I will do the bare minimum instead of fighting to win like some other solicitors.' Thomas cleared his throat. 'It also means I can give her advice that maybe another solicitor wouldn't.'

Leo's eyebrows shot up. 'But that's—'

'Unethical, completely unprofessional? I could lose my licence? Yes, you're right. But maybe I can fight for something good and right for a change. Isla keeping that house is the right thing. Hand on heart, if Sadie was to go to court with any solicitor, any half decent judge wouldn't give her half the value of the house and I told her that. She paid two thousand pounds towards the deposit of the house and Matthew paid three thousand. She didn't work in the months after they bought it because she was looking after Elliot so she didn't contribute to any of the bills and then she left. I also know that she stole four thousand pounds from her and Matthew's joint account to go to Australia. She doesn't know I know that, but Matthew came to see me after she left to ask about removing her name from the deeds and he told me all this. But that's something you might want to tell your solicitor, make sure the judge is aware of it too.'

Leo didn't know whether to be a bit disappointed that Thomas was not a good solicitor or be relieved and pleased that he was on their side. He'd always respected him for being an upstanding member of the community, but maybe loyalty was a much worthier attribute to be respected.

'Honestly, I don't think she has a cat in hell's chance,' Thomas went on. 'Especially as there is a child involved. Selling the house would effectively make Isla and Elliot homeless and the judge would take that into consideration. And Elliot is Sadie's son.

That looks even worse for her. I'll do everything I can to get the best result for you. Taking her case means I can also keep you in the loop as well. But you understand that you can't tell anyone about this meeting, about anything we've discussed. My name will probably be mud anyway in this village for taking the case but I can't tell anyone why – my reputation will be in tatters if I do, and I'd quite like to retire gracefully.'

'You have my word. But can I tell Isla? I'm sure she will be relieved to know you're fighting on our side,' Leo said.

'Yes, but make it clear it can't go any further.'

Leo nodded. 'So what happens now?'

'I've told Sadie to think about it. I've told her my fees and she wasn't impressed but I know I'm the cheapest in the area. I explained that going to court is going to be a long and expensive battle and I don't think she's here for the long term. I've told her to think about considering an out-of-court settlement, my fees for that would be a lot less. But I think you would have to offer her a fairly decent amount to agree to have her name taken off the deeds. If we went to court the judge might award her anywhere between ten and twenty-five percent and I told her that as well. Well, I told her she might get ten percent if she was lucky.'

Leo smirked slightly at the underhand tactics.

'We have another issue,' Leo said, the smile falling off his face. 'We're worried about Elliot. We're moving to formally adopt him but this could throw a spanner in the works. We really need her to agree to give parental responsibility to Isla.'

Thomas pulled a face. 'She could use that as leverage.'

'Did she mention him at all?' Leo asked.

'No, she didn't, so I can't see that's a priority for her. But once she knows that's an issue for you guys she might try to push for more money. Maybe I'll mention that she'll have to start paying child maintenance if she doesn't sign over parental responsibility.'

'I think Isla would quite like it if we didn't mention Elliot at all. She doesn't want Sadie anywhere near him.'

'OK, maybe I'll add that in at the end of the process. Who are you going to get to represent you?'

Leo felt bad that he hadn't thought of Thomas, but he'd considered him to be soft and with a good heart when it came to his cases, whereas Kim was the hard-assed, take-no-prisoners sort that would grab a case by the jugular. Exactly what he needed to fight Sadie.

'Kim Nash.'

'Ah, I like her, she reminds me of me in my youth. I think it's best that any further contact will be between me and her so you won't hear from me, but I may contact you surreptitiously with any updates you need to know.' He tapped his nose. 'Keep it under your hat.'

'I will, thanks Thomas.'

He nodded and Leo stood up and shook his hand. 'We'll sort this out and hopefully Sadie will disappear back off to where she came from.'

'Let's hope so.'

Leo left, feeling slightly better about this nightmare already.

CHAPTER 12

Isla hurried along the beach to meet Melody and Tori for the golden acorn hunt – or rather she was dragged along by Elliot, who was beyond excited.

She couldn't help thinking she should be doing something to deal with this Sadie situation rather than going out and enjoying herself. But Leo had insisted that she take Elliot to the acorn hunt, practically pushing her out the house. She knew he didn't want her to worry and he was trying to ease some of that stress by taking care of the solicitors himself. Although she was quite capable of dealing with that on her own, she was pretty happy to share the load, and she had enough on her plate at the moment trying to sort out what they would do about the adoption.

Ahead of her on the beach, she saw Melody and Jamie, Tori and Aidan, Emily and her daughter Marigold, Agatha and Isla's mum Carolyn. Isla forced a smile on her face as she approached. Melody and Tori greeted her with a kiss and hug and Carolyn embraced her too.

Melody gathered her nephew up in a big hug. 'Are you ready for the acorn hunt, little man?'

'Have you seen the prizes? If we find all the acorns we get a chocolate one. Leo says I'm to keep my eyes peeled,' Elliot said, holding his eyes wide open with his fingers.

'We're going to make sure that we find all those acorns. We have the map, we have our fabulous team, are you ready to get going?' Melody asked.

'YES!' Elliot cheered.

'Go and say hello to Marigold,' Melody said, gesturing towards Elliot's best friend who was a little way ahead and already studiously looking at the map with Emily. She put him down and he raced over to join them. The kids dragged Emily ahead of the group as they searched for the golden acorn cards that were hidden among the trees.

'You OK?' Melody said to Isla. 'You look like you haven't slept.'

Isla knew she had slept only a few hours the night before, partly because she was so worried and partly because she had spent many hours kissing Leo like her life depended on it. She smiled slightly at that wonderful memory.

'She hasn't slept because she spent the night at Leo's last night,' Agatha said, waggling her eyebrows mischievously. 'And my spies tell me that the light in the guest room that Isla normally sleeps in didn't come on all night.'

Isla stared at her in shock. How could she possibly know that? And then she remembered that Elsie West from the chemist, one of Agatha's best friends, lived opposite Leo. But surely she hadn't been watching the house that closely over the last year that she would know which room Isla normally slept in when she stayed over?

Melody and Tori's faces lit up at this exciting news. Even Carolyn seemed delighted.

Isla decided to try to change the subject. 'And have your spies told you that Sadie Norton is back in town?'

All of their smiles disappeared. They all knew what that meant: Elliot's adoption, her house, it was all up in the air now.

'Normally the town grapevine is a lot better at keeping us informed.' Melody looked at Agatha accusingly. But Agatha shrugged; she clearly hadn't heard either.

'When did she arrive?' Carolyn asked.

'Last night. She came to my house,' Isla said.

'What does she want?' Tori said as they started making their way down the beach, the kids racing on ahead.

'At the moment she just wants the house but I'm scared she'll want to see Elliot. I'm petrified she'll fall in love with him if she does.'

'She left because she had no interest in being a mum,' Aidan said.

'And she was completely useless at being a mum when she was here,' Jamie said.

'But what if she left because she couldn't cope with the sleepless nights and the crying?' Isla said. 'I know Matthew found that first year hard, any parent would. But Elliot is past all that now and he's cute and funny and kind and wonderful. What happens if she meets him and sees how amazing he is and wants to be part of his life again?'

God, the thought of that almost brought her back to tears again. She couldn't lose him and she had no idea what Karie was going to say about it all this afternoon, although she hadn't been particularly overjoyed by the news when Isla had phoned her earlier.

'That's not going to happen, dear,' Agatha said, all humour vanished now. 'There's no judge in the land that would award sole custody to a woman who has been absent from Elliot's life for four years.'

Isla liked her optimism but she knew that wasn't necessarily the case. The reason that the adoption had taken so long to go through was because the powers that be didn't want to strip the parental responsibility from Sadie. In their eyes, the fact that she was Elliot's mother superseded everything and everyone else. According to the authorities, taking Sadie's maternal rights away would be a violation of her human rights, despite the fact that she had abandoned Elliot completely.

'You know Leo has a plan to take you to Canada if Sadie ever returned?' Jamie said.

'I know, bless him, and I'm very very tempted to say to hell with it, throw our belongings in a suitcase and follow him to the Canadian wilds, but I don't think running away is the answer.'

'Then hide him away,' Carolyn said, a note of panic entering her voice. 'Don't let her see him.'

'That's part of the reason we are staying at Leo's for a few days. But I'm not keeping him locked in the house. If the house business goes to court Sadie could be here for weeks or months, and at some point Karie will need to discuss giving me parental responsibility with her. Now Sadie's crawled out of her hole, she's going to have to give consent before the adoption will be allowed to go ahead. Even if she does have no interest in him, I can't see her handing that over willingly, not without some kind of monetary compensation.'

'God, what a mess,' Tori said.

'I know.'

Carolyn took her arm and gave it a squeeze. 'If there's anything I can do, you just need to ask.'

'Thanks, Mum.'

'Even if it's money for tickets to Canada.'

Isla smiled. 'I'll bear that in mind.'

'I can always set Dobby on her,' Jamie said and Isla smiled at the thought of Jamie's pet turkey chasing Sadie down the street.

'Very tempting,' Isla said. 'Leo is going to talk to a solicitor this morning and I'm talking to Karie, my social worker, this afternoon so we will have a better idea where we stand then. Until then we are acorn hunting.'

Melody looked like she was going to ask her more questions but Isla stilled her with a hand on her arm. 'Can we talk about something else? If I think about it too much I will break down again and I really don't want Elliot to see me cry.'

Melody squeezed her hand and nodded.

'Tori, I meant to ask, how was your scan?' Isla said, hoping to change the subject completely.

Tori's face filled with happiness. 'It was amazing, we could see his hands, his head, his heartbeat. I'm pretty much in love with him already.'

'Him?' Isla asked.

'The nurse wouldn't tell us but there was a trainee with her and she was asking lots of questions and the trainee mentioned *he* and *him* several times while they were looking so we think it might be.' Tori looked over at Aidan with an expression of complete love on her face. 'Can you imagine a little boy that looks like him?'

Isla smiled with happiness for her.

Elliot came running back to them then with Marigold at his side.

'We found an acorn!' he said. 'It's hanging from the tree over there.'

'Good job. OK, we need to take a photo of it as evidence,' Isla said.

'Mummy hasn't got her phone,' Marigold said.

'Here, we can use mine,' Jamie said.

Marigold took his hand and ran over towards the trees.

'So you're staying at Leo's for a few days?' Agatha said to Elliot, openly fishing for gossip again.

'Yes, because we have problems with the house and because Isla is sad. Last night Isla was so sad she had to have a cuddle in bed with Leo,' Elliot said and Isla couldn't help but burst out laughing at being dropped in it by her nephew. Nothing stayed private in this village.

'Oh, did she?' Agatha said, smiling at Isla knowingly. 'That's interesting.'

'She was lying on his chest this morning like he was a big squishy pillow,' Elliot continued, pleased to be the bearer of such exciting news. Isla knew her face was burning bright red but she couldn't help but smile at Elliot's excitement.

'That's very interesting,' Agatha said.

Melody giggled.

'What else happened?' Agatha asked.

'We had pancakes for breakfast.'

Isla grinned at his priorities.

'What did you have on your pancakes?' Carolyn asked, clearly trying to help Isla out of this embarrassing hole.

'Bananas and maple syrup,' Elliot said. 'We always have maple syrup when we go to Leo's house because he lives in Maple Cottage.'

Isla smirked at that logic, although they did drink a lot of hot chocolate at Hot Chocolate Cottage so maybe there was some truth in it, after all.

'Anything else happen between Isla and Leo?' Agatha fished. It was obvious she was trying to get the subject back on track before they moved on to other pancake toppings.

Elliot thought about this for a moment. 'No. He did hug her for a really long time before we came to the acorn hunt and then he kissed her on the cheek and then on the lips and Isla stroked his cheek and said she was really looking forward to tonight.'

Oh god. He really was going to tell Agatha every single detail.

Tori and Aidan laughed.

'And what's happening tonight?' Agatha asked.

'Isla said that we would decorate my bedroom for Halloween,' Elliot said.

'That's right, we are,' Isla said. 'Now, shall we have a look at that map and see where the next acorn is supposed to be?'

She was hoping she could change the subject, but the cat was already out of the bag now.

'Do you think Isla will be having cuddles with Leo in his bed again?' Agatha said, rubbing her hands together with visible glee.

Elliot shrugged. 'Probably. They do like to hug quite a lot. And this morning when they were in bed and I was brushing my teeth I heard them say they would need to practise for when they get married.'

Oh my god. He had heard that too? She had told Leo off the night before for giving Elliot false promises and then he'd heard her talking about getting married as well.

'Oh honey, we were just joking, just being silly,' Isla said. Maybe they would need to start communicating in a foreign language while little ears were around. Her French was quite good, she wondered if Leo spoke any French.

'This just keeps getting better and better,' Agatha said.

'Marigold said you were cuddling in bed because you love each other, is that true?' Elliot said.

'We both care about each other a great deal,' Isla said, carefully. She didn't want to encourage him into thinking this was going to lead to marriage and happy ever afters, and she didn't want to encourage Agatha either.

'And you love each other like you love chocolate?'

Isla smiled. 'Yes, something like that.'

'Marigold says that adults who love each other cuddle in bed a lot. Will you be cuddling Leo in bed again tonight?'

It seemed the whole group waited with bated breath for her answer. Isla cleared her throat. 'We might be.'

Carolyn suppressed a laugh. Melody gave a little squeal. Agatha clapped her hands together with joy.

'Or we might not,' Isla tried. 'See how we feel.'

'If you feel sad again?' Elliot said, taking her hand.

'Or happy, sometimes it's nice to cuddle when we're happy.'

'Cuddling can make men and women very happy,' Agatha said, cryptically.

Jamie came back over, holding hands with Marigold again. 'Do I want to know what you guys are talking about?'

Melody shook her head.

'Where's the next acorn?' Isla said, deciding this was enough for Elliot to hear for now.

'I don't know, I'll look at the map,' Elliot said.

'Oh, take Agatha with you, she's desperate to find the acorns too,' Isla said.

'Oh no…' Agatha tried but Elliot was already grabbing her hand and tugging her along the beach to join Emily and Marigold.

'Aren't you worried what Elliot will tell her?' Tori asked.

'I think he's already told her all of it,' Isla said.

Carolyn linked arms with her. 'So, is this… is something really happening between you two?'

Isla sighed. 'I don't know what it is. Yesterday I thought there was no hope and then last night he comes round and tells me he has feelings for me too.'

'He said he loved you?' Tori asked.

'No, he didn't say that.'

'Of course he didn't,' Aidan said dryly. 'I apologise for my brother, he has trouble expressing his emotions.'

'I know. And now I have no idea if those feelings are just lust or something more.' She really needed to talk to him.

'So you spent the night together?' Melody nudged.

'No, well yes, but not like that. I was so upset after Sadie left and Leo was trying to comfort me and he was holding me and telling me it was going to be OK and then suddenly we're kissing.'

Tori gasped and Melody let out a tiny squeal of excitement.

'What was it like?' Melody asked.

Isla sighed happily. 'As magical as the first time, better actually.'

'The first time?!' Tori said, incredulously. 'When was there a first time?'

Oh god. All the secrets were coming out today.

'There was a thing, once, many, many years ago,' Isla tried to dismiss it but she had everyone's interest now. 'It was one night.'

'Why did I not know this?' Tori asked. She turned to Aidan. 'Did you know this?'

He shook his head. 'No, but…'

'But what?' Melody said.

'There was a time that Leo stopped dating and seeing random women. I'd be at the pub with him and women would come up to him as normal, but he turned them all down. He wasn't interested, which was odd for him. When I asked him about it after a few beers, he said he was in love. But he wouldn't tell me who it was.

Though I did suspect it might have been you. This was around the time of Elliot's christening and on that day, when he was with you, I've never seen him so happy. Is that when it happened?'

Isla felt an ache in her heart as she nodded. 'The night before the christening.'

'But nothing ever happened between you after?' Tori asked.

'No, I just figured… I was one of many.'

'It was more than that,' Aidan said. 'You were different.'

'Leo said that too,' Isla said, quietly. Had she really thrown away her chance of being with this wonderful man all those years before? Had he really loved her? Was that love still there now?

'So last night you kissed at your house, went to Leo's and ended up in his bed?' Melody said.

'It was a comfort thing, we both knew that. I was a bit of a mess.'

'So nothing happened?'

'We kissed again. That was it. I don't know where I stand with him. I know he'd quite like to recreate that night four years ago but I don't know if it's more than that. I feel like he's holding back. I need to talk to him, preferably without little flapping ears who will repeat everything. You know what else Leo said to me last night? That he feels guilty for being with me because he feels like he's benefitting from Matthew's death. What kind of messed-up logic is that?'

'He blames himself for Matthew's death,' Jamie said.

There was silence for a few moments.

'What?' Isla said in shock.

Jamie winced. 'It's not my place to tell you that – he should tell you himself why he carries this guilt around with him – but it breaks my heart that he is holding himself back from living his life because of it. He was so messed up over our dad dying when we were kids, taking all that on himself, he went down a bad path for a while. I worried he would start to go the same way after Matthew died. Fortunately, he had you and Elliot to live for. You probably saved him more than you think. But I suggest you talk to him about it. He shouldn't keep it bottled up inside.'

'I will.'

She walked along in silence. There were quite a few things she wanted to talk to Leo Jackson about.

CHAPTER 13

The acorn hunt had taken a lot longer than Isla would have liked. Finding some of them around the village was like finding a needle in the haystack. So she arrived back at Leo's with only fifteen minutes left until Karie Matthews arrived.

She walked into Leo's to find him making lunch in the kitchen, singing to himself as he listened to the radio.

Luke ran past her to greet Elliot outside and she smiled as they romped around the garden together, despite the cold weather.

She turned back to Leo, who hadn't even noticed their arrival. 'Leo.'

He turned with a start and then his face split into a huge smile at seeing her. He moved towards her, cupped her face and kissed her briefly on the lips.

She frowned. She had no idea where she stood with this man. He smiled at her expression. 'Too soon?'

'I don't know. Probably not, seeing as we spent the whole night kissing in bed. I'm just not sure what this is.'

'It's a welcome home kiss.'

Home?

'Our relationship feels like it's suddenly progressed very quickly,' Isla said.

'Depends on your perspective. We've known each other for about five or six years.'

She smiled. He did have a point.

She glanced over at Elliot. Now was not the time to talk, especially as Karie would be here soon.

'You seem happy,' she said.

'I spent the night kissing the most incredible woman in my bed, that's a lot to be happy about. But actually I feel a bit more positive about the whole Sadie debacle.'

'I'm glad you do, I feel sick worrying about what Karie is going to say this afternoon. What's put you in such a good mood?'

'Well, I spoke to my solicitor, Kim, and not only is she really confident that Sadie wouldn't get half the value of the house should it go to court, but she also said she's happy to represent us against Sadie over custody of Elliot too. She doesn't think the judge could possibly award custody to a woman who abandoned her son. We had a long chat about it and she was really positive. Kim's a great solicitor, she's one of those "grab them by the balls" types. Also… batting for Sadie is my godfather Thomas.'

'What? Why?' Isla couldn't believe that. She'd met him several times and he always seemed nice, in a grandfatherly way. Surely, he didn't need the money so badly that he'd take any case?

'OK, you can't tell anyone this, but he's fighting for us and feels he can do it better from her side of the fence.'

She was stunned by that; it was such a risk for him. 'Wow. That's a big thing from him, he's been a solicitor for years, hasn't he?'

'Pretty much his entire adult life. He's retiring. I think he considers this his swan song.'

Isla smiled. This news did make her feel mildly better. Although her nerves came flooding back as she saw Karie coming up the drive.

Leo squeezed her shoulders. 'It's going to be OK.'

Isla nodded and then went to open the door. Karie greeted her with a small smile and a hug.

'It's OK, don't worry,' Karie said and Isla couldn't help the tears that formed in her eyes at her words. Karie knew how much Elliot meant to her. She also had the power to take Elliot from

her on the fact that she was fighting on their side made her feel
a little bit better.

'Can I get you a tea, Karie?' Leo said and Isla was relieved to
see that some of his nerves had returned too. It wasn't just her
being overdramatic.

'Yes please.'

Leo set about putting the kettle on and Karie gestured for Isla
to sit down at the dining table.

Isla looked out the window at Elliot but he was too busy
playing with Luke.

'So tell me what she said last night,' Karie said. 'Did she
mention Elliot at all?'

Isla shook her head. 'As far as I can tell she was only interested
in the house. You'd think, after four years of not seeing him, that
she would at least ask after him, even if she has no interest in
raising him. Even to be polite.'

Leo snorted, probably at the thought of Sadie being polite.

'OK, well this could be a lot more straightforward than we
thought. She might be more than willing to sign over parental
responsibility, especially if I mention that if she doesn't she would
be liable for child maintenance costs. If she gives her consent,
then the adoption can go through as planned.'

Isla liked that Karie thought it would all be that simple.
Although, in her heart, she knew that it wouldn't.

Leo brought the teas over and then sat down at the table with
them. 'What if she refuses? Her solicitor, I mean my solicitor…'
he quickly amended, 'thought that she would go after monetary
compensation to sign him over.'

Karie sniffed her disapproval. 'The sale of children is against
the law and she should not receive any money in return for
his adoption. That being said, I can see how she could easily
and legally incorporate that fee into the money she wants for
the house.'

'What if she wants custody?' Isla said, hating the wobble in her voice. Leo put his arm around her and kissed her head.

Karie didn't bat an eye at this sign of affection.

'Then we have a problem. But it's a bump in the road, that's all. I'm Elliot's social worker and my opinion would far outweigh anything she has to say. The judge will decide what is best for the child and being settled, happy, loved and well taken care of, as he is now, is going to be a priority for Elliot. It would be too disruptive for him to live with her when he has already lost his dad and has no memory of who she is. I would push for him staying with you and the judge will listen to that. It would stop the adoption going ahead and at worst I think he would award her regular visiting rights. Supervised visits at first but if she proves to be responsible then the supervision will stop, unless you can prove that she is abusive or alcohol or drugs are involved.'

'What about neglectful? Surely the fact that she abandoned him has to count for something?' Isla said.

'It will, but she could argue that she wasn't in the right frame of mind then, but she is in a much better place now. She could say that Matthew drove her away and he's not even here to defend himself. Her solicitor could advise her to come up with any cock and bull story to win the judge over.'

Isla felt relieved that Sadie's solicitor was Thomas. He would never suggest Sadie do something like that.

'This is all hypothetical, though,' Leo said. 'She has no interest in Elliot, she just wants the money. If I was coming back to fight for my son after four years away from him, those would be the first words out of my mouth, but she didn't even mention him.'

'No, I'd have to agree. Elliot is not a priority at all for her. I really need to talk to her,' Karie said.

'Do you have to?' Isla said, knowing that her protests were futile. 'I don't want to mention Elliot at all to her, then we can just focus on the house.'

'Getting her consent for the adoption is going to be the best thing for us now she's back,' Karie said. 'And our meeting will be solely about that, I won't mention her having custody at all. Do you know where she's staying?'

'Yes, Clover Hill Hotel,' Leo said. 'Her solicitor contacted mine this morning while I was there to give her the details. Her solicitor is Thomas Kent, he has an office just off the village green.'

Karie nodded. 'It might be a good idea if he was there in the meeting. Have you told Elliot anything about this?'

Isla shook her head. She was scared enough about Sadie wanting to see Elliot, she didn't think her heart could cope if Elliot wanted to see Sadie.

'I didn't know what the best thing would be to say to him. I don't want to confuse or worry him unnecessarily. I have no idea what Matthew even told him about her. Elliot's never mentioned her to me.'

'That makes it even trickier to bring it up,' Karie agreed. 'I still think Elliot should be told, or at least some of it.'

'Tell me what?' Elliot said, appearing at the back door. 'Is it something cool?'

'Hey Elliot, good to see you. Why don't you come over here and draw me a picture?' Karie said, pulling some paper and crayons from her bag with impeccable timing.

Elliot came running over, Luke hot on his heels. If there was one thing he loved it was drawing.

'What shall I draw?' Elliot asked, grabbing a blue crayon.

'How about a picture of your mum and dad?'

Isla waited, wondering what he would do.

Elliot thought about it for a moment and then got to work.

'Are you looking forward to Halloween?' Karie asked.

'Yes, especially the Trickle Treat.'

Isla smiled and didn't bother to correct him.

'And are you dressing up?'

'Yes, but it's a secret,' Elliot said, sticking his tongue out as he picked up a yellow crayon and started drawing hair on one of the stickmen.

'Is it?' Leo asked. 'I thought we were going as Batman and Robin?'

Elliot shook his head. 'I have a better idea. There, finished.'

He handed over his piece of paper with a flourish and Isla smiled at the blonde stickwoman and the two stickmen.

'Who are these?' Karie asked.

'That's Isla,' he pointed to the blonde woman. 'And that's Leo,' he pointed to one of the men who was holding the stickwoman's hand. 'And that's my real daddy,' he pointed to the other man.

God, her heart swelled with love for this little man. She looked at Leo's reaction at being labelled *daddy*. If anything, he seemed quite choked up by it.

'And what about your real mummy?' Karie asked, gently.

Elliot pulled a face as if he didn't really understand. 'Isla's my mummy.'

'Do you have any other mummies?' Karie tried again.

'Do you mean the lady that had me in her belly?'

'Yes.'

'Daddy said she left when I was very young. He said she couldn't be my mummy any more and she moved very far away.'

'Do you know anything else about her? Have you ever seen any photos?'

'No, but Marigold says she's not very nice and Emily thinks that me and Daddy had a lucky escape when she left. That's what Marigold told me. What does that mean?'

Karie smirked and Isla wondered how she would play this professionally.

'It means that you and Daddy were very lucky to have each other. Do you think that you'd like to meet her one day?'

'No. If she's not nice then I don't think I would like her very much.'

'No, fair point,' Karie said, smiling. 'Your mum might want to see you again one day but if she did then I would be there and probably Isla and Leo too. Would that be OK?'

Elliot shrugged. 'I suppose. Can I go and play in my room now?'

'Sure you can,' Isla said.

'Bye Karie, you can keep the picture,' Elliot said, racing out of the room.

'Thank you, but I think I might pin it up on Leo's fridge next to that very interesting picture that's already there.'

Isla looked up at the picture of her and Leo in bed that Elliot had drawn that morning and felt her cheeks flame red. 'That's—'

'That's absolutely none of my business,' Karie said. Smiling, she gave Isla a wink. 'I'll speak to Sadie and I'll get back to you.'

Isla stood up and hugged Karie goodbye. After she left she turned back to face Leo.

'Well, that sounded positive, didn't it?' she asked, wondering if she was just trying to convince herself.

'She doesn't think Sadie would get custody either, that's massively positive,' Leo said. 'And that's if Sadie even wants custody, which she clearly doesn't. But think about it, why would any judge give Elliot to someone he doesn't even know? They're not just going to take him off you and give him to her. He's settled here, happy, even Karie can see that.'

'No, you're right,' Isla said. She did feel slightly better after that meeting. 'Although I still don't feel happy that she'd get visiting rights.'

'If she had any interest in visiting Elliot, in being a part of his life at all, no matter how small, she would have stayed in touch. She's not going to stay here in Sandcastle Bay, not long term. My bet is she'll get the money from the house and run back to Australia or whichever hole she's crawled out from. She left because life in a small village wasn't enough for her, that's unlikely to have changed.'

Isla nodded, still not entirely sure it was going to be such smooth running as Leo and Karie thought.

'Look, why don't I go and speak to Sadie, off the record? No solicitors or social workers. I know her well from when she was with Matthew,' Leo said.

God, that was the last thing she wanted. Leo was so protective of her and Elliot, she didn't think any conversation between Leo and Sadie would be polite. He was likely to go in there like a bull in a china shop and what if his antagonistic attitude made Sadie defensive and angry? It was hardly going to have a positive result.

'I don't think that's a good idea,' Isla said, diplomatically. 'You were the one that said that she should get a solicitor and do this properly, I don't think confronting her behind their back is going to help.'

'I didn't say confront, I said talk. We used to get on OK. Maybe we don't need all these legal channels, maybe just a sensible conversation…' he trailed off as he could clearly see the doubt on her face. 'OK, maybe not.'

'I just don't want to do anything wrong. What if this goes to court and she claims we've been harassing her? I want to do everything by the book for now, and then if it all goes wrong then that cabin in Canada might be a serious option.'

He nodded. 'OK.'

She could see he wasn't happy with the decision so she cast around for a suitable change in subject. Her eyes fell on the picture of the two of them in bed. 'I can't believe she saw that picture.'

Leo grinned. 'There are no secrets around here.'

'No, and we really need to talk… about us, without flapping ears.' She looked across at the picture Elliot had drawn of his family. 'Though in Elliot's mind it's already a foregone conclusion. How do you feel about being called Daddy?'

Leo's smile was the only answer she needed. 'I love it. And I'm glad he drew me and Matthew. I can never replace Matthew and I wouldn't want to, but hopefully I can make a half decent substitute.'

'You're more than half decent in his eyes,' Isla said. 'And in mine.'

He frowned as if he didn't believe her. 'I'm not but I'm trying to be.'

'You don't have to try to be anything, you're already a wonderful man,' Isla said, resting her hands on his chest. He wrapped his hands round her waist and leaned his forehead against hers.

'Isla—'

'Are we having lunch soon, my tummy's rumbling,' Elliot said as he ran back into the kitchen with Luke trailing in his wake. 'Luke says he's hungry too.'

'Well, we can't have that.' Leo stepped back out of Isla's embrace, giving her a wink and turning back to the food he had been preparing before Karie arrived. 'Let's see what we have.'

Isla watched them as Elliot stood next to Leo and helped put food onto plates. They were going to have that conversation at some point but maybe now, with everything that was happening with Sadie, wasn't the best time.

CHAPTER 14

Leo had popped into work that afternoon while Isla and Elliot had spent the time decorating Elliot's bedroom with all kinds of Halloween paraphernalia. She felt bad that on her second day at her new job she hadn't even made it into the office, but Leo insisted that she stayed with Elliot. She had compromised a little and had answered quite a few of the emails that had come into The Big Bang account while helping Elliot make some of the decorations.

Melody rang just as Luke was attempting to attack the spider conkers they'd made for the end of Elliot's bed.

'Hello,' Isla said, laughing as Elliot made the spider crawl up her arm.

'Are you free tonight?' Melody said, sounding a bit rushed and nervous. Or was it excited? 'Please say yes.'

'Um, yes, do you want to come over?'

'No, Jamie and I are having a meal at the Golden Bridge tonight, we're inviting all of our friends and family.'

The Golden Bridge was a very classy and glamorous place to eat on the cliff tops just outside the village. Isla had been in there a few times for coffee but never to eat. It struck her as the kind of place you went to for very special occasions. Her heart leapt. 'Is it... a special occasion?'

'I can't say, will you come?'

Oh god, her little sister had got engaged, that's what this was, surely.

'Of course.'

'Emily has said Elliot is welcome to come round and have a sleepover with Marigold tonight and Luke as well, so you don't need to worry about coming back early.'

'Oh great, Elliot will love that. But isn't Emily coming to the Golden Bridge too?'

'She is, Stanley is looking after the kids. Apparently, Marigold has already insisted they are going to watch *Beauty and the Beast*.'

'Elliot, want a sleepover with Marigold tonight?'

'Yay!' Elliot said, leaping onto the bed and punching the air. Isla laughed. 'I think that's a yes.'

'Can Luke come too?'

'He normally does when you sleep over with Marigold,' Isla said. Elliot was obviously happy with this and went back to his Halloween decorations as Isla carried on talking to Melody. 'OK, what time?'

'Seven thirty at the restaurant, table will be booked under my name. Stanley will come and collect Elliot around quarter past.'

'OK, great, looking forward to it,' Isla said, her voice barely able to contain her excitement. She had to rein it in, it might not be engagement news at all. But what else could it be? She couldn't think of any other reason why Jamie and Melody would want to go to the Golden Bridge with all their family and friends. God, if there was a time she really needed some good news, it was today.

They said their goodbyes and Isla hung up.

'Why are you so happy?' Elliot asked.

'I'm… just… happy about how your room looks,' Isla lied and felt instantly bad about it. But she couldn't tell Elliot that she thought Melody was engaged because he would tell Marigold and half the town would know before the end of the day tomorrow and it might not even be true.

She heard the door open downstairs and Leo called up to her.

'Yay! Leo's home,' Elliot said, running out of the room and down the stairs before Isla had even got up off her knees.

She walked downstairs and found Elliot wrapped around Leo like a monkey, Leo holding him tight.

'Will you come and see my room?' Elliot asked. 'It's very spooky.'

'I will in a few minutes, me and Isla just have to make a really important phone call first and then I'll be up to see all the scariness.'

He put Elliot down and gave her a meaningful look.

'Elliot, why don't you finish putting the cobwebs around the room and we'll be up in a minute.'

'OK, but be prepared to be very very scared,' Elliot said, putting on a spooky voice as he ran out the room.

'What's up? Have you heard from Jamie about tonight?' Isla asked.

'Yes, do you think they're engaged?' Leo said.

'That's what I was thinking. Melody wouldn't tell me either.'

'OK, hold that thought for a few minutes. Thomas called me earlier and he's about to call again in a few minutes. He's going into a meeting with Sadie and Karie and says he's going to FaceTime us in surreptitiously.'

'How is he going to do that without Sadie or Karie knowing?'

'Well, he'll FaceTime us, then switch to the back camera and put his phone in his top pocket so they won't see us. I've also told him to turn the volume down on his phone so they won't hear us either, but it's probably best if we don't speak, or speak quietly just to be on the safe side.'

Isla bit her lip. 'Isn't this really dodgy? I'm worried we're going to get caught.'

'I know, but it would be really good if we can see what Sadie has to say about Elliot.'

'I'm sure Karie will tell us all about it after.'

'I'm sure she will. Look, if you don't want to go ahead with this…'

The phone rang in Leo's hand.

'Shall I ignore it?' Leo said.

Isla stared at the phone for a moment. 'Answer it.'

Leo moved closer to Isla and answered the video call. Thomas's face appeared on the screen.

'Hello,' he whispered. Evidently, he was in the toilet.

Leo waved a hello.

'Thomas, are you sure this is a good idea?' Isla whispered back, feeling like they were undertaking some big spy operation.

'They'll never know,' Thomas said.

'Are you in the toilet?' Leo asked.

'Yes, it's OK, no one else is in here. Sadie is waiting outside and I've come in here while we wait for Karie to arrive. Right, I'm going to switch the camera round now so you'll be looking out of the back camera.'

Isla wondered if she should stop him, but she didn't.

Their view changed to that of Thomas in the mirror of the toilets as he held up the phone.

'Is that OK, can you see that?'

'Yes, we can,' Leo said. 'Now turn down the volume and put the phone in your pocket.'

Thomas did as he was asked and placed the phone in his suit pocket so that just the top of the camera was peeping out. He gave them a thumbs up and then left the bathroom.

It was just like watching *The Blair Witch Project* with the shaky camera work as Thomas returned to Sadie in what was quite clearly the bar area of the hotel she was staying in. Isla saw Sadie sitting at a table waiting for him. Thomas sat down opposite Sadie and Isla noticed she looked on edge, nervous, agitated.

'Thank you for agreeing to meet with me and Karie today,' Thomas said, his voice betraying his nerves slightly too. He knew what was at stake if he was caught.

'I'm not sure why we need a meeting with social services at all,' Sadie said. 'What's this got to do with my half of the house?'

'You have a responsibility to Elliot, whether you want that or not. As the only living parent there are certain things you have to do if you want to be absolved of all responsibility in the future, including any financial implications for child maintenance for example. Sorting out this… technicality will make the court case for the house go a lot smoother,' Thomas said.

'I don't need some lecture from some stuck-up social worker, telling me what a neglectful mum I am. I already know that, I don't need it rubbed in my face,' Sadie said, fingering her box of cigarettes nervously.

'That's not what this is, I assure you. Karie just wants the best for Elliot, I'm sure we all do.'

'I should never have come back,' Sadie muttered.

Thomas paused for a moment. 'Why did you?' Sadie flashed him a defensive look and Isla saw Thomas hold his hands up. 'I mean no disrespect but you've been gone four years and the courts have been trying to trace you since Matthew died over a year ago with no success. Why did you come back now?'

Isla was pleased he asked that question, it was something she wanted to know herself.

Sadie paused in tapping the cigarette box on the table. 'I needed the money,' she said, bluntly.

'Did you know about Matthew's death?'

Sadie shook her head and Isla saw a glimmer of remorse there. 'Not until recently. I didn't know anyone was looking for me, why would they? When I left foster care at eighteen I think everyone was glad to see the back of me. I drifted round the country for the next few years, I never tied myself to anywhere, never put down roots or made any friends. I bet Matthew was glad to see the back of me too. I couldn't do the girlfriend thing and I definitely couldn't do the mother thing. He picked the wrong girl for that.'

'Where did you go?' Thomas asked.

'Australia, New Zealand, Thailand, India. I travelled all over. I lived hand to mouth. Working in a bar for a few nights before moving on to the next place where I might pick up some cleaning work. I've hitchhiked, I've slept on beaches or benches. I've slept in filthy hostels, or sometimes I've been lucky enough to be able to afford a beach hut or cabana for the night. It's no way to live, is it, never knowing if you're going to be eating that night or not?'

'I suppose not,' Thomas said.

'I've met someone. Jim. We've talked about getting a house. He seems nice, most of the time, and I'd quite like to stand still for a while. And then unbelievably I actually bumped into someone from Sandcastle Bay, in a bar in Goa, of all places. Sally Fitzpatrick. I think she was screwing around with Leo Jackson for a while, well she was when I was there...'

Isla looked at Leo. 'Ex-girlfriend?' she whispered.

'Hardly,' he muttered.

'.. Anyway, she told me about Matthew. It was such a shock. I was gutted for him.'

'And for the people he left behind?' Thomas said, meaningfully. Had Sadie considered for one second what it would be like for Elliot to lose the only parent he'd ever known?

'Yes, I imagine he was sorely missed,' Sadie said, a trace of bitterness in her voice, probably because no one would ever have missed her when she was gone, at least in her mind.

'It's been hard, for all of them,' Thomas said. 'But for Isla especially, raising Elliot while dealing with her own grief and his.'

Sadie looked up from the table. 'Are you friendly with Isla?'

Crap. Isla didn't need Sadie to worry about the possible connections between Thomas and Leo and herself.

'No, I'm just telling you what anyone in the village would tell you, it hasn't been easy. I barely know the woman. She's not exactly in my social circles, I'm a bit old for that,' Thomas said.

'Well, it got me thinking. Of all the bars in the world, Sally happens to walk into the one where I'm working. Maybe it was fate. We needed the cash and, with Matthew dead, there was the house here to think about. Maybe this was the break we needed. There's a house we've seen, not far from the beach in Goa, has its own swimming pool. In English money, it's only about a hundred and fifty thousand. With the sale from Matthew's house, that would pay for everything, pay all Jim's debts. Jim wants to start his own diving school so that would pay for that too. I really didn't want to come back at all, I have no good memories of this country, no place to call home, but Jim persuaded me it would be for the best, we can start over. We managed to scrape together the money for my plane ticket and, well, here I am.'

Isla couldn't help thinking that Jim sounded like a bit of an arse, pushing his girlfriend to do something she didn't want to do. And why did she have a suspicion that Jim would probably do a runner as soon as Sadie came back with the cash?

'And what of Elliot in all of this?' Thomas asked.

Sadie flashed him a glare.

'I'm just asking what the judge will ask. If this goes to court, the judge will consider everything, including that selling Isla's home would effectively make Isla and Elliot homeless.'

'They have family, friends, people who love them, I'm sure they will be just fine,' Sadie said, bitterly.

'Christ, she wants everything,' Isla whispered.

'She doesn't want Elliot, though,' Leo said. 'We can work something out with the house and the money, the most important thing is that she doesn't get Elliot.'

Isla nodded her agreement, though that still didn't stop her worrying. It was clear Sadie was not going to settle for a few thousand pounds and if Isla was to sell the house to pay her off, where would she and Elliot live then?

Sadie tapped her cigarette box again and looked at her watch as if she would rather be anywhere but there.

'What's the minimum you'd settle for?' Thomas asked.

'As much as I can possibly get.'

'Realistically?'

Sadie sighed. 'Right now, I'd settle for a few thousand so I can get back to Goa. Coming here was a mistake.'

Thomas didn't say anything for a while then he stood up. 'Let me go and get some drinks. Coffee OK?'

'Yes, and if you want to put a shot of something stronger in it, I wouldn't mind.'

Isla watched as Thomas headed over to the bar and placed an order for two coffees, one of them Irish.

The barman moved away to make the order.

'Well, I think that's positive,' Thomas whispered into the top of the phone. 'She'd probably take an out-of-court settlement by the sounds of it.'

The barman looked over. 'Sorry sir, did you say something?'

'No, just… thinking out loud.'

The barman turned away and the coffee machine hissed and billowed with steam.

'Anyone else think this Jim sounds like a douche?' Thomas said.

The barman looked over again and Isla giggled.

As Thomas came back to the table carrying the drinks, Isla saw Karie come over and join them. He shook her hand, made polite introductions, offered to get Karie a coffee which she declined, and then Karie sat down opposite Sadie. This was obviously not in his plan at all as Isla saw him hesitate before he sat down next to Sadie. Now they had an excellent view of Karie but not of Sadie. Thomas seemed to angle his body a little to try to capture Sadie on the camera but all he succeeded in doing was showing them a close-up of a nearby plant.

Isla stifled a giggle. Well, if nothing else, they'd be able to hear them. Except the phone had now shifted a little and was bumping up against a pen or something else in Thomas's pocket. Every time he moved, even slightly, the pen rattled against the phone and it seemed that Thomas's heart was beating so loudly that Isla caught only a few snatched words from Karie and the reason for her visit.

Leo shook his head fondly. Poor Thomas, this clearly hadn't been what he'd planned at all.

Thomas visibly shifted in his seat and the phone slipped sideways in his shirt pocket so for a few seconds the plant was at a severe angle before the phone slipped completely inside the pocket. All they were left with was a close-up of the blue stitching and material of the shirt pocket and the bottom of the pen.

Leo smiled.

'This surveillance is going well,' Isla whispered.

'I don't think Thomas is cut out to be a spy,' Leo said.

The audio was even more muffled now. Coupled with the sound of Thomas's heartbeat, material shifting against the speakers of the phone, the phone still moving against the pen and muted voices beyond the shirt, they could barely hear anything.

Isla distinctly heard the word *Elliot* and it sounded like it had come from Karie. She quickly grabbed Leo's hand, all humour now gone, but try as she might she couldn't make out what Karie and Sadie were saying. The voices went back and forth but apart from the odd word it was impossible to hear how the conversation was going.

'Do you have any interest in the boy?' Thomas said, his voice so much louder than normal.

Isla held her breath.

'No,' Sadie said, clear as day, and Isla nearly sagged with relief.

Then Karie said something else which Isla couldn't hear.

'I agree,' Thomas said. 'If the boy isn't a factor, sign the form giving away your parental responsibility and then we can concentrate on the house without any other annoyances getting in the way.'

Isla didn't like that Thomas had just called Elliot an annoyance but she knew he was only saying that to persuade Sadie that her son was a thing to be got rid of. If it worked, Thomas could call Elliot whatever he liked.

There was silence while Sadie presumably thought about what he was saying.

'I think if the ownership of the house goes to court, the judge will look more favourably on your case if you were not to stand in the way of Elliot's adoption. It makes the case a lot less complicated too,' Thomas said.

There were a few more mumbles from Sadie and Karie.

'OK, let me just check my diary,' Thomas said and the phone was suddenly pulled from his pocket. They had a brief few seconds of seeing Karie, then he must have pressed a button that switched their view to the front-facing camera. They saw Thomas's confused face as he tried to work out how to continue with the phone call and bring up his calendar at the same time, then the phone call ended abruptly. He had probably accidentally pressed the call end button.

Isla looked at Leo. 'That went well.'

'Well, one thing came out of it. We know for a fact that Sadie has no interest in Elliot.'

Isla smiled, cautiously. 'I know, that's wonderful. I mean, I feel really bad for Elliot that his mum wants nothing to do with him, but I'm also so relieved and happy. I don't want her in his life.'

'Don't feel bad. Elliot has you. He's the luckiest little boy in the world to have you in his life, he doesn't need Sadie adding pain and confusion to it. If he never sees her again that will be fine by me,' Leo said.

'I agree. Do you think she signed the paperwork?'

'Hopefully, if Karie and Thomas are on her case to do it, she might. But I think maybe we can have a small glass of wine to celebrate this evening.'

Isla suddenly remembered. 'Yes, at the Golden Bridge. What did Jamie say to you about it?'

'Just that they were meeting friends and family for dinner tonight and he wanted me there. I suppose I better dig out my suit and tie, the Golden Bridge is a bit fancy.'

Isla laughed. 'Being a mum to a five-year-old, there isn't much cause for fancy dresses and glamorous occasions, but I'm sure I have something semi-smart in my wardrobe.' She felt the smile fall off her face. 'At my house.'

'I'll go and grab something,' Leo said, instinctively knowing that Isla wouldn't want to go back to her house just yet in case she ran into Sadie again. 'I'll just go and be suitably scared of Elliot's room and then I'll pop out.'

'Thank you.'

Leo picked up the walkie-talkie and pressed the button, putting on a scary voice. 'Elliot, I'm coming.'

Upstairs, Elliot squealed with delight and she heard Luke join in with the excitement.

Leo left the kitchen and a few moments later she heard his high-pitched and over-the-top scream as he hammed it up for Elliot's benefit, followed by a thunder of feet as he ran back down the stairs.

He grinned as he came back into the kitchen and she could hear Elliot's laughter from upstairs. 'I won't be long.'

He gave her a brief kiss on the mouth and left.

She smiled as she watched him go. Elliot was the luckiest boy in the world to have Leo in his life as well. And she knew she was pretty damned lucky to have him too.

CHAPTER 15

Isla had decided to have a bubble bath in preparation for her glamorous evening. Leo had a big hot-tub-style bath with jets and she had been dying to try it out for some time. She needed this distraction tonight – the bath, going out, celebrating with Melody. Sitting at home gave her too much time to think and worry. Of course, the bath hadn't been as relaxing as Isla had hoped for as Elliot had insisted on joining her too and a T-rex, a rubber rocket, a water pistol and a few Lego men had also made it into the bath tub with them, many of them floating up her end as she lay in the warm water.

'This bath is way more fun than ours,' Elliot said as he pressed the button for the jets for the umpteenth time. 'When you get married and we live here, we can go in this bath every day.'

'That would be cool, but sometimes if you do something that's fun every day, then it stops becoming fun,' Isla said.

Elliot wrinkled up his nose as if he didn't understand.

'Don't listen to her, buddy,' Leo said, walking into the bathroom. 'There are some things I could do every single day and never ever get bored of it.'

'Like what?' Elliot said.

Leo grabbed the little bathrobe he had bought for Elliot off the back of the door and held it out for him. Elliot stepped up onto the side of the bath and held out his arms as if he was a king about to be dressed.

Leo flashed Isla a glance that was dark and laced with intent. 'Like hugging Isla. I could do that all day, every day, and it'd never be enough.'

Isla smirked, knowing full well he wasn't talking about hugging.

Leo wrapped the robe around him, then scooped Elliot up and threw him over his shoulder.

'I like hugging Isla too,' Elliot said, as he hung upside down.

'Let's get you dressed and then you can give Isla a big hug before you go off to Marigold's shortly,' Leo said. He turned back to Isla before he left. 'Your dress is on the bed and we have about half an hour before we have to leave.'

'I'll be ready.'

Leo left her alone in the bathroom and she relished in the quiet for a few moments, the bubbles trickling through her toes, before she got out, patted herself dry and pulled on her robe.

She paused for a second outside the bathroom, wondering which bed Leo had meant. She peered round the door of Leo's bedroom and her heart leapt when she spotted a gold dress on the bed. Mainly because it wasn't hers. She stepped closer and saw it was a fifties-style gown with a flared skirt. The bodice and shoulders were almost completely covered gold sequins which faded out into the lower part of the dress. It was beautiful and entirely unlike anything else she owned. There was even a pair of shoes to match. Leo had bought this for her. God, she loved this man.

She quickly got dried and was just pulling it on when he walked into the room.

He was wearing a suit and her words disappeared in her throat as she stared at him. He looked divine, the suit jacket moulded to his broad shoulders. He was quite simply the sexiest man she had ever seen.

'Does it fit OK?' he asked.

'I… I haven't zipped it up yet.'

'Here, let me,' he said, moving behind her, his fingers brushing against her bare back as he slowly zipped her up. His touch made goosebumps erupt across her body.

He looked at her in the mirror, his hands on her shoulders. 'You look beautiful.'

'Thank you for this,' Isla said, staring at their reflection. 'You didn't have to buy me a dress, I have lots of semi-smart things I could have worn.'

'You said you never have a reason to wear fancy dresses or enjoy glamorous occasions. I thought we should make the most of tonight.'

'Thank you.'

He kissed her shoulder and then whispered in her ear. 'Maybe you'll let me take it off you one day.'

She watched the blush spread across her cheeks. God, she really wanted that. Right now she had no idea why she was holding back from that.

'Marigold's here,' Elliot yelled up the stairs.

She turned round to face Leo and kissed him on the lips. 'Maybe I'll let you take it off tonight.'

He stared at her and she stepped out of his arms and wandered downstairs to say goodbye to Elliot.

'Wow, Isla, you look really pretty,' Elliot said when he saw her.

She hugged him. 'Thank you beautiful boy, you have a good night with Marigold.'

There was a knock on the door and Isla grabbed Elliot's rucksack and opened it to find Stanley and Marigold on the doorstep.

'Hi Isla, you look nice,' Stanley said.

'You look like a princess,' Marigold said, stepping forward and feeling the dress.

'Thank you. Do *you* two have any idea what tonight's about?' Isla asked, hoping Stanley might have some insight.

'No clue. Emily just said we're having Elliot. It's fine by me, it keeps Marigold entertained,' Stanley said.

'Emily said Leo's going to get lucky tonight,' Marigold said.

Isla laughed. 'Did she?'

Stanley cleared his throat awkwardly. 'Shall we go?'

'What's Leo going to be lucky at?' Elliot asked.

'He's, um…' Stanley was obviously struggling.

'I'm just lucky to be spending the night with such a beautiful woman,' Leo said, appearing behind Isla. He swept Elliot up in his arms and gave him a big hug. 'See you tomorrow buddy, love you.'

'Goodnight Leo, love you too.'

Isla stared at them, feeling like her heart might burst.

Leo passed him to Isla and she hugged him tight too.

'Love you,' Isla said and she smiled when Elliot squeezed her a little bit tighter.

She placed him down and he immediately took Marigold's hand and they ran out to the car, closely followed by Luke.

Stanley cleared his throat awkwardly. 'Um, have a good night.'

Isla smirked and watched him go.

'Right, shall we head off?' Leo said as the car drove away.

She looked at him and something passed between them. A shiver of excitement at what the evening would hold slid down her spine.

She nodded.

He held out her coat for her and she relished in his brief gentle touch as his fingers grazed her neck and then he escorted her out to his car.

The chemistry sparked in the air between them. Truth be told, it had been sparking between them for years, but now it seemed to have turned into an explosive firework. They didn't talk on the short drive to the restaurant but as the car moved along the coastal road, capturing the moon sparkling over the waves, Leo put his hand on the inside of her knee, stroking his fingers round the crease at the back of her leg.

Her breath caught in her throat. Kissing him the night before had been everything but this felt so much more intimate and sexy. And even though his hand never went any higher than her knee, it was like the wonderful prelude to something more.

They arrived at the Golden Bridge and the sky was a glorious inky blue that seemed to go on forever as it stretched out over the sea.

Leo got out and she stayed in the car for a few seconds to catch her breath. She smiled when he came to open the door for her. To her surprise he took her hand as they walked towards the restaurant.

She looked up at him and he smiled. 'I really am the luckiest man alive to have you with me tonight.'

She smiled, still not entirely sure where she stood with him but by then she was caring less and less. Maybe she would see where the evening took them without worrying about defining it.

He held the restaurant door open for her and she was greeted by a woman in a smart black suit.

'Hello, we have a table booked under the name of Melody Rosewood,' Isla said, looking round the restaurant to see if she could see her sister.

The woman checked her book and nodded.

'Of course, right this way,' the woman said, grabbing two menus and walking off towards the far side of the restaurant. It was such a glamorous place, all black sparkly walls, gold waterfall walls and marble floors. It was not like any other place she had ever been to.

The woman stopped by a small candlelit table overlooking the bay. The view of Sandcastle Bay was incredible, the houses twinkling in the darkness, the moon lighting up the sea beyond, laying a shimmering path out towards the horizon. However, as the woman placed the menus down on the table and waited for them to take their seats, Isla realised there had been a mistake; this wasn't their table at all.

'Oh no, we're part of the Melody Rosewood and Jamie Jackson party. There's a big group of us,' Isla said.

The woman's smile faltered.

'I'm pretty sure this is the table that Melody booked, I spoke to her myself.'

Isla frowned in confusion. Maybe the table was booked under another name. 'Is there not a big party booked in for tonight?'

'I don't think so, let me go and check.'

The woman wandered off and Isla turned to Leo.

'What's going on? How can they not have a big party booking? There's going to be at least seven of us, plus a few friends, Jamie's friend Klaus maybe, Agatha and Carolyn too. Melody said it was going to be all their friends and family. What if the restaurant screwed up?' She looked around; could they squeeze in a table for eight or nine people? It looked pretty busy. But where was everyone else? She looked at her watch to see that they were a few minutes early. Perhaps everyone else was still on their way.

'Maybe you should call Melody,' Leo suggested.

The restaurant was very quiet, people talking in low voices at their tables, so Isla decided to text her instead.

> *We're at the restaurant and they have given us a table for two, how many people are coming?*

The reply was instant.

> *Just you two. Thought you could do with a night out and maybe a chance to talk. Have a good night.* Followed by a winky smiley face.

She stared at the text in confusion just as the woman returned. 'I've checked the booking and it was definitely a table for two. It came with instructions for the most romantic table in the restaurant.'

Leo stared at the woman and then at the table and the incredible romantic view. 'We've been set up.'

Isla passed him the phone so he could read Melody's message. 'It seems that way.'

The woman hovered for a moment. 'Is the table OK?'

'Yes, it's fine, thank you,' Leo said and the woman left them alone. 'It seems we have ourselves a date.'

Isla smirked and shook her head. She couldn't be angry over Melody's choice of timing. Melody would have known that Isla would have just sat at home and worried and overanalysed everything surrounding Sadie. She looked across at Leo and couldn't think of a nicer way to be distracted. And Isla herself had said she wanted time to talk to Leo properly. Melody had given her that.

'Wow, it seems our families are going all out to get us together.'

Leo held her chair out for her and she quirked her eyebrow at him. In her entire life, no one had held her chair out for her.

'Well, if we're on a date, I should do dately things,' he said.

She sat down, shaking her head fondly, and he sat down opposite her. To her surprise, he took her hand again.

'I'm sorry, this is kind of my fault,' Isla said.

'Bloody hell, don't apologise. I get to be on a date with the most incredible woman I've ever met.'

She stared at him, her heart racing as he looked at her with complete adoration.

'And no, I don't say that to all the women,' Leo said.

She smiled and looked out over the view, playing for time. She had no idea what to say to that wonderful compliment.

'Why is this your fault?' Leo said, stroking his fingers gently over the back of her hand. It was the exact same pressure he had used on the back of her leg in the car on the drive over and she suddenly wanted him to stroke her like that all over her body.

Isla swallowed and started caressing the palm of his hand with her thumb. 'Because I said I wanted time to talk to you.'

He looked down at where their hands were touching and he nodded. 'Talking is very important,' his voice was strained. 'Right now, I could think of quite a few things I'd like to do on our date later on and talking isn't one of them. But we're here at this lovely restaurant at this romantic table with that amazing view, what would you like to talk about?'

He moved her hand to his mouth and kissed across her knuckles. His hot breath on her skin was heavenly.

'I have absolutely no idea,' Isla said, her breathing heavy. 'But I'd quite like to know about those things you want to do on our date later.'

His mouth twitched into a smile. 'I'd rather show you those things.'

She couldn't take her eyes off him. Her heart was thundering in her chest, blood roaring in her ears.

She placed her menu down on the table and stood up, offering out her hand. 'Then let's go.'

He frowned slightly. 'Wait, I'm just teasing you. Well, of course I want that but we don't have to do that now. Wouldn't you prefer to have your glamorous date, here, overlooking the sea?'

'There is nothing I'd rather be doing right now than being with you again like we were four years ago.'

He didn't hesitate this time. He stood up and took her hand. 'Let's go home.'

He marched out of the restaurant and she followed in his wake. He didn't even break his stride when he approached the woman who had shown them to the table.

'Sorry, change of plan,' Leo said and Isla giggled as he tugged her outside into the car park.

As they approached his car, Leo stopped and pulled her into his arms and kissed her hard. His large hands spanned her back, holding her close against his body. His touch was gentle, almost reverential, but his kiss was so much more. It was sensual, dark, sexy as hell. It took her breath away. God, his house was suddenly too far away. If he tried to push her back against the side of his car and take her there and then, she wouldn't even stop him.

He pulled back abruptly. 'We need to go home, now.'

She nodded and he grabbed her car door and yanked it open, probably a bit too hard. She quickly got inside as he ran round to the driver's side. She had to laugh at his urgency.

He started the car, slammed it into gear and took off in a wheel spin, with gravel flying behind them in a cloud of dust. Although to his credit, once he hit the road, he drove a bit more sedately. She had noticed that he was a very safe driver, though maybe that was an after-effect of Matthew's accident.

She placed her hand on the inside of his leg this time, giving it a little squeeze, and she smirked when he swerved a little.

She inched it a little higher and he captured it with his own, raised it to his mouth to kiss and then pushed it back towards her. 'Let's save that for the bedroom or I don't think we'll be arriving back home in one piece.'

They pulled into the secluded drive in front of his house, the lights shining from the windows welcoming them home. He quickly unclipped his seatbelt and she laughed when he unclipped hers too. He moved to get out but she caught his shoulder and held him back, nerves suddenly getting the better of her.

He looked at her in concern.

She stroked his face to soften the blow of what she was about to say. 'Promise me something.'

'Anything.'

'Promise me, that whatever happens between us, it won't affect what you have with Elliot. He needs you more than I do and I never want to do anything to ruin the beautiful relationship you two have.'

He smiled and shook his head.

'I love him. I never wanted children and I was scared about the responsibility of being his godfather but now, god, I love him so much and that is never going to change. I'm not going anywhere.'

'Even if we hate each other and don't want to talk to one another any more?'

'That will never happen. We'll always be best friends. But when I said I'm not going anywhere, I meant for you too. I'll always be here for you.'

She smiled, her doubts and fears fading away, at least for tonight.

She leaned over and kissed him and he stroked her face, his gentle fingers caressing down her throat and then sliding her dress strap off her shoulder. She felt the bodice of the dress slip down a little and his hand skated down her chest and inside her bra, touching her nipple with the lightest of touches.

It was like her body was suddenly coming alive again, as if it recognised his touch and was waking up after four long years of hibernation. Sex with her ex had always been good but it was never like this.

She let out a sigh of need as Leo stroked her and she pushed him back in his seat. She quickly wiggled out of her knickers and then climbed over the handbrake and straddled him, kissing him again as his hands pushed her dress down to her waist and explored her body. He took both breasts in his hands, running his thumbs over her nipples. He knew exactly where to touch her to make her gasp.

She yanked the tie from his neck and undid his shirt buttons, stroking across his strong hard chest.

He lowered his lips to her breast, sucking her into his hot mouth, and she moaned as she wrapped her hands round his neck and kissed the top of his head.

He slipped his hand between her legs and it was mere seconds before waves of pleasure rocked through her. She clung to him, her breath accelerated and unsteady.

She was vaguely aware he was undoing his trousers and rolling on a condom. She shifted to her knees so she was raised above him but her legs were shaking like jelly.

He leaned up and kissed her, cupping her face and gently taking his time as if he was in no rush. She slowly moved down on top of him and he shifted his hands to her hips, guiding her so she took him inside her. He pulled her tighter against him, so he was deeper inside her and she gasped against his lips. It was as if something had been missing from her life for far too long, and it wasn't sex, it was him.

They started to move against each other. It was gentle at first as if they wanted to take the time to rediscover each other but pretty soon it became hard and urgent and needful as they grabbed at each other, kissing hard, tasting and exploring. It was hot and sweaty and their bodies sliding together as one was so incredibly erotic that she was soon shouting out his name as her orgasm hit her with the force of a double-decker bus. He let out a noise that sounded like a roar as he kissed her hard, and then she slumped against him, resting her head on his shoulder as she tried to catch her breath.

He stroked his hands down her damp back soothingly and she sat up to look at him, her whole body shaking. He smoothed her hair from her face and gave her a brief kiss on the lips.

'So, shall we go inside now?' Leo said.

She laughed and nodded.

He ran his hands up her thighs, stroking that sensitive area at the top of her legs. 'We have lots more to *talk* about.'

She kissed him. 'I agree. I hope you have more condoms because I have a feeling we'll be *talking* all night.'

He grinned. 'I came prepared.'

'I'm so glad.'

CHAPTER 16

Leo watched Isla as the light from the log fire flickered across her face. She was wearing only her bathrobe as she sat on his lap, twisting her damp hair round her finger as she stared at the flames. She leaned back, resting her head on his shoulder, slipping her arm round his stomach. He wrapped his arm around her shoulder and held her against him, kissing her forehead. She had a peaceful, contented expression on her face. He couldn't really believe he had put that look there. The women he had been with in the past always looked at him as if they were waiting for him to leave after they'd spent the night together. There had never been any cuddling like this, it had always just been sex. In fact, if any of them had cuddled up with him like this he would have run a mile. But it was different with Isla, it had always been different with her.

'We should have done this a long time ago,' Isla said, quietly.

'What, shower sex?' he teased. 'Yes, that was one place we never ticked off our list last time. We pretty much stayed in bed the whole night.'

She giggled. 'No, this – us.'

He leaned his head on top of hers and let out a sigh.

'Maybe it wasn't the right time,' Leo said. When was the right time to make a move on his best friend's sister when she was grieving the loss of her brother and trying to raise her nephew at the same time? Especially when it was partly his fault that her whole life had been turned upside down. A wave of guilt surged through him but he pushed it back down. Even though he knew this wasn't the moment to tell her what he did, or rather didn't do, he still cursed himself for being a coward.

She looked up at him. 'Is it the right time now?'

He stared at her. 'God, I hope so.'

She smiled and kissed him briefly before cuddling back up to him again.

It had been an incredible night so far. After coming in from the car, they'd kissed for the longest time, against the wall, on the sofa and then in the shower, where things had progressed to the best sex he'd ever had. He smiled; every time with Isla was the best sex he'd ever had. In fact, that night had probably been the best night of his life, and although he'd said that about the first night they'd spent together, this was infinitely better. Probably because he loved her completely and because he'd never thought this would really happen for them. She had turned his marriage proposals down more times than he could count. He'd always thought it was because she didn't like him that way. Until recently, he'd had no idea that she had feelings for him too.

And he'd nearly screwed it all up that day that the truth about how she felt about him came out. He'd walked away from her. But he had her now and he wasn't going to let her go.

'What did you want to talk to me about tonight?' Leo asked, tracing his fingers down her back.

She sat up and smiled at him. 'We never got the chance to finish our conversation yesterday. You said you had feelings for me but I wasn't sure if you meant sex and lust or… something more.'

'Ah, I never made myself clear.'

'No, you didn't. But it's OK, I know now,' Isla said.

'You do?' She couldn't possibly know how deep his feelings ran for her.

'You feel the same way I do.'

He smiled; they were both skirting around those words.

'I really do, with everything I have.'

She pushed apart the top of his robe and placed a kiss over his heart. 'It's this I like the most.'

'My pecs?'

She laughed. 'Those too.'

'Was that the only thing you wanted to talk to me about?'

She frowned, as if trying to decide whether to talk to him about something. 'Jamie says you blame yourself for Matthew's death?'

He swore under his breath. Talk about a mood killer. He couldn't do it. He couldn't bear to see the love for him that was shining from her face fade away. He knew he would have to tell her at some point but he didn't want to destroy what they had, not when he'd just got her back after all this time.

'That's not... I... Let's not talk about that tonight.'

She stroked his face, her eyes clouded with concern. 'We don't have to talk about it now but if this is holding you back then you need to let go of it at some point. And talking it through with me might help.'

'You will hate me,' Leo said, quietly.

'That's not possible. Best friends forever, remember.'

'I'm not a good man.'

'But you are, you are wonderful and generous and loyal. There is no one else in this world that I would rather raise Elliot with. I don't care about the man that you were. Who you are now is the man I've fallen for.'

He stared at her. She saw something incredible in him and maybe it was time he started believing in that person too.

He kissed her hard, cupping the back of her head. She tasted divine. She slipped her hand underneath his robe, stroking across his shoulder and chest. As the kiss continued, he slid his hand between her legs, caressing her in that place that made her moan against his lips. That moan sent a kick of desire straight to his gut. He needed her now.

He quickly brought her tumbling over the edge. As she was trying to catch her breath, he wrestled a condom from the pocket of his robe but to his immense frustration she suddenly stood up and climbed off his lap.

He watched as she slipped out of her robe, letting it fall to the floor. She looked magnificent, her damp hair tumbling down her back, her skin all pink and flushed from the orgasm he'd just given her.

She held out her hand. 'Join me.'

He scrambled out of his chair faster than he'd ever stood up in his life. He took her hand and she lay down on the rug, pulling him down next to her. He wrestled himself out of his robe and kissed her again, rolling on top of her and pinning her to the floor. He snatched his mouth from hers for a second as he tore the condom open with his teeth and quickly rolled it on and as he kissed her again he slid carefully inside her. Her kisses became frantic and urgent, her hands down his back urging him on. He pulled back slightly to watch her come undone, capturing her hands and pinning them over her head, her fingers clasped tightly between his. She wrapped her legs around his hips, pulling him in deeper, but it was the look of complete love in her eyes that brought him to the very edge.

From here on in, he was going to believe in the man she saw. He was going to let go of his past and move forward with his future. She was his future now and he was going to take it.

'Marry me?' he said.

She smiled, tears welling in her eyes. 'Don't stop asking me, Leo Jackson. One day soon, I'm going to say yes.'

He'd take that.

He kissed her, moving against her harder and faster, and he felt her body tremble beneath him as she cried out his name and then his orgasm was ripping through him too.

He collapsed on top of her and couldn't help smiling against her neck. One day soon, she was going to be his wife.

Isla woke the next day with Leo's arms wrapped tightly round her, and his hand stroking through her hair.

'What a lovely way to wake up,' Isla murmured.

'Were you sad again last night, Isla?' Elliot said.

Isla's eyes flew open. She saw Elliot standing next to the bed and realised it was him stroking her hair.

Crap.

They were going to scar this poor boy for life. Even worse, she and Leo were both stark naked and the only thing preserving their modesty was a thin bit of sheet that felt like it was barely covering her bum.

'Morning beautiful boy,' Isla said. 'No, I wasn't sad last night.'

'Then why are you in bed with Leo again?'

'Because cuddling Leo makes me happy,' Isla said.

'It makes me very happy too,' Leo said, clearly just waking up himself. 'Hey buddy.'

'Why are you both naked?' Elliot asked.

'Um, we got a bit hot last night?' Isla said, which was the truth, although no need to explain quite why they were hot and sweaty. She could see that Leo was suppressing a smile.

'What's this?' Elliot picked up a condom in its foil packet from the top of the bedside drawers. 'It's squishy.'

Oh god.

'That's, erm...' Isla started but she literally had nothing.

'Elliot!' came Emily's voice as she walked along the hall. 'I don't think they're here.'

Oh crap, this was just getting worse. Isla fumbled around for the sheet but it was caught up between their legs and a second later Emily appeared in the doorway, followed by Luke.

'Oh shit, sorry.' Emily quickly shielded her eyes and turned away.

Elliot giggled. 'Emily swore.'

'Sorry,' Emily said. 'We thought we'd give you guys a bit of a lie-in this morning. I didn't think you'd still be in bed at this time.'

Isla frowned and looked at the clock. It was already half past ten. She had never slept that late, well at least not since she had started looking after Elliot. Although the night before had been quite... energetic.

'Elliot, why don't you show me your room and how you've decorated it for Halloween and we can leave Isla and Leo to finish off... I mean, finish getting ready,' Emily said.

Elliot was easily distracted and he quickly ran out the room to show Emily his Halloween paraphernalia, although to Isla's horror, he took the condom with him.

'What's this, Emily?' Elliot asked, proffering the treasure up in the air.

Isla giggled at Emily's mortified expression as she ushered Elliot and Luke out of the room.

'That's... um. Actually, I'm not really sure, probably best to ask Isla about it later on. Come on, which one is your room?'

Elliot's voice faded away as he took her to the room down the hall and Isla propped herself up to look at Leo.

'Wow. We're never going to live that down.'

'I don't even care,' Leo said, a wonderful relaxed smile on his face. 'I had the best night of my life and nothing is going to change my good mood this morning.'

Isla smiled. But despite the wonderful night they had spent together, it still hadn't come with any kind of declaration of love. She'd told herself she didn't need to hear the words, she knew how Leo felt, but in reality she did need confirmation of his feelings. But she couldn't exactly be angry that he hadn't said what she wanted to hear when she hadn't managed to say the words herself.

Her relationship with Daniel had hurt a lot more than she acknowledged. He had let her down spectacularly and he had often told her he loved her. But what kind of love meant you could walk away from someone so abruptly? They hadn't fallen out of love with each other, in fact the night before Matthew had died they had made love and it had been as good as always. There had been no affair or arguments. But a life with a child that wasn't his was not the life he wanted. For Daniel, he clearly didn't believe in for better or worse, and for the longest time after they'd broken up she just didn't know what to do with that.

If he could walk away from her so easily, then maybe he had never loved her at all. She was scared of handing her heart over on a plate to someone only to have it thrown back in her face again.

She trusted Leo and in her heart she knew he loved her, but everything was suddenly happening so quickly. She felt like she needed some confirmation that she was doing the right thing.

He stroked down her back, his face suddenly filling with concern. 'Listen, last night, Thomas texted me. Sadie didn't sign the consent form, giving parental responsibility to you.'

Her heart leapt in chest. 'She didn't? But she said she had no interest in Elliot. Why would she not sign?'

'She said she wanted to think about it.'

'What is there to think about?'

'Probably how much money she can gain from this.'

She sighed and got out of bed. She looked around frantically for some clothes, that sense of panic that had faded away the night before well and truly back now. Sadie really was like those characters in the horror films, she kept coming back to take more of her pound of flesh. And where the bloody hell were her clothes?

Leo was suddenly there, jeans on, passing her one of his shirts, which made it look really bloody obvious that they had spent the night getting up to all sorts. Though as Emily had already caught them naked in bed together there was no point in being coy now.

She yanked it on, doing up the buttons on the shirt wrong in her haste.

Christ, she would just go down to the bank and remortgage her house and give Sadie half in return for giving her parental responsibility and pissing off for good. Quite how she was going to pay back the monthly mortgage she didn't know, but she had a job now. It was a regular salary even if her part-time hours meant that there wouldn't be much coming in. She hadn't even talked about a salary with Leo. God, what if the bank looked at her finances and decided she wasn't earning enough to give her a new mortgage? Maybe she should sell the house instead.

But could she really move in here? Would Leo really want her to? Being a full-time dad was a big responsibility. Leo was wonderful with Elliot but there was a big difference between having Elliot stay over for a few days or once a week and having him here all the time. Her nephew had so much stuff, so many toys and it seemed to spread out from his bedroom and take over the whole house. If Daniel didn't want the responsibility of raising a child with her after two and half years together, would Leo really want that when they'd only been together in reality for one night? Was it too much to ask? But Leo had asked her to marry him so many times with that end in mind. Maybe he *had* considered what life would be like. He'd said the night before how much he loved Elliot. Maybe he really did want this life with her. She shook her head. But in reality, she didn't need Leo. Her half of the money would be enough to get her a tiny one-bedroom flat on the furthest reaches of town, or if she went further inland, left Sandcastle Bay, she might be able to afford something a little bigger. It would be a small price to pay as long as she was able to keep Elliot.

'Stop panicking,' Leo said, gently.

'This is Elliot, for Christ's sake,' Isla snapped. 'I don't care about the house, I just want him.' She knew she was being unfair to Leo, but fear was taking over and she couldn't think rationally.

'You don't need to tell me what's at stake here. There's not one single thing I wouldn't do to protect him,' Leo said.

'When did you know about Sadie not signing the form?'

Leo let out a little sigh. 'Last night before we went to the restaurant.'

'And you didn't think to tell me?' Isla protested.

'I did think about it, but it's not like we could do anything about it last night and I thought it would be nice for you not to worry for a few hours.'

'So you could get laid,' Isla said and regretted it immediately. His face turned to thunder.

'No, so you could enjoy a nice meal out with friends. I didn't realise we would end up in bed, that wasn't part of my agenda at all.'

'I'm sorry,' Isla said, quietly.

'I have to go to work. I'll let you know if I hear any more updates from Thomas,' Leo said. With that he left the room, without so much as a kiss goodbye.

God, she was a cow. This whole thing with Sadie was stressing her out completely and now she was lashing out at the people she loved.

She would apologise to him later when she went into work. She'd already asked her mum if she would look after Elliot that afternoon.

She quickly found a pair of Leo's shorts and went off to find Elliot and excuse Emily from any more awkward questions.

She found them in Elliot's room.

'And this spider bounces, look,' Elliot said, giving the spider a tug and then watching it bounce up on its spring. To Isla's embarrassment, Elliot was still clutching the condom in his other hand. Obviously he wasn't going to let that conversation go any time soon.

'Hey Emily, thank you for having Elliot last night,' Isla said as nonchalantly as she could, given only minutes ago Emily had walked in and found Isla and Leo naked in bed together.

Emily turned round. 'Oh, no problem. We had a lot of fun, though clearly not as much fun as you two.'

Isla cleared her throat. 'It was a very… enjoyable evening.'

'I bet it was. I better go, I need to be at the café soon. Pop in later and maybe you might want to share a few more details.'

'I think I've shared enough this morning to last a lifetime.'

Emily grinned, gave her a hug and walked out.

Isla turned back to Elliot. 'Shall we have a bath in the hot tub again?'

'Yay!' Elliot said and she gave a little sigh of relief that he might be suitably distracted. 'Isla, what's this?' He offered out the condom again.

'It's a condom,' she said. She saw him wrinkle his little face up as he tried to remember if he'd come across that word before.

Isla sighed and scooped him up and sat him on her lap on his bed.

'You know how Emily is carrying a baby in her belly.'

'Yes, Stanley gave her the baby.'

'That's right, he did. Well sometimes, when a man and a woman cuddle together in bed, the man might wear this to stop him accidentally giving her babies if she doesn't want one.'

Elliot wrinkled his little nose. She wasn't sure if this was too much information, but as he had asked the question she knew she had to give him an honest answer.

'Do you not want Leo to give you a baby?' Elliot asked.

God, this was getting worse. How was she supposed to answer that question? Because in reality she wanted that with Leo, to be married to him, make a proper family with him, Elliot and maybe children of their own one day.

'Maybe, sometime in the future, I might have a baby. But now is not the right time.'

'When is the right time?'

'If Leo and I get married one day, then we might have a baby together then.'

'When are you getting married?'

'I'm not sure, we're both a bit busy at the moment,' Isla tried.

'I'd like a baby sister,' Elliot said.

'I know you would,' Isla said. It was something he had mentioned before.

'So you need to hurry up and get married,' Elliot said.

She smiled. 'I'll do my best.'

Elliot was clearly happy with this answer as he dumped the condom on the bed and ran out the bedroom, stripping clothes off as he headed for the bathroom.

CHAPTER 17

Isla pushed open the door to The Cherry on Top and let Elliot run on ahead of her. Her mum, Carolyn, was waiting for her at a table, reading a book and looking... contented. It had been a long time since she had seen her mum look so peaceful and she liked seeing her that way. Obviously Trevor was having a positive influence on her.

To her confusion, Elliot ran straight towards the counter instead of towards Carolyn. There was no sign of Marigold, so he couldn't be running off to see her.

'Elliot, where are you going? Your nan is over here,' Isla pointed.

'I'm just going to tell Emily what a condom is, she didn't know when I asked her before.'

Isla blinked.

'Oh, I don't think that's necessary, Emily is very busy...' she trailed off as Elliot ran round the back of the counter.

Emily was busy making a milkshake for Mary Nightingale. Emily glanced over at the new arrival. 'Oh hey, Elliot.'

'Hey. I found out what a condom is, that squishy thing I found in Leo's room. Men use it to stop giving babies to women,' Elliot announced loudly.

There were a few giggles from the people waiting at the counter as Isla stood there powerless to stop the car crash from happening.

Emily blushed. 'Oh, thanks Elliot, good to know.'

'Oh, that *is* interesting,' Mary Nightingale said, waggling her eyebrows in Isla's direction. Isla sighed. As Mary was one of

Agatha's closest friends, this information was definitely getting back to her and probably to the rest of the village as well. 'And you say that you found this *condom* in Leo's room?'

'Yes,' Elliot said, keenly.

'Was Isla in the bedroom with him when you found this condom?' Mary Nightingale went on.

'Yes, they were naked in bed together,' Elliot said. 'Isla said they were naked because they got very hot the night before.'

'Ooh, I bet they did,' Mary chortled.

This was just getting worse and worse.

'Isla says that she wants Leo to give her a baby but they can't have one until they're married and Leo isn't going to marry her yet because he doesn't love her enough, he only loves her like he loves chocolate which is a lot but not enough to get married so Leo has to use the condom so he doesn't accidentally give Isla a baby when he cuddles her in bed,' Elliot said.

Wow, it had just got a lot worse.

'No, honey, that's not…' Isla trailed off. Everyone was staring at them now, some of them were even looking at her with pity. Elliot hadn't painted Leo in the best light there, but bless him, he was just repeating everything she and Leo had said to him in the last few days, even if things had definitely moved on since she'd told Elliot that Leo loved her like chocolate. 'That's not how it is,' Isla said, not really wanting to go into the specifics of her relationship with the whole village.

'I'm going to say hello to Frankie,' Elliot said, oblivious to the impact of his announcement. 'Oh and Emily, if you don't want any more babies, you need to get Stanley to wear a condom *all* the time.'

Emily suppressed a smile. 'I'll pass that on.'

Elliot pushed the door open on the kitchen and disappeared inside.

'Well, that was certainly enlightening,' Mary Nightingale said, her eyebrows still waggling mischievously.

'I think Elliot misunderstood,' Isla said, lamely.

'No, he seems to have perfectly understood what a condom is for,' Mary said.

She looked around the café at all the faces watching her, some with amusement, some with sadness.

'Me and Leo are doing fine, but it's very early days yet,' Isla said and then moved to the counter. 'I'll have a hot chocolate when you're ready, Emily, and one for Elliot too.' She turned round to address her mum. 'Did you want anything?' Her mum shook her head and Isla was thankful that conversation seemed to resume amongst the customers, even if she was quite sure that some of that conversation might be to do with her.

Mary took her milkshake and went and sat down and Isla gave a little sigh of relief that the attention was over, at least for now.

Emily clearly decided to give her a pass on quizzing her for more details after that embarrassing debacle and handed over the hot chocolates without any further comment.

Isla went and sat down with her mum.

'Your little man does make me laugh,' Carolyn said as Isla leaned over and gave her a kiss on the cheek.

'He has no filter and then just repeats everything he's heard and not necessarily in the right order or context.' Isla shook her head fondly, deposited her coat over the back of the chair and took a long sip of creamy hot chocolate.

'How are things going with Sadie and the house and the adoption?' Carolyn asked, placing her bookmark in her book and slipping it into her bag.

'Good and bad, I suppose. She has no interest in Elliot, which is something of a relief. I couldn't bear to go through a whole custody battle for him, but she has so far not been willing to sign the paperwork giving me full parental responsibility. Leo thinks she's just stalling to play for more money.'

'Bitch.'

Isla smirked at hearing her mum curse like that then she sighed. 'I'm actually starting to feel a little sorry for her.'

'Really?' Carolyn stared at her incredulously.

She nodded as she took another sip. 'I mean, I know she is completely ruining my attempt to adopt Elliot and I may have to sell the house to pay her off, which would technically make us homeless, but… she has no one. She grew up in foster care, several foster homes actually. She has no friends, no family and has been practically homeless for the last few years, scraping together enough money to eat and occasionally get a bed for the night. By the sounds of it, she's hooked up with an arsehole of a boyfriend who pushed her into coming back here to get the money. I don't think she's in a good place.'

'Maybe she should have thought of that before she left Matthew and their son and the home they had bought together. Who walks away from their only child?'

Isla shrugged. 'Parenthood isn't for everyone. I'm not saying we're going to become friends or that I even like the woman. I'm just saying I feel sorry for her and I understand desperate times call for desperate measures.'

'So what are you going to do?' Carolyn said.

'I know her solicitor is pushing for an out-of-court settlement, but we're still waiting to see what Sadie wants. I'd like this whole debacle over with as quickly as possible. I can't wait around for this to go to court. Elliot's adoption hearing is in two weeks and I'd quite like matters sorted before then, at least where he is concerned, even if the house business isn't finished. The last thing I want is to put the hearing back. She just wants money so I'm going to go down to the bank this morning and ask to remortgage my house to get half the value. Hopefully that will be enough to get her to sign the paperwork for Elliot's adoption and go back to where she came from. I have a job now, albeit a part-time one, so I should be able to afford the repayments. That's if they'll let me do it.'

'And if they don't?'

Isla sighed. 'Then I guess we'll have to sell. But I should be able to afford a small flat with my half of the money. It's not ideal but at least I'll have Elliot and that's the most important thing.'

Carolyn shook her head, angrily. 'It's not fair.'

'No, it isn't.'

They sat in silence for a while as they contemplated the mess that Sadie had created.

'And things are finally happening between you and Leo?' Carolyn asked, quietly.

Isla couldn't help the smile from spreading across her face.

'Yes, it's crazy. I'm completely in love with him, have been for some time if truth be told, and I'm pretty sure he feels the same way. He has all this guilt over the idea that he feels he is benefitting from Matthew's death by us being together, but I think he is slowly getting past that.'

'I'm happy for you, he's a good man,' Carolyn said.

'Yes, he is. He doesn't see himself that way, but he really is. And how are things going with you and Trevor?'

Her mum smiled. 'Really good. I never thought I'd be in love again but here I am.'

Isla smiled. 'Good things happen when you open yourself up to new possibilities.'

Her mum nodded.

Isla drained her cup. 'I better go. I need to go to the bank shortly and I promised Leo I'd be at the office this afternoon. I'll pick Elliot up after work.'

'OK, no rush.'

'Thanks Mum, see you later.' She gave her a kiss on the cheek and stood up just as Sadie walked into the café.

Within seconds, the whole café fell silent, everyone staring at the new arrival with complete contempt. Isla was quite sure that everyone in the village had heard that Sadie was back and was trying to kick Isla and Elliot out of their home. She was definitely not going to receive a royal welcome.

Sadie stopped halfway between the door and the counter as she realised everyone was staring at her.

She spotted Isla and shifted awkwardly.

'I just want a ham sandwich,' Sadie addressed the café at large.

'Not from here you don't,' Emily said. 'I'm not serving you.'

Sadie stared at her in shock. Even Isla was a little stunned by this. She knew the villagers were loyal but she hadn't expected this.

Sadie looked around the café again, clearly seeing the hatred there, then turned and quickly walked out.

Isla hesitated for a moment or two as conversation between the villagers slowly resumed and then walked up to the counter. 'Can I get a ham sandwich to go?'

Emily narrowed her eyes. 'Is it for her?'

'Let's say I'm trying the good cop, bad cop approach.'

Emily sighed. 'Fine.'

She took one from the fridge and rang it through the till. 'It's yesterday's one so I hope it's all stale and dry.'

Isla smirked, knowing that would be very unlikely.

She waved goodbye to her mum and went outside. Sadie was sitting on the sea wall, staring down at the phone in her hand and chatting to someone.

'I just want to come home, Jim,' Sadie said, sadly.

Isla could hear his reply; clearly Sadie had him on speaker-phone.

'You're not coming back here without that money,' Jim snapped.

'Everyone hates me, and you know what, I'm starting to hate myself. This was a mistake.'

'If you walk away from there with a hundred and fifty thousand pounds, they can hate you as much as they want. You'll be out of there soon, who gives a shit what they think of you?' Jim said.

'If we have to go to court, it could take months. You're not here having to deal with all this. I'm pretty sure a waitress at the hotel yesterday spat in my food. And a bloody turkey chased me down the road this morning.'

Isla smirked at the vision of Dobby chasing Sadie – it was his usual trick if anyone was walking past Jamie's house, but she wouldn't put it past Jamie to have set Dobby on her as he'd said he would the day before.

'I'm running out of money to pay for the hotel and for food too and now I can't even get served to buy a bloody ham sandwich,' Sadie went on.

'If you come home without that money, then it's over between us. In fact, don't even bother coming back to Goa without it.'

The phone went dead and Isla watched Sadie for a moment. She looked utterly defeated, as if she hadn't slept properly in years. Isla took a breath and walked over.

Sadie leapt up as Isla approached, looking ready to defend herself in a fight. Isla offered out the sandwich and Sadie looked at it suspiciously.

'Did you put poison in it?'

Isla shrugged. 'If you don't want it, don't eat it. Feed it to the birds, I'm sure they'll appreciate it.'

Sadie sighed, her shoulders slumping as she took the sandwich. 'Thanks.'

She sat down on the sea wall, unwrapped the clingfilm and took a bite.

'Why are you being nice to me?'

Isla hesitated, not sure whether to say anything but then decided it couldn't do any more harm.

'Look, I understand you're desperate for cash. The only thing I'm desperate for is to adopt Elliot. Sign the form to give me consent to adopt him, please. It's a child's life you're playing with, *your* child's life.'

Sadie looked at her and then bit into her sandwich. She didn't say anything but Isla could see she was thinking about it. Isla decided to let it go for now. She certainly didn't want to be accused of harassing her.

'So you've travelled around a bit for the last few years?' Isla asked.

Sadie nodded as she ate; she wasn't much good at this conversation malarkey. She hadn't always been like this. Isla had met her only a few times after Elliot was born and she'd come across as quiet but nice. Now she seemed permanently on edge, looking at the world as if she was a dog waiting for the next beating.

'What was your favourite place?' Isla asked.

'New Zealand... it's so peaceful and beautiful.'

'Maybe, when you get the money from the house, however much it is, you could go there instead of going back to Goa,' Isla said, meaningfully.

Sadie's head whipped up as she took in what Isla meant. It didn't look like that piece of advice had been well received.

Isla shrugged. 'Just a thought.'

She walked away, hoping she hadn't just done more harm than good.

Leo walked towards The Cherry on Top with the intention of buying lunch and cake for Isla. She was right, he should have told her the night before that Sadie hadn't signed the papers, not kept it from her. And he should have stayed this morning when she was stressing out, even if the only thing he could offer her as support was a warm hug. He needed her to know she was not facing this alone. He wasn't great at this relationship thing and he needed to be. He wanted this to work more than anything.

He saw Carolyn up ahead on the beach with Elliot making sandcastles, despite the coolness of the day. Carolyn was talking to two women he recognised from the village. Frances Cook used to live next to his mum and dad when he was little and Betty Lucas was her sister who lived down the road. Frances had never had much time for him when he was a kid, she was always coming round to complain to his mum about his behaviour. For the most part, his mum, bless her, would listen patiently to what Frances would moan about and, as soon as she was gone, just laugh it off.

He moved closer to say hello to Carolyn and play with Elliot for a few minutes when he heard them talking.

'You must be so worried about your Isla,' Frances said.

'I know, this whole situation with Sadie Norton is a complete nightmare,' Carolyn said.

'Well yes, of course,' Betty said. 'But we meant about her relationship with that Leo Jackson.'

He stopped. *That* Leo Jackson?

'What's wrong with Leo?' Carolyn said, defensively. 'I think he's wonderful with Isla and Elliot.'

He smiled, slightly.

'He's rotten, that one,' Frances said.

'And did you hear what Elliot said back there, that he's only using her for sex?' Betty said. 'He has no intention of marrying her.'

'That's not true, he's proposed to her many many times,' Carolyn said.

'Oh well, you have to ask yourself why Isla has said no so many times. She obviously knows he isn't the marrying kind. Do you know how many women he's slept with?' Betty asked.

'Do you?' Carolyn said, pointedly.

'I bet even Leo Jackson has no idea how many women he's slept with,' Frances said.

Leo shoved his hands into his pockets. That was probably true.

'You know he got into trouble with the police when he was younger,' Betty said.

'Got into lots of fights too,' Frances said.

'Everyone knows a leopard never changes his spots.'

'He's self-absorbed, only looks out for himself.'

'Isla will realise the truth soon enough and send him packing.'

'Do you really want a man like that raising your grandchild?'

'A man that's kind and generous?' Carolyn snapped. 'A man that's redecorated one of his bedrooms with planets and stars so that Elliot has in his own room every time he stays over? A man that's been there for Isla and Elliot every single day since Matthew died? I think I'll take my chances.'

Elliot suddenly leapt up from his sandcastle-building. 'Leo is not a leopard and he doesn't fight with anyone and he's the best dad in the whole world and I love him and you are all being very mean and I don't like it.'

Elliot ran off the beach, heading straight for the road. Thankfully there were no cars coming but Leo got to him before he could step one foot off the pavement. He caught him round the middle and scooped him up, holding him tight as his godson wrapped his arms around his neck and cried.

'Hey, it's OK,' Leo soothed, stroking his back. He moved a little further away from the café and Frances and Betty, just in case they had any more mean things to say that he didn't want Elliot to overhear.

'They're being mean,' Elliot said.

'I know.'

Carolyn moved quickly over to them. 'Leo, I'm so sorry, I had no idea you were there.'

'I think you did a pretty good job of fighting my corner,' Leo said.

'I'm sorry, Elliot,' Carolyn said. 'I shouldn't have let them say nasty things about Leo in front of you.'

'Carolyn, it's not your fault people are small-minded,' Leo said 'Or that they chose to say those things in front of Elliot. Elliot's fine, aren't you, buddy?'

Elliot pulled back to look at him, and Leo wiped the tears from his cheeks. He sniffled a bit but giggled when Leo tweaked his nose.

'You're not sad?' Elliot asked.

'Not one bit,' Leo said, though the ache in his heart said otherwise. Did everyone in the village really think that of him? Did everyone look at Isla sympathetically and shake their heads at her getting involved with him? Would he really lose Isla and Elliot one day when she came to her senses and realised what kind of man he truly was? Someone so self-absorbed that he did nothing to stop his best friend from being killed.

'I love you,' Elliot said and then held his arms out really wide. 'This much.'

Leo swallowed down the emotion that had caught in his throat and stuck one arm out, which reached a lot further than Elliot's arm. 'I love you this much.'

Elliot giggled as he tried to reach down to Leo's hand but it was too far away.

'And Isla loves you very much too,' Elliot said.

'And that's all that matters,' Carolyn said, meaningfully.

Leo looked at her and nodded. It didn't matter what anyone else thought. His family were loyal to him, he knew that, and beyond that Elliot and Isla were the only ones who were important. Isla saw something in him that was wonderful so he would trust in her that he was good enough for them. Everyone else could go to hell.

He kissed Elliot on the head and tried to ignore the ache in his heart that refused to go away.

CHAPTER 18

Isla arrived at work at lunchtime but there was no sign of Leo in the office. Not wanting to prolong the argument any longer, she went off to the warehouse to look for him. She found him checking fireworks from a large crate off a list on his clipboard. Loud music was playing and he obviously hadn't heard her come in.

She walked up to him, slipped her arms around his stomach and pressed a kiss onto his back. He jumped a little at her touch and then held his hands over hers. She sighed with relief.

He turned round and she opened her mouth to apologise but he captured the words on her lips as he kissed her.

'I'm sorry,' she giggled against his lips as he continued to pepper her with kisses.

'I'm sorry too,' he said. 'I should have told you last night, not kept it from you. I just didn't want you to worry. But it was wrong of me to keep it from you.'

She pulled back slightly, wrapping her hands round his neck. 'I'm sorry I snapped at you. I'm just getting so stressed out about this whole Sadie debacle and—'

'It's fine, don't worry.'

Isla sighed. 'I spoke to the bank this morning about remortgaging the house so I can release some capital for Sadie and—'

'Don't do anything hasty, this is far from over yet,' Leo said.

'I know, but whatever happens, whether we settle out of court or let the solicitors fight it out in front of a judge, Sadie is still walking away from this with some cash in her pocket. There is no way, despite the circumstances, that any judge is going to award me the cost of the whole house. Her name is on the deeds and if it was that simple to remove her we would have done that already. I'm not sure how much Hot Chocolate Cottage is worth but if she gets ten percent, that's still at least twenty to thirty thousand pounds. I don't have that. My funds are running out fast. And I don't want to go to court, I don't want this to drag on for months with Sadie hanging around like a bad smell. If I can pay her off now then I will. Sadly, though, the bank won't let me remortgage. I haven't had a job for over a year and that's kind of frowned upon.'

Leo stroked his hands up her back. 'OK, we can figure this out, we can—'

'I'm going to sell the house. There's these estate agents who will buy the house off you for less than market value but the house sale will then go through relatively quickly.'

He let out a heavy breath. 'I don't want you to do that, that's your home.'

'I don't have much choice.'

'OK. So you'll move in with me into Maple Cottage. Elliot already has his own room—'

Isla shook her head. 'No, I was considering renting, but the rent on properties round here is sky high and it just feels like wasted money. So I'm going to buy a small flat on the other side of town.'

He frowned. 'Why would you not want to move in with me? Elliot's happy there and we're getting on OK.'

She grinned. 'More than OK. But we're not there yet, me and you. To go from young, free and single to living under the same roof and raising a child together in a matter of weeks is a huge leap. I don't want to do anything to risk us or put pressure on what we have.'

'You don't think I'd cope being a dad?'

'I think you'd cope just fine, you're a wonderful dad to Elliot and he loves you. But I'd quite like to focus on us as a couple for a while, not us as parents. If this was anyone else you were dating, you wouldn't be asking her to move in after one amazing night.'

'This is not anyone else, this is you,' Leo said, softly.

'When I move in with you, I want it to happen because it's the right time for us, not because I'm being forced to.'

He shook his head, smiling fondly at her. 'You're a stubborn woman. Why won't you accept help when you need it? You don't have to do this alone.'

'I know. And you're amazing. You've done so so much for me already but I want this to work between us. You have no idea how badly I want this to work, but let's take it slow and not rush into anything.'

He frowned, clearly not happy about this decision.

'And not to add any pressure to our relationship, but Elliot wants us to hurry up and get married so you can give me a baby.'

Leo's eyebrows shot up. 'No pressure at all then.'

She laughed. 'None whatsoever.'

He kissed her and then eased her back against the wall. 'I think we need some baby-making practice.'

'I have work to do,' Isla only half protested.

'I can be quick,' Leo said, undoing the buttons on her shirt.

She laughed. 'That's not a selling point.'

But what he did next with his tongue most definitely was.

─────

Isla was just shutting down her computer and getting ready to leave the office when Leo walked in from the warehouse.

'Thomas wants to meet with us,' Leo said, grabbing her bag and holding out her coat.

'Now?'

'Yes, and we're to meet him up in Clover Woods, so no one will see us together,' Leo said, a smile playing on his lips. It was clear Thomas was loving all this incognito stuff.

'Do we need to wear a rose in our lapel so Thomas will recognise us, or take a decoy briefcase?' Isla asked.

He smiled. 'I don't think so.'

'Then let's go,' Isla said.

'Let's go in my car. I can drop you back here after to pick up yours,' Leo said.

She followed him outside, locked the office door and got into his car.

'Did Thomas say what it was about?' Isla asked as Leo negotiated the car down the long driveway.

He shook his head. 'Just that he'd had a meeting with Sadie and he wanted to discuss the results.'

Isla sighed. Whatever it was, it wasn't going to be good, and she hoped she hadn't made things worse with her interfering earlier that day. But just as long as Sadie hadn't changed her mind about Elliot, she could cope with anything else.

Leo placed his hand on her knee, but it wasn't sexual this time, it was purely a comforting thing. 'It's going to be OK, I promise you.'

She nodded, even though she couldn't really find any solace in his words.

He pulled up his car in the little car park next to the path that went through the woods. Thomas's car was already there, which might have looked a bit suspicious if anyone had been watching them. Luckily this wasn't a Hollywood movie and the FBI weren't watching because Thomas wasn't the best at this spy game stuff.

They started walking through the woods, Leo taking her hand. It was still fairly light, although the nights were drawing in now and the muted twilight lent an eerie air to the proceedings. As the trees cleared, they saw a bench in a little glade and sitting on it was Thomas, actually in disguise, wearing a full-length trench coat, a fake moustache, a trilby hat and big black sunglasses. He was even reading a newspaper to finish the look. He looked so ridiculously out of place that if anyone was passing they wouldn't be able to help but think Thomas was up to no good. The whole thing was such a farce that Isla wanted to laugh but the subject of the meeting prevented that.

Leo sat down next to Thomas and Isla joined them. Thomas brought his newspaper up so if anyone was watching they wouldn't be able to tell he was talking to them.

'Thank you for meeting me. I had a meeting with my client today. I'm afraid to say she wants seventy-five thousand and then she will sign over her half of the house and give you full parental responsibility.'

Isla's heart sank. That was so much more money than she'd hoped. She had spent a while looking at small houses and flats near to the village today and they were a lot more expensive than she'd first thought. If she gave seventy-five thousand to Sadie, she wouldn't have anywhere near enough left to get even the cheapest of flats. She'd have to go further inland, but then that would make taking Elliot to school every day tricky. She'd be further away from all her friends and family, too.

'That's ridiculous,' Leo said. 'Tell her to go to hell.'

Thomas lowered the newspaper, giving up all pretence. 'I told her if it was to go to court she would be unlikely to get half of that amount but she's obviously done her homework on what the houses round here are worth. She knows seventy-five thousand isn't half the value of the house so she believes this to be a fair deal. She also knows how much you want to keep Elliot so she's holding that over your heads too.'

Isla groaned. She'd laid her cards on the table with Sadie earlier that day, about how much she wanted Elliot, and Sadie had used that against her.

'I say we call her bluff, take her to court, let's see how much the judge gives her,' Leo said.

'I don't want to do that, I want her gone. It will take months to sort out if we go to court,' Isla said.

'She won't want to do that either, it would mean hanging around here for months, living out of a hotel when she probably wants to go back to Goa or wherever,' Leo said. 'She's playing us, she knows we want this resolved quickly and we don't want to go to court either. She's banking on us wanting this done with as soon as possible.'

'But if she thinks she's going to get seventy-five thousand pounds or more out of it, waiting around for a few months is no great hardship for her,' Isla said.

'Maybe you come back with a counter-offer,' Thomas suggested. 'Through your solicitor obviously.'

'Five thousand pounds and the promise we won't go to the police because she's trying to sell her child,' Leo said.

Thomas tilted his head as if he agreed with that sentiment. 'You could certainly try that. I mean, I think you'll have to up your offer significantly but you're right, her offer to sign over parental responsibility of her child in return for monetary gains is actually illegal. I did tell her that it makes it far more complicated if she wants to include Elliot in her offer. If it goes to court the judge would throw that part of the agreement out completely but that would have a negative impact on your side of things. She'd get the money that the judge awards her and she would still have parental responsibility over Elliot with no need to sign it over to you.'

Isla groaned. It was all so complicated. 'What do you suggest, Thomas?'

'I think you need to go away and work out what you could reasonably afford to pay, come back with a counter-offer. I'd suggest something like twenty-five thousand as a starting point and then hopefully she can be negotiated down to forty or fifty thousand. Legally, Elliot won't be part of the formal agreement but I'm going to make damned sure she signs that parental responsibility form before she gets a single penny. I've also pointed out that if she refuses to sign him over to you, you could reasonably sue for four years' child maintenance costs, which would be expensive for her.'

'OK, and if she refuses to budge from seventy-five?' Isla asked.

'Then I agree with Leo. Take her to court and let the judge decide. I certainly wouldn't give her seventy-five thousand pounds. And at the very least calling her bluff may make her reconsider. But she's in this for the most money she can possibly get so court may be the only option at the end of the day.'

Isla sighed.

Thomas stood up and folded his newspaper. 'And of course, you didn't hear any of this from me. I'll speak to Kim tomorrow and let her know the results from my meeting, so act surprised when Kim tells you. I'll be in touch if I hear any more.'

He moved to leave and then placed a hand on Isla's shoulder. 'We'll sort this out, love.'

She smiled weakly and nodded and he left them alone in the darkening woods.

Isla sat back and stared up at the stars starting to pepper the sky above them.

'Matthew, you've left a right mess behind, I don't mind telling you. If there's any divine intervention you can offer, I'd be eternally grateful.'

Leo put his arm round her and she leaned into his shoulder. She looked up at him and he kissed her briefly on the lips. She smiled and gazed back up at the stars again as she snuggled into Leo's side.

'Though I am very grateful for this gift you sent me,' Isla said, placing a hand over Leo's heart.

He smiled and kissed her forehead. 'Come on, let's go home.'

Leo pulled into his driveway knowing that Isla wouldn't be far behind. He'd dropped her off at her car and she'd gone off to pick up Elliot, while he'd stayed behind for a while at the office.

He'd gone through all his bank accounts to see how much money he could reasonably take out and give to Isla. The problem being that since he had started taking a step back at work so he could be there more for Isla and Elliot over the last year, he'd taken on more staff to pick up his shortfall. He had three teams now who took care of all the displays, four pyrotechnicians in each team. They all needed paying as did Annie, his office manager, which was now Isla's job and his own wages. The company made good money from firework displays, but once fourteen people's wages had been factored in, plus the ongoing outlay for new fireworks and equipment, there wasn't a great deal left over.

He had recently managed to pay off his mortgage in full so had been putting quite a bit into his savings each month. He now had ten thousand put aside which he would give to Isla in a heartbeat but it wasn't enough. Knowing Sadie as he did, she wasn't going to back down from her offer. And if Isla thought she would have enough left over after selling the cottage to buy somewhere small in Sandcastle Bay, she was sorely mistaken. He didn't know what the answer was. The obvious answer was for her to move in with him but he did understand why she didn't want to do that yet.

The drive looped round itself in a steep circle and he was surprised to see all the cars that were at the top when he pulled up outside his house.

He smiled to himself when he realised it was Jamie, Melody, Aidan, Tori, Emily and Marigold. In times of crisis his family were always there and this was a time of crisis. They would no doubt have heard by now what was happening with Sadie and were here to offer emotional support if nothing else.

He got out of his car and Marigold came running to greet him. He scooped her up and she gave him a big hug.

'What a lovely welcome,' Leo said, hugging her and then tickling her ribs, which sent her into peals of giggles.

'We're here to stage an invention,' Marigold said.

Leo suppressed a smile. 'An invention? That sounds wonderful. What are we inventing?'

'Something that gets rid of witches,' Emily said, coming over and giving him a hug.

'Well I definitely need one of those,' Leo said.

'Do you have a witch here?' Marigold's eyes glittered with excitement at the possibility of a real-life witch. This was a girl who wasn't scared of anything.

'Apparently there's one nearby,' Leo said theatrically. 'She has a green face and warts on her nose.'

'And she's called Sadie,' Emily said.

Leo smiled. 'Why don't we go inside and get warm and, when Elliot gets here, you two can make a magic potion for getting rid of witches.'

'Yay!' Marigold cheered.

He popped her down and went to open the front door. Luke greeted them all with a bark and Marigold scooped him up and carried him off to the kitchen, telling him he was going to be her assistant.

'So, good night last night?' Aidan said, clapping Leo on the back.

'Yes, thank you for interfering with my life so spectacularly,' Leo said, dryly.

'By all accounts, our interfering worked out pretty damned fine,' Melody said.

'We were just cuddling in bed, nothing more,' Leo said, truthfully, because at the moment that Emily had seen them, that's exactly what they had been doing.

'Sure you were, that's why you were stark naked and Elliot found a condom on your bedside drawers,' Emily said, following them into the house and clapping her hands together to keep them warm.

There was nothing he could say to that. Everyone here knew what he'd been doing with Isla the night before and, almost certainly by now, Agatha and therefore the rest of the village knew too.

'Well, as our last lot of interfering worked so well, you won't mind us interfering again,' Tori said, taking off her coat and scarf.

'I'm sure Isla might mind,' Leo said, indicating the headlights pulling into the drive.

A few seconds later, Elliot burst into the house and ran straight into the kitchen to play with Marigold.

Isla appeared in the doorway and looked around at all the faces waiting for her. 'Are we having a party?'

'Apparently so,' Leo said.

'That explains why Mum wanted to come back with me.' Isla nodded her head outside and a few seconds later Carolyn walked in stamping her feet from the cold.

'We want to know what's going on with Sadie and Elliot,' Emily said.

'And most importantly what we can do to help,' Melody said.

Isla let out a hollow laugh. 'Do you have a spare seventy-five thousand pounds?'

'Is that what she wants?' Jamie asked.

Isla shut the door behind her and gestured for them to go in the lounge so they couldn't be overheard from the kitchen.

'I'll just go and check on the kids,' Emily said. 'Don't say anything until I get back.'

Everyone settled themselves on chairs and sofas. Leo sat down and pulled Isla down on his lap just as Emily came waddling back into the room.

'They're busy making a magic potion out of water, flour and glitter. I think they'll be busy for a while, though I don't think your kitchen will be clean and tidy afterwards,' Emily said, lowering herself into a chair. 'So, tell us everything.'

Isla took a deep breath and explained what had happened so far: Sadie turning up on her doorstep, hiding out at Leo's so Sadie wouldn't see Elliot, the fact that Sadie had no interest in Elliot at all, and now this ridiculous request for seventy-five thousand pounds in return for signing over Elliot and Sadie's half of the house.

'I can't believe she has no interest in her own son,' Tori said, rubbing her belly protectively, as if the thought of abandoning her child was not one she could possibly comprehend. Thankfully most mothers felt the same.

'I know, it makes my heart ache just thinking about it, and also how Elliot will react to that when he's older and able to understand all this,' Isla said. 'I love this little man with my whole heart, I just can't see how she could walk away from him. But in many ways, I'm glad she doesn't want him. I can deal with losing money, I can't deal with losing him.'

'So what are you going to do?' Melody asked.

'I can't remortgage – not having a job for the last year is not looked on favourably by the bank. I'm going to have to sell Hot Chocolate Cottage but I don't think there'll be enough left over for me to get anywhere in Sandcastle Bay. I may have to buy a place further inland, away from the beach. Elliot will be gutted.'

Six confused faces stared back at them.

'But, why wouldn't you just move in here?' Melody asked as if it was the most obvious answer in the world.

Isla let out a little sigh. 'Because... it's not fair on Leo.'

They still looked confused. Leo tried to find the words to defend her decision but he didn't like it either. She belonged here at Maple Cottage.

'We've had one date. Would any of you move in with someone after one date?' Isla tried again.

'But you've known each other for years,' Melody said.

'To be fair, we've known each other for years,' Jamie said to Melody. 'We've been going out for three months and we haven't moved in together yet.'

'Well, no,' Melody conceded.

'It took me two years to move in with Stanley,' Emily said. 'I'd have run a mile if he'd asked me to move in with him after one date.'

'I just don't want to move in with Leo because I have to. I want to move in with him when the time is right for us, because we love each other and we see a future together. Not because I'm going to be homeless.'

Was that what this was? Was she just waiting for him to tell her he loved her? Was that all it would take? Hell, he'd tell her he loved her now if she'd agree to forget this nonsense and move in with him.

'You won't be homeless, you can move in with me,' Melody said.

'Or me,' Carolyn said.

'I have Elliot and he comes with a ton of toys and you both only have one bedroom. But thank you and, no, I won't be homeless, but I will have to make some sacrifices and leaving Sandcastle Bay will probably be one of them.'

'Would you move schools? Marigold will be distraught if she can't see Elliot every day,' Emily said.

'I don't want you to leave,' Melody said.

'I don't want to leave either but I have to be practical. And I wouldn't be too far away, maybe only half an hour in the car. We'd still see each other,' Isla said.

'There has to be another option,' Tori said, looking at Aidan for help.

'Look, we need to go back with a counter-offer first,' Leo said. 'We'll offer her twenty-five thousand and see if she'll take that. I have ten thousand in my savings, you can have that, and I'm sure we could find another fifteen from somewhere and you wouldn't have to sell your home at all.'

'I have three thousand in my savings,' Melody said, immediately. 'You can have that.'

'I've just sold one of my big sculptures to one of those posh hotels in the next town. I got five thousand for that, you can have it,' Jamie said, without any hesitation.

'I probably have four thousand you can have,' Carolyn added. 'I have a lump sum from my pension, it's just sitting there in my account. I was thinking I might put it towards a conservatory but, hell, it's not something I need.'

'We don't have a ton of money as we're saving for the baby and the wedding but we could probably spare a couple of thousand,' Aidan said.

'We're saving for the baby too, but I could give you five hundred pounds. It's not much but if it helps I'd gladly give it to you,' Emily said.

'No, wait, I can't take your money,' Isla said. 'Thank you, that's very kind, but you all work damned hard for that money and I'm not going to take it from you.'

'Why not?' Melody said. 'You'd do the same for us if we were in trouble.'

'I would but this isn't fair.'

'None of this is fair,' Tori said. 'If it was fair, Sadie would never have come back at all and she certainly wouldn't be holding the future of your child to ransom, what kind of asshole does that? But as it's quite clear she has no scruples and as we all love you and want to help you, you'll take the money.'

Isla sighed, her shoulders slumping. She looked utterly defeated and not just by this conversation but this whole situation. Leo just wanted to take all this away from her.

He stroked down her back. 'Come on, let's make a start on dinner. That's if my kitchen isn't covered in glitter.'

'Good luck with that,' Emily said.

He smiled as he stood. He'd take all the glitter in the world if it meant having Isla and Elliot in his home where they belonged.

CHAPTER 19

Isla stared at the envelopes of money on the table. She had refused to give her friends and family her bank details because she still didn't feel right taking the money from them. So envelopes stuffed with cash had all arrived this morning from Aidan, Tori, Jamie, Melody, Emily, Carolyn and even Agatha, who had no doubt been informed of the situation.

She felt awful that so many people were freely giving her their hard-earned cash when all of this could have been solved if she just moved in with Leo.

She thought back to the night before and how he'd made love to her. It wasn't rushed and passionate like it had been before, it had been slow, gentle, languid. The way he had stroked and caressed her like she was someone to be cherished and adored. And the way he had looked into her eyes as they'd made love, she knew that he loved her as much as she loved him. She wondered why she was holding back from this. He was her forever, why didn't she just grab hold of this opportunity now?

But in her heart, she knew it was the right decision not to move in with him, not yet. She wanted it to work with Leo more than anything and turning up on his doorstep with all her worldly goods and five tons of toys for Elliot just seemed like it would be too much too soon. She didn't want to scare him away.

But nothing seemed to faze him. Elliot had had nightmares the night before, waking them both up with his screams. Leo had been on his feet and out the door before Isla could even get out of bed. He'd brought a crying Elliot back into bed with

them and cuddled him between them until Elliot had gone
back to sleep. Isla had thought Leo would take Elliot back to
his own room after that but he didn't. With one arm round Isla
and Elliot fast asleep on his chest, they'd spent the rest of the
night like that, all entwined together like a proper family. And
even this morning, when Leo was woken by a fist in the face
and a heel to the stomach as Elliot starfished across the bed, it
didn't seem to bother him.

Leo walked into the kitchen wearing jeans and a thick jumper.
With his dark curly hair slightly damp from the shower they'd
shared this morning, he looked like he'd just stepped off the pages
of a catalogue.

He dropped a kiss on her head and then stole a slice of banana
from Elliot's plate.

'Hey!' Elliot said, indignantly.

'Nice smiley face.' Leo indicated the French toast on Elliot's
plate which Isla had cut into two eyes, chocolate sauce for the
spiky hair and the chopped banana arranged into a big smile.

'You stole his nose,' Elliot giggled. 'That's the best bit.'

Leo moved another slice of banana from the smile to take up
the nose position and Elliot seemed happy with that.

'Are we ready for the Great Pumpkin-Carving competition?'
Leo said.

'Yay!' Elliot cheered. Obviously the nightmares of the night
before had been completely forgotten this morning.

Leo sat down next to him. 'Are we going to do it as a team or
do you want to do one on your own? Me and Isla can help with
some of the cutting.'

'Can we do one together as a family?' Elliot said.

'Of course we can, buddy,' Leo said.

Elliot took a bite of his French toast, kicking his legs happily.
'Marigold says we're going to get married soon.'

Isla had to smile at that. *We're* going to get married. As if it would be a group activity, which she supposed in some way it would be.

'Did she?' Leo said, again unfazed as he grabbed a piece of toast and started buttering it.

'Because we've now moved in with you,' Elliot said.

'We haven't moved in with Leo,' Isla quickly corrected. 'We're just staying with him for a few days.'

'But you are getting married?' Elliot said.

'Maybe,' Isla said, carefully.

'Yes,' Leo said, at the same time.

Isla supposed she should be annoyed that Leo was offering Elliot empty promises again but they no longer felt like vague pledges that would never happen. She knew they would end up there and probably sooner rather than later. He loved her and, although he hadn't said it yet, they were clearly on the same page now.

'I think… it's very likely that we will but now isn't the right time.'

'And when you get married, then we'll move in here?' Elliot said, not to be deterred.

'That's right, buddy,' Leo said. 'We'll be a proper family and one of those spare rooms upstairs will be your toy room.'

'Which one?'

'The big room.'

'But that's Isla's room,' Elliot said, in confusion.

'When we get married, we'll be sharing a bedroom,' Leo explained patiently.

'Oh. Will I still have my own room?'

'Of course.'

'And Luke will live here too.'

'Yes, we couldn't leave him behind.'

Elliot popped another piece of banana in his mouth.

'And I'll get a baby sister?'

Leo grinned. 'We're going to do our very best on that one.'

Isla wanted to be angry that her whole life was being planned out for her but she wanted that life so much: marriage, living here with Elliot as a family, maybe having children of their own one day. And it sounded like Leo wanted all of that too.

So why the hell was she holding back? Relationships didn't move to a given schedule, there were no rules that said when the right time was to move in with someone. She had known Leo for years, they had been best friends, seeing each other every day for the past year, and she'd been in love with him for too many months to count. He had proved, time and time again, that he was here for her, that he adored Elliot. So what was she waiting for? And maybe everything that was happening with Sadie had brought it all to a head, but it had been bubbling there for some time. She knew it probably wasn't the right time to make decisions about her future with everything else up in the air, but maybe actually it was the perfect time. Maybe when her back was against the wall and she could see that Leo was still there for her, holding her hand, she needed to take a step towards the future she wanted. Maybe something positive should come from this.

She looked at the money on the table. 'I can't take this.'

The smile fell from Leo's face. 'Yes you can. People want to help and we need all the help we can get at the moment.'

She shook her head. 'No, you don't understand, I don't need it—'

'We do, I've already spoken to Kim this morning. She let me know officially about the request for seventy-five thousand and I've offered a counter-offer of twenty-five. With this money and my ten grand, we'd have twenty-five. If she accepts then you wouldn't need to sell the house.'

Elliot looked between them with wide eyes. 'We're selling our home?'

'Yes,' Isla said. Suddenly she'd never been so sure of anything in her entire life.

'No, you're not,' Leo said firmly. 'You belong here in Sandcastle Bay; your family is here. Stop being so bloody stubborn and independent and let your friends and family help you for once.'

Elliot giggled. 'You said bloody.'

'Sorry buddy, I did, but your mum's being infuriating,' Leo said.

Elliot shook his head at Isla. 'Silly Mummy.'

Her heart leapt. He'd never called her that. He had kept saying, *Isla is like my mummy*, and when he'd drawn pictures of his family, Isla was always the mummy, but he'd never actually called her that. It was always Isla. She hadn't realised how much she would like being called *Mummy* before.

'Yes she is, isn't she? She…' Leo trailed off as he too realised what Elliot had said. He looked over at Isla and his face softened.

She cleared her throat. 'And your dad won't listen to me.'

Leo quirked an eyebrow.

'Silly Daddy,' Elliot said, wagging a finger at Leo. And then giggled as if he liked trying these new words on for size.

The whole of Leo's face lit up. He cleared his throat but when he spoke his voice was thick with emotion. 'We need to get ready, we need to be at the pumpkin-carving competition in half an hour.'

He stood up and kissed Elliot on the head. 'Love you,' he said and left the room.

Elliot stared after him. 'Did I make him sad?'

'I think you just made him very happy,' Isla said.

⁂

The rules for the pumpkin-carving competition were quite strict and there were lots of them. Everyone had been asked to bring their own pumpkin that fell within a certain size bracket so that all competition entries could be judged equally. They were allowed to bring their own cutting tools, but props and stencils were strictly forbidden. All pumpkins had to be checked to make sure that there were no pencil marks or holes premade on the pumpkin so everyone was starting from a clean slate.

It all seemed a bit over the top to Leo for what was supposed to be a family event, but that didn't stop the families and teams signing up in their droves as they struggled in with their pumpkins and waited patiently while they were measured and checked. Tori and Aidan were there a few tables down, as were Jamie and Melody. Emily and Stanley were on the other side of the village hall with Marigold, who was determined to win and appeared to be giving her parents strict instructions.

Agatha was also here and surprisingly appeared to be in a team with Stefano from the Italian restaurant. She had been trying to get him to agree to go on a date with her for months – had he finally succumbed? Although Stefano didn't look entirely thrilled about his new team mate, as they were clearly arguing over what they were going to carve. But they were here together, which was a start.

This was the first year that Leo had entered, as it was more an event for families or couples than individuals. This was the first year he had a family of his own. He swallowed down the lump of emotion in his throat as he thought about that, how utterly complete his life was now.

'It's a bit serious, isn't it?' Isla whispered as one of the judges walked past with their clipboards, giving them the beady eye to make sure they hadn't started yet.

'You know Sandcastle Bay, we take all our competitions and festivals very seriously,' Leo said, examining their pumpkin. 'So what are we going to make?'

'Batman,' Elliot said, excitedly.

Leo looked at their pumpkin and tried to work out how he would achieve that.

'We could do Batman's head or the Batman logo,' Leo said. Normally he had a lot more time to plan out what he was going to do in these kind of competitions, and normally the work was all done at home weeks in advance. However, with everything that had happened over the last few days, he hadn't really given this much thought so he really was starting from scratch.

Isla picked up the long list of rules and flicked through them.

Leo looked at the spare pumpkin they'd brought along, just in case Elliot decided he wanted to do his own pumpkin after all. A lot of the kids were doing their own and Isla thought once Elliot saw the other children working by themselves he might want to do that too.

'Elliot, are you sure you want to work with us?' Leo said. 'Because I might have use for your spare pumpkin.'

'I want to work together as a family,' Elliot said.

Leo smiled. He loved that Elliot had called him *Daddy* that morning. It had been a silly, off-hand comment but it had filled his heart.

'OK, Isla, anything in those rules that says we can't use more than one?'

Isla scanned through the list, flicking the sheet over to check the rules on the other side too. 'Surprisingly not.'

'OK, so we can use the slightly smaller one as Batman's head and the bigger one as his body with the cloak and utility belt,' Leo said.

Elliot jumped up and down with excitement. 'It's going to be amazing.'

Leo swung him up onto his hip and Elliot kissed him on the cheek and gave him a big hug.

Leo looked over at Isla to see if she agreed with the Batman plan and realised she was staring at them. He looped an arm round her shoulders, bringing her into the group hug, and she slipped an arm round his stomach and leaned into him.

'You OK?' he said softly.

She nodded but she didn't say anything.

'Can I go and see Marigold?' Elliot said.

Leo placed him down on the floor and he ran off.

Immediately Leo pulled Isla back into a hug and kissed her on the head.

'What's wrong?'

She clung onto him for a second as if she wanted to hold him close and then she leaned back slightly to look at him. He watched her visibly take a deep breath as if about to say something terrible but then she seemed to change her mind. He realised she was trembling slightly in his arms. Then her face set with determination and she took another deep breath. What the hell was she going to say to him because it didn't look like it was going to be anything positive?

'I love you,' Isla said and his heart roared to life in his chest. 'I know this is definitely not the right time to tell you, in a hall full of people and with all this mess with Sadie going on, but I wanted you to know. I love you. In fact, I've been in love with you for some time. You are the most incredible, amazing man I've ever met and I'm head over heels in love with you.'

Leo stared at her. His mouth was dry and there were no words in his head at all.

She loved him.

He knew she had feelings for him and he'd hoped and thought that she might love him, but to actually hear her say it was something else entirely. If he'd thought he had felt complete this morning when Elliot had called him *Daddy*, this was another league of happiness.

Christ, why did she have to tell him here, in front of all these people? He wanted to kiss her, pin her to the nearest hard surface and make love to her.

He realised he still hadn't spoken. He needed to tell her how he felt too, how much joy she brought him. What were the words he should use? He needed to get this right and simply to say, 'I love you,' suddenly felt wildly inadequate.

'I—'

She put her fingers to his lips. 'I don't need you to say it back, that's not what this is. I just wanted you to know how I felt.'

'Ladies and gentlemen, thank you all for coming today, and welcome to the fifth annual Great Pumpkin-Carving Competition.' The voice of the mayor came over the loudspeaker, interrupting this wonderful moment. Everyone started cheering and clapping.

Damn it. He couldn't concentrate on a bloody stupid pumpkin competition now. He wanted to take her somewhere quiet and tell her everything that was in his heart. Except his godson was running back across the hall towards them, a huge excited grin on his face. There was no way they could leave now, Elliot would be distraught.

Isla pulled away from him and swept Elliot up in her arms, peppering his face with kisses.

'I hope you all have been reading the rules,' the mayor went on and everyone groaned playfully.

Leo couldn't take his eyes off Isla. She had told him she loved him and he'd said nothing. Not one word. That wasn't how he imagined it going down at all. Not even close.

'Are you ready, beautiful boy?' Isla said and Elliot cheered.

'So, as you know because you've all read the rules,' the mayor teased. 'You have thirty minutes to create your pumpkin masterpieces. There is a prize for the best child's pumpkin and a prize for the best team pumpkin. May the best carver win. Everyone, to your pumpkins. We'll start the competition in ten, nine, eight…'

Elliot slipped his hand into Leo's, distracting him from his thoughts.

'Are we going to win, Daddy?' Elliot said.

God, his heart felt fit to burst. He didn't deserve any of this. What was a man like him doing with this perfect, ready-made family who loved him?

'Hell yeah, we're going to win,' Leo said, his voice thick.

' three, two, one,' the mayor said over the microphone.

An air horn filled the air and suddenly there was a flurry of activity.

'OK, I'm going to chop the lid off this one. Isla, can you chop the lid off that one and then, Elliot, you can help us get the goo and slime out.'

'Yes, I love goo and slime!' Elliot said.

Leo was aware those were the first words he'd spoken to Isla since she'd told him she loved him but she didn't seem to care. She picked up the pumpkin and started chopping around the stalk to get a lid. He did the same on his pumpkin and then he and Elliot started scooping out the insides, Elliot giggling over how slimy it was.

'Right, keep going on this one, buddy. I'm going to give Isla a hand.'

Elliot started using an ice cream scooper to get out the straggly bits around the edges as Leo moved over to Isla's pumpkin.

'We need to talk later,' Leo said, his hand grazing hers as he reached inside to get the flesh out.

She smiled up at him. 'There's no need. Don't get yourself in a flap over this. I just wanted you to know. It doesn't change anything between us.'

'It changes everything,' Leo said, gruffly.

She frowned. 'It really doesn't. I love you, you care about me a great deal. You've given me everything. I don't need anything more than that.'

He opened his mouth to speak and she reached up and stroked his face with a slimy hand. The cold of it was something of a shock. She giggled slightly as she realised what she'd done. 'You don't need to make this into a big deal. Don't freak out.'

'I'm not freaking out.'

'You are a little,' Isla said, turning her attention back to the pumpkin.

'I'm really not. I'm just… I'm not getting a chance to tell you—'

'You don't need to tell me anything,' Isla said, gently.

Leo groaned in frustration. 'What kind of person tells someone else they love them for the first time at a bloody pumpkin-carving competition? Couldn't you have told me at home this morning, or even in bed last night?'

'I'm sorry if my timing isn't convenient for you,' Isla said.

'It's not bloody convenient. Because all I want to do right now is take you back to bed and make love to you for the rest of the day and instead I have to carve the best god damn pumpkin I've ever carved.'

She smirked. 'Well, you'll just have to wait until later.'

'And before that you're going to let me talk, whether you like it or not,' Leo said.

'OK,' Isla nodded.

'Good.'

Isla passed him a knife. 'Now, less talking and more carving. You don't want to disappoint your *son*.'

Christ. *His son.*

He looked over at Elliot who had his tongue sticking out of the corner of his mouth as he scraped the last bits of flesh from inside the pumpkin.

'No, I bloody don't.'

He turned the pumpkin around to see where the best place would be to start carving and then he started cutting the pattern of Batman's mask. Isla stood and watched him for a while and then, while his hands were occupied, she leaned up and kissed him on the cheek.

'I love you,' she whispered in his ear.

He grunted, knowing she was doing it now to tease him, but before he could say anything else, she moved over to help Elliot.

These thirty minutes were going to be the longest of his life and then he needed to go somewhere quiet with Isla. He wondered if he could get Melody or Aidan to look after Elliot for him for a few hours so he could talk to Isla properly, and then spend the rest of the afternoon celebrating their love for each other in bed.

He slipped with the knife and stabbed himself in the finger. He quickly sucked the cut in his mouth but thankfully it was only small. Damn it, he really needed to concentrate on the task in hand and not what the rest of his day might look like.

'You have fifteen minutes left,' the mayor said over the loudspeaker.

'What kind of thing do you want over here, can we do anything?' Isla said, meaningfully, and Leo looked over at Elliot bouncing up and down impatiently.

'Yes, you could start carving out a belt shape in the middle, about this wide.' Leo showed them with his fingers. 'Don't worry about any kind of detail, just a belt all the way round. Try not to go all the way through with the knife, just score the skin.'

He watched as Isla guided Elliot to cut very carefully along the middle of the pumpkin and he returned his attention back to his own pumpkin, carving out the thin triangular eyes and then the bottom half of the face. Satisfied with the head, he joined Isla and Elliot to help them with theirs. He scored the Batman logo on the chest of the pumpkin and then helped Elliot to cut along the lines so that the bat was removed completely. Elliot started playing with the bat, swooping it around Isla and Leo as they carried on cutting. Leo cut out triangular bits from the back for the cloak and Isla added detail to the utility belt.

'You have one minute left,' the mayor said.

There was a last frantic attempt from all the teams to get their pumpkins finished, theirs included, although Elliot was still busy playing with his pumpkin bat, and then the air horn sounded.

'OK, ladies and gentlemen, your time is up. We are now going to dim the lights and you can put your candles inside and then the judges will come by each pumpkin to decide on the winner.'

The blinds were drawn and the lights flicked off, plunging the whole room into semi-darkness. There were *oooohs* as the room went dark and then lots of whispering as if the darkness commanded that everyone went quiet. Candles were lit and placed inside the pumpkins and golden orbs of light slowly filled the room. Leo and Isla put their tealights inside the two pumpkins and then Leo carefully lifted the head onto the body. They all stepped back to admire their handiwork.

Leo looked down at Elliot, who was beaming hugely.

'I think our pumpkin Batman is the best pumpkin in the whole village,' Elliot declared loudly.

Leo smiled. They hadn't seen any of the others yet and Leo suspected some of the carvings would be amazing, but if Elliot thought theirs was the best, that was good enough for him.

'Two pumpkins,' Tori said, as she came over with Aidan to admire Leo's creation. 'Surely that's against the rules?'

'Actually, it's not,' Leo said. 'We checked, it doesn't mention anything about the use of multiple pumpkins.'

'I think they'll probably add that rule in for next time,' Aidan said. 'That list of rules seems to be getting bigger every year.'

Leo noted the judges coming round and making notes on each entry.

'Love your Batman,' Jamie said as he came over with Melody.

'Even if he is a bit on the tubby side for a superhero,' Melody said. She had a point; with the roundness of the pumpkin, their Batman did look like he had been feasting on all the cakes.

'Shall we go and see what everyone else has done?' Leo suggested to Elliot and he nodded keenly.

They first wandered over to see Aidan and Tori's pumpkin, which was a really cool spider on a web. Leo didn't know if he wanted to look at Jamie's as he was a brilliant sculptor and it would certainly put his to shame. Sure enough, he had carved the shape of an amazing dragon. They wandered over to Emily next, who had carved a ghost into her family's entry.

Agatha and Stefano had done the pizza logo for Stefano's restaurant. Nothing like a bit of free advertising, though Leo was slightly disappointed that Agatha had done something so normal. But as the kids hurried on to look at the next pumpkin, Agatha turned their pumpkin around to show a couple in the throes of sex. It was a very basic stickman-like recreation but there was no doubt what they were doing. Agatha winked at him and he burst out laughing. It seemed that Agatha and Stefano had both carved their own design after failing to agree on what to carve as a team. Stefano quickly turned the pumpkin back around so the pizza design was facing outwards as the judges walked past, clearly a bit embarrassed by what Agatha had done. If Stefano had finally succumbed to Agatha's advances and agreed to go on a date with her, he would soon find out that that level of naughtiness was just the tip of the iceberg.

They moved around the rest of the hall and saw witches, cats, haunted houses, owls and a multitude of scary faces.

There was a lot of talk up near the stage as the judges made their decision and then the microphone squeaked to life.

'We have seen some very impressive entries this year, a much higher standard than last year. First of all, we are going to announce the runner-up and winner of the team competition. The runner-up caused a lot of discussion between the judges but it was a unanimous decision that it should go to the Jackson family with their fabulous Batman.'

Everyone clapped, though there were a few boos, which Leo strongly suspected had come from his own family.

He gave Elliot and Isla a hug as one of the organisers came over and presented Elliot with a little trophy – so tiny that Leo thought they might need a magnifying glass to see it – and a box of chocolates.

Elliot ran off to show Marigold his trophy just as Leo's phone beeped in his pocket with a text message and he quickly fished it out. It was from Thomas. He was vaguely aware of the mayor announcing the other winners as he opened the text.

Sadie has agreed to go down to sixty-five thousand, but says she won't go any lower than that.

He sighed. It was still too much.

Isla's phone beeped in her pocket and she dug it out too.

'Thomas has just texted me,' Leo said. 'He says Sadie will do sixty-five, but she won't go any lower than that.'

Isla pulled a face as she swiped open her phone. 'There was no way she was going to accept twenty-five. I'm surprised actually that she agreed to come down from seventy-five.'

'I still think we should take this to court,' Leo said as Isla pressed a few buttons to open up her own text message.

Tears suddenly filled Isla's eyes as she read the message.

'Shit, what's wrong?' Leo said.

She passed him the phone and his heart sank as he read the text message from Karie.

I tried to call you but I couldn't reach you. I think we may have to postpone the adoption hearing in a few weeks. Now Sadie is back, I'm afraid we cannot go ahead with the adoption without her consent. I'm going to talk to my boss about this on Monday and after talking to Sadie I feel sure we can get her consent soon so please don't worry. It will happen, just not when we hoped it would. Call me if you want to talk it through, if not I'll speak to you on Monday when I've spoken to my boss.

He wrapped his arm around her and held her against him. 'Look, it's OK, it's just going to be postponed, it's not cancelled for good. This is just a blip, a bump in the road.'

Isla wiped her tears from her face. 'God, this is such a mess. It feels like one step forward, three steps back. I just want Elliot and to not have the threat of losing him hanging over our heads. I'd give her the whole god damn house if it meant she would give us consent to adopt Elliot. I just want him with us, where he belongs.'

'He will be soon, you have my word,' Leo said, holding her tight.

Enough was enough. He was going to sort this out once and for all.

CHAPTER 20

Leo walked into the hotel where Sadie was staying and straight up to the reception. He knew the receptionist, Steve, in fact he had played football with him a few years before.

'Hey mate, how you doing?' Leo said, forcing a bright smile onto his face.

'Leo, good to see you. Haven't seen you for ages.'

'I know, I've been busy. How's the wife?'

'Pregnant with her third child,' Steve said.

'Wow, you didn't hang about, you guys only got married…'

'Two years ago, I know, she's a baby-making machine. How're things going with Isla?'

'Good, really good in fact,' Leo said, not at all surprised that Steve had heard they were together. Nothing was a secret, even for those who didn't live in the village any more.

Steve nodded. 'What can I do for you today?'

'Can you give me Sadie Norton's room number?' Leo said, keeping his voice as casual and light as he possibly could.

Steve narrowed his eyes slightly. 'I heard what she's doing to you and Isla, I think it's disgusting. Everyone does actually.' He checked on his computer, writing a room number on a slip of paper, and made to pass it over the counter. He held onto it as Leo made a move to take it. 'Leo, I need this job, more than ever with the baby on the way. Tell me I'm not going to regret giving you her number.'

Christ, what kind of monster did Steve think he was? He had a bad reputation for being a bit of an ass in his teenage years, got into a few fights, but surely Steve couldn't think that he was going to hurt her?

'I just want to talk to her, that's all,' Leo said.

Steve hesitated for a moment and then passed him the number. 'You didn't get it from me. Take the lift to the third floor and then follow the hall to the left.'

Leo nodded and took the slip of paper before Steve could change his mind.

He took the lift, his heart racing in his chest. He had to do this. He found her hotel room and knocked on the door. After a few moments Sadie answered it.

She looked startled at seeing him there.

'Bloody hell, Leo, have you come to kill me?' she said dryly.

'I'd be lying if I said I hadn't thought about it,' Leo said.

She hesitated then stepped back. 'You better come in then.'

He moved into the room and she closed the door behind him. 'Drink?'

'No thanks,' Leo said, coolly. 'Bit early in the day for me.'

He watched her move to the minibar and pour herself a gin, straight, no ice. She looked… haggard, there was no other way to describe it. Her face showed a lot more wrinkles than he remembered, her face was puffy in parts and he wondered if that was due to too many years partying too hard. She'd always liked a drink, but then so had he. He'd always liked Sadie, he'd had a good laugh with her when he'd gone to the pub with her and Matthew. She was completely useless at being a mum, but he'd never thought less of her because of it. Some people were just not cut out to be a parent and he'd often thought, back then, that if he had been forced into parenthood, he would be as rubbish as she was at it. And though it would be a push to say she was forced into it, she had definitely been… coerced into keeping the baby when she'd found out she was pregnant. She had never wanted a child, but Matthew had been over the moon. Even still, Leo was stunned when she had walked out on Elliot and Matthew shortly after Elliot's first birthday, but in his heart he had known it was for the best and he'd wondered if Sadie had thought that as well. And though his opinion of her had slipped quite considerably because of it, he had never thought she was a nasty person. That was until she came back and ruined everything. She had changed over the years, become harder, he could see that. She wasn't the same person who had walked out of Sandcastle Bay over four years earlier.

'I thought we could talk, no lawyers, no more going back and forth.'

'OK,' Sadie said, hesitantly. She took a big swig of her gin.

'You need to leave Elliot out of all this.'

She cocked her head on one side, her face hard and resolute. 'Why would I do that?'

'Because that's not why you're here. You want money, that's all. And I get that, I really do, but in all this mess, you're ruining a little boy's life, your son's.'

'All Isla has to do is pay me sixty-five thousand pounds and I'm gone, the house is hers, the boy is hers, and I disappear. I think I'm being more than fair, sixty-five is nowhere near half the value of the house. If she really loves him, surely that's a small price to pay.'

'She has to sell the house to get that money, and she has nowhere to go. You're making your son homeless.'

She shrugged. 'That really isn't my problem. I'm sure someone will come to her rescue. You're a big strong man, Leo, I'm sure you'll swoop in and save her.'

'Wow. I took you for a lot of things but I never thought you were such a heartless bitch. Clearly, I was wrong,' Leo said and then cursed inwardly. He hadn't come here to insult her, that wasn't going to curry any favour with her. This was exactly why Isla hadn't wanted him to talk to Sadie in the first place. She would kill him if she knew he was here, he had to get a good result from this.

Sadie put her drink down and folded her arms across her chest. 'I think I'd like you to leave now.'

'Wait, I'm sorry. I'm finding all of this so hard. I'm Elliot's godfather and I'm supposed to protect him, but I can't protect him from this. Have you thought about Elliot in any of this? Have you thought for one second what his life was like when you left?'

'A thousand times better than when I was here, I suspect,' Sadie said, bitterly.

He was going to come back to that, that was his way in.

'I don't suppose he has any recollection of you, he was still a baby when you walked out of his life. It was just him and Matthew for three years. They were so close, thicker than thieves. Elliot adored his dad, anyone could see that,' Leo said, his voice choking unexpectedly. 'And then, one day, Matthew was gone and we had to tell Elliot that Daddy was never coming home. Do you know how hard that was for him? He was four years old and he had to accept that he was never going to see his dad again, never play with him or have him read him a bedtime story again. It destroyed him.'

He looked out the window a moment; he had to keep this together.

'Isla upended her entire life to come here and look after him. She left her home, she left London where she had spent her entire life, quit her job, even left a boyfriend behind to be here for Elliot, to raise him. Elliot was content and settled again. Of course he misses his dad, but he is confident, brave, kind, and most importantly happy, and that is all down to Isla. She was the mum he never had.'

Sadie narrowed her eyes and he wondered if he had gone too far with that comment.

'All Isla has wanted since Matthew died was to adopt Elliot formally, to provide him with security, a home with her and not lose him to foster care or to someone who doesn't love him as much as she does. Every step of the way, this adoption has been blocked because no one could find you. To adopt him we needed your consent. And finally, *finally*, last week, the adoption was given the go-ahead. The courts had made every effort to find you and decided to let the adoption process be completed. We were due to go to court in a few weeks for the final time for the adoption to be made official. But now you've come back, it's ruined all of that. Because you won't give consent, the adoption hearing has been cancelled and… it's broken Isla. She's scared she's going to lose him and I've never seen her so utterly defeated before. Her brother died, her boyfriend dumped her when she agreed to take on Elliot and none of that broke her, but this… She can't lose Elliot and I dread to think what that poor boy will go through if he is taken away from her.'

He knew there was no threat of that, but he wanted to lay it on as thick as possible. He needed to pull on Sadie's heart strings and he was going to do everything he could to get the result he wanted, including lie and beg.

And it seemed to be working, her face had softened. There *was* a heart beating inside this ice queen.

'Isla doesn't care about the house,' Leo went on. 'I mean, of course it has sentimental attachments for her and Elliot. It was Matthew's home, it was where Elliot has his only memories of his dad. But Isla just wants to keep Elliot safe, she doesn't care about the money. If you want the money, then let's go to court, let's do this fairly. Let a judge decide how much your claim is worth, we'll pay you whatever the judge decides. But please, I beg you, leave Elliot out of this.'

Sadie sighed and sat down on the bed. She was silent for the longest time.

'I was a terrible mum to Elliot. I often wondered if that was because I didn't have any good role models myself growing up.

I was a kid lost to the foster system too. I had twenty-three different foster homes. Safe to say, I was a difficult child. When I
had Elliot, I didn't have a clue what I was doing. All these other
mums that had children around the same time as me seemed to
be absolute naturals at it. I was rubbish. I didn't feel this huge
surge of love for him that other mums said they did. Did you
know I dropped him?'

Leo did know. 'That wasn't your fault, it was an accident.'

'Of course it was, I didn't do it deliberately, but I felt awful.
What kind of mum actually drops their baby?'

'I'd imagine a lot more than you'd think,' Leo said.

Sadie took another swig of her gin. 'When I left, I honestly
thought it was the best thing for Elliot. He didn't need me
screwing up his life.'

'I don't know if it was the best thing for him, he probably
missed out a lot on having a mum there. But you can do the
best thing for him now. He has a mum now, a wonderful one
who loves him very much. Don't take that away from him. Sign
the consent form, giving Isla permission to adopt your son, give
Elliot the family he deserves to have.'

Sadie considered this for a moment. 'My life in foster care
was crap, I'm not going to condemn my son to that. I'll sign the
form. I'll give Karie a call now and tell her.'

Leo let out a huge sigh of relief, 'Thank you.'

'I still want my money,' Sadie said, her shutters going back up.

He smiled, slightly. 'Then we'll see you in court.'

She nodded.

He moved to the door and she followed him.

'Thank you for this. It's the right thing to do.'

She nodded. 'I know.'

He left the room and closed the door behind him. As soon
as he was out in the corridor he sagged against the wall in relief.
It was over.

Isla smiled as she watched Elliot carefully trying to pipe a scary face onto the last pumpkin cupcake on the tray. He had more icing round his face than on the cakes, and somehow Luke had got pretty covered too, but it didn't matter, Elliot was enjoying himself.

She had needed something to distract her from this mess that Sadie had made and cupcake-making seemed to be just the thing. Karie had phoned three times that night, but she hadn't been able to face speaking to her. She definitely didn't want to do so in front of Elliot because it was very likely she would cry and she didn't want to upset him.

'What are we doing tomorrow?' Elliot yawned sleepily as he put the piping bag down.

It was a little later than his normal bedtime, but as he was on holiday it didn't really matter. He wanted to wait up until Leo got home, so he could say goodnight to him. She smiled and shook her head, fondly. She wasn't sure how they had got to the stage of playing happy families but she liked it. She checked her watch; Leo had told her he was going to work straight after the pumpkin-carving competition, but he had been gone a while now. They had already eaten their dinner as Leo had texted telling them not to wait.

'You're going to be with Leo tomorrow, for the morning at least. I have to be measured up for my bridesmaid dress for Tori's wedding,' Isla said.

'Yay, I get to spend the day with Leo. I love Leo.'

'I know you do and he loves you too, very much,' Isla said.

'It's true, I do,' Leo said, appearing in the kitchen door right on cue.

'Leo!' Elliot said, getting down from his stool and running towards him as if he had been parted from him for days, not just a few hours.

Leo swung him up onto his hip and hugged him tight. He moved towards Isla and as he held onto Elliot he leaned down and kissed her cheek.

'Shall I put you to bed?' Leo said.

'Will you read me a story?' Elliot said.

'Of course, which one would you like?'

'The one about the Gruffalo's Child,' Elliot said.

'That's one of my favourites.' He winked at Isla. 'I'll be down in a few minutes, and then we can talk,' he said meaningfully.

Her heart leapt. She had no idea what Leo wanted to say but, after the day she'd had, it had better be good.

Leo passed her Elliot so she could say goodnight and she hugged him tight. 'Love you, beautiful boy.'

'Love you too,' Elliot said.

She smiled and then passed him back to Leo.

'We might need to wash your face before we get you into your pyjamas, you have a teeny tiny bit of icing on your cheeks,' Leo said, as he carried Elliot out of the room.

'That's because I kept licking the icing,' Elliot whispered.

'Luke will probably need a wash too,' Isla called as the puppy followed them out of the room.

Leo gasped in mock shock as he spotted the dog. 'How did Luke get so covered in icing?'

'Because he kept eating the icing too,' Elliot laughed and their voices faded away as they went upstairs.

Isla smiled and started tidying away all the cake bowls and stowing them in the dishwasher. She put all the cupcakes inside cake tins. That made her smile – that in Leo's kitchen there were cake tins and other cake-making tools and ingredients. The Leo Jackson she had met five years ago would never have had cake-making stuff in his house. He also wouldn't have converted one of his bedrooms into a little boy's room and painted planets and stars all over the walls. A lot had changed over the last five years. But, quite honestly, she couldn't imagine her life without Leo in it.

When everything was tidied away, Isla sat down at the kitchen table and decided to give Karie a call. Although what was there left to say? Karie had said it all in her text.

Karie answered after the first ring. 'Jesus, Isla, I've been trying to get hold of you all night.'

'I know, sorry, I was busy,' Isla said, quietly, not wanting to admit she had been avoiding her.

'Listen, I have news, bloody brilliant news,' Karie said. 'Sadie called me this afternoon and said she was happy to give consent for the adoption to go ahead. She came in and signed all the paperwork.'

Isla didn't say anything for a moment, her heart roaring in her chest.

'Isla, did you hear me? Elliot's officially yours. Well, it will all be official once the adoption hearing is out the way. But now Sadie has given her consent, it will just be a case of going before the judge to put the official stamp on it. It's over.'

'Oh my god,' Isla breathed. 'I can't believe it.'

'No, I couldn't either. I mean, in that first meeting she made it clear that she wasn't interested in Elliot at all but she was dragging her heels over signing him over and I didn't know why.'

'She wanted more money,' Isla said.

'Yeah, I figured as much. This was a very sudden about-turn,' Karie said.

'Why the sudden change of heart?' Isla asked.

'I have no idea, she just said this was the right thing to do.'

'So that's it, she can't change her mind again?' Isla said, barely daring to believe it was really over.

'No, that's it. The court hearing will go ahead as planned and then he'll be yours, but you can definitely celebrate tonight.'

'Oh, thank god,' Isla said and felt the tears welling in her eyes.

Karie promised to be in touch to go over the court case and then Isla said her goodbyes and disconnected the call with shaky fingers.

Tears fell down her cheeks. Elliot was hers.

She had to tell Leo.

She pushed the chair back and ran upstairs, just stopping herself from shouting out his name. She didn't want to wake Elliot up if he was already in bed.

Leo came out of his bedroom and stopped when he saw her crying. He quickly moved towards her, his hands on her shoulders.

'What's the matter, what's wrong?'

She could barely speak, she was crying so much. 'It's over.'

'What is?' Leo said.

'Sadie came in to see Karie this afternoon and signed the consent form allowing the adoption to go ahead. Elliot's now ours.'

Leo hesitated, no doubt processing all of this. 'Are you serious?'

Isla nodded. She had never felt relief like it.

Leo hugged her tight and she felt him laugh with relief. 'Oh god, that is wonderful news. I can't believe it.'

'The adoption hearing will go ahead but now it will just be a case of crossing the T's and dotting the I's. Karie didn't mention the house or the money, but I imagine that Sadie will still want her cash, but I don't care about any of that. Elliot is the only thing I care about.'

Leo pulled back slightly and wiped the tears from her face. 'You have no idea how happy this makes me.'

He bent his head and kissed her and she laughed and cried against him.

He pulled back. 'Listen, we need to talk.'

She nodded, because whatever he wanted to say now, nothing was going to wipe the smile from her face.

He took her hand, tugging her into his bedroom where she was surprised to see candles dotting the surfaces.

'I wish I'd had time to plan this properly but you kind of surprised me with your declaration this morning. I never thought a man like me would ever have someone like you fall in love with me. You see something in me that I've never seen in myself. This morning, when you told me, I wanted to find the right words to tell you how I felt but really I just needed to say the words that I've never said to anyone, the words that have been in my heart for the last four years. I love you Isla Rosewood. You will never know how completely and utterly happy you and Elliot have made me but I'm going to work every day for the rest of our lives to make you just as happy as you make me.'

Isla stared at him in shock, her heart thundering in her chest.

'I'm going to ask you one more time, and not because of Sadie or because I want to take care of you, but because you and Elliot belong here with me, because I love you both so much, you fill my heart.' He dropped to one knee and offered out a ring box, opening it. She stared at the yellow stone that sparkled in the candlelight. 'It's a yellow sapphire, which is rare and unusual, just like you. I saw this and was instantly reminded of the sunshine and light you have brought into my life. Will you marry me?'

Isla dropped to her knees in front of him, new tears falling down her cheeks now. The lump of emotion in her throat was so big she could barely breathe. She nodded because she couldn't talk and he smiled and took the ring from the box, sliding it onto her finger. Oh god, she was so happy right now she thought her heart would burst.

She leaned over and kissed him, hard.

'I love you,' she whispered against his lips. 'I love you so much.'

He kissed her as if he couldn't take enough, his hands spanning her back, and without taking his mouth from hers, he eased her back onto the floor.

The kiss continued, his hands caressing everywhere, his tongue in her mouth, his body against hers. Clothes were removed, his, hers, until they were both naked, his wonderful, warm body pinning her to the floor. He kissed her throat, her shoulder, and then slipped her breast inside his mouth, driving her to the very edge as she writhed on the floor desperate for that release.

He paused long enough to tear open a condom and then he was inside her. He stilled as she wrapped her legs around him, stroking her hands down his back and shoulders as he simply stared at her.

'You're going to be my wife,' he whispered, staring at her in awe.

She smiled and nodded.

He kissed her and started to move against her and that feeling started to build inside her, just there but out of reach.

'I promise to love and cherish you.' He kissed her. 'I will be there for the good times and bad, for better and worse, I will love, honour and respect you,' He kissed her again and she ran her fingers into the hair at the back of his neck. 'I promise to help you raise our children together, to be your best friend for as long as we both shall live.'

She kissed him and it was the thought of forever with this wonderful man that sent her roaring over the edge.

CHAPTER 21

Isla woke to the sound of laughter and hushed whispers and she opened one eye to see Elliot sitting on Leo's lap as they chatted happily, Elliot showing Leo some toy and how to use it. Luke was also on the bed, chewing happily on one of his dog toys.

God, her heart felt so full with love for her boys and now they were going to be together as a proper family.

'Hey beautiful boy,' Isla said, stroking a finger down Elliot's arm.

He grinned when he saw she was awake and Leo immediately leaned over and kissed her on the lips. Just a brief kiss but she wondered idly what Elliot would make of it. But Elliot didn't even blink, just carried on playing with his toy as if it was the most normal thing in the world.

'Morning,' Elliot said. 'That's a nice ring.'

She smiled; he was so observant.

She sat up and Elliot scrambled over onto her lap for a cuddle.

'This is an engagement ring,' Isla said, turning her hand so the ring sparkled. She checked with Leo that she was doing the right thing in telling him, but Leo was smiling. 'It means me and Leo are going to get married.'

'Yay!' Elliot said, wriggling around on her lap in excitement. 'When are we getting married?'

'Soon,' Leo said, before Isla could speak. 'Probably before Christmas.'

Isla smiled at Leo and shook her head at him fondly.

He grinned. 'There's no point hanging around.'

'No, I think we've done enough of that over the last few years,' Isla said. She checked her watch. 'I better get ready. What are your plans today?'

'I thought we'd dig out the old go-kart, see if it still works, and yes we'll make sure Elliot wears his helmet,' Leo said, instinctively.

Isla smiled. 'I know he's in very safe hands.'

She leaned over and kissed Leo and then shifted Elliot back onto his lap. She watched them chatting for a moment. As much as she was looking forward to spending the day with Tori and Melody, getting all excited about Tori's wedding and telling them her own exciting news, she would much rather stay here with her own little family. She placed another kiss on Leo's shoulder, dropped one on Elliot's head, and then slipped from the bed and padded off to the bathroom, knowing she would have a huge smile on her face all day. Nothing was going to ruin her mood today. Right now she was happier than she'd ever been.

⚜

'OK, are we ready to go?' Leo said.

'Yay!!' Elliot danced up and down on the spot.

'OK, let's run through our checklist. Is the go-kart ready?'

'Yes!'

Leo knew it was, they'd spent the morning cleaning it and Leo had meticulously checked the wheels, the brakes, the steering. Although it hadn't been used for several months, it was in tip-top condition.

'Helmet on securely?' Leo checked the straps and could see that it was.

'Yes!' Elliot said, giving it a little tap.

'Super-grip racing gloves?' Leo asked.

Elliot giggled as he wiggled his fingers to show that he had his gloves on.

'Then I think we're ready.'

Elliot quickly moved round to the seat, climbed in and put his hands on the steering wheel.

'Seatbelt,' Leo reminded him. Elliot quickly did his seatbelt up.

Leo moved round the back and started rocking the car back and forth. 'Three, two, one…' He pushed the car down the curving driveway and Elliot steered it. Leo had a good hold of the back of the seat and used his weight to give a bit of guidance to the direction of travel. Elliot whooped and laughed all the way down to the bottom where Leo let the car come to a stop.

'That was brilliant!' Elliot said. 'We went so fast.'

Leo smiled, knowing that he had barely picked up speed at all. 'Want to go again?'

'Yes!'

'Out you hop then.'

Elliot undid his seatbelt and climbed out and Leo picked the go-kart up and started carrying it up the hill.

'Are you OK about me and Isla getting married? Leo asked.

'Yes, it's very exciting. Me and Marigold have been practising.'

'You've been practising getting married?'

'Yes, we take it in turns to be the bride and groom. The bride gets to carry pretty flowers, which I like, and wear a pretty dress, which I didn't really like wearing but Marigold said I had to. And the priest, which was Stanley last time we played weddings, says do you Marigold take you Elliot to be your awfully wedded wife and then she says I do and Stanley asks me if I want to be Marigold's awfully wedded husband and I say I do and then Stanley says that we can kiss but Marigold won't let me do that bit. Will you kiss Isla on your wedding day?'

'Yes, I will.'

'And what will I have to say?'

Leo smiled. 'I'm sure there will be something you will say in the ceremony. We will speak to the registrar and they will tell us all what we need to say.'

'And will I carry pretty flowers?'

'If you want to.'

'I'd like that.'

'OK,' Leo said.

'I don't think I'll wear a dress though.'

'You can wear whatever you want.'

'My Batman costume?'

Leo cleared his throat as he imagined the wedding photos and what Isla would make of Batman attending their special day.

'Why don't we talk to Isla about what you should wear? Maybe you could wear your best clothes.'

Elliot wrinkled his nose.

'Well, I'm sure we can find something to wear that makes you and Isla happy. Are you OK about moving out of Hot Chocolate Cottage and moving in here?'

'I like the idea of having a toy room. And when I have a baby sister she will need her own room too.'

'That's right, she will,' Leo said.

'And we don't have room for that at Hot Chocolate Cottage.'

'No.'

Elliot was quiet for a moment. 'I think I will be a bit sad. Me and Daddy painted my bedroom together.'

Leo knew what he was trying to say but perhaps couldn't find the words. He had memories of his time with Matthew there and he would be sad to leave those behind.

'And Marshmallow Cottage,' Elliot said.

'Your treehouse?'

'Yes, Daddy made that.'

'We could bring Marshmallow Cottage here. Take it apart very carefully and put it back together.'

'Can we?'

'Yes, of course.' He put the go-kart down at the top of the hill and squatted down to face Elliot. 'Just because we move away from Daddy's home doesn't mean we'll forget about him. We have photos and videos of him we can look at any time.'

'I miss him sometimes,' Elliot said.

'I do too, very much. And I know living with me will never be the same as living with Daddy but I'm going to try my best to make you happy.'

Elliot smiled. 'You do make me happy. I love you. This much.'

He held out his arms really wide.

Leo did the same. 'I love you this much.'

Elliot laughed and then moved back to sit in the go-kart again. He put his seatbelt on and Leo started rocking the car back and forth a second time.

'Three, two, one,' Leo said and then started running forward, pushing the go-kart.

Elliot turned the wheel as they approached the corner but then Leo stumbled on a small bit of branch that was in the driveway, his feet tangled up in it as he went down. Leo hit the ground but as he was still holding onto the back of the go-kart he managed to turn it around. To his horror the go-kart ripped out of his hand, and flipped over, rolling sideways down the hill. Leo scrabbled to his feet as the go-kart came to a stop on its side in the grass and bushes.

As he ran towards the go-kart, the only thought that kept screaming through his mind was that there was no sound from Elliot at all.

CHAPTER 22

'You're engaged!' Melody exclaimed, spotting the ring almost as soon as Isla got out of the car.

Isla laughed and nodded.

'What?' Tori's head snapped up. She'd been making lists in her notebook as they sat outside the wedding shop waiting for her. 'Show me the ring.'

Isla stuck out her hand as the girls admired it with *ooohs* and *ahhhs*.

'When did this happen?'

'Last night. I have so much to tell you,' Isla said.

'But I thought you were taking things slow. It's only been a few days since you got together,' Tori said.

'I know, but Melody was right, we've known each other for years. I've loved him for a long time and he loves me too. There doesn't seem much point in waiting around. We were meant to be together, you guys know that.'

Melody squealed with happiness. 'I can't believe this, I'm so happy for the two of you.'

She got up and hugged Isla tight.

'Tell me everything,' Melody said.

'Don't we need to go into the wedding shop for our fitting?' Isla asked.

'We have time,' Tori said. 'Besides, this is more important. How did it happen? He's proposed to you so many times.'

'Well, actually I have news which is equally as important. Sadie has signed to say she is happy for the adoption to go ahead.'

They stared at her.

'What?' Melody said, looking even more happy at this news.

'It happened yesterday afternoon, Karie called me. I have no idea why Sadie decided to do it. I'm not sure if Karie or even Thomas had some part to play in this but, apparently, she thought it was the right thing to do. So we have our court hearing as planned in a few weeks but that's just a formality now.'

'That's brilliant, so he will officially be yours?' Tori said.

Isla nodded. 'I can't tell you how relieved I am. So while we were celebrating that last night, Leo told me he loved me and he wanted to marry me. There was not a single doubt in my heart that this was the right thing.'

Tori hugged her. 'Ah, I'm so pleased for you.'

'Yes, this is wonderful news,' Melody said. 'We'll have to go for lunch after to celebrate.'

Isla smiled. 'I'll check with Leo, he has Elliot, he might need to get into work. Although I didn't give him a specific time I'd be back.'

She pulled her phone out of her bag.

'Ah, no reception,' Isla said.

'No, you won't get any here, we're in this weird pocket of the world where mobile phones don't exist,' Tori said.

'I'll try and phone him after,' Isla said, slipping her phone back into her bag. 'Let's go try on our dresses, Tori. I can't wait to see yours again.'

'You'll have to have a look for yourself while you're here,' Melody said. 'At least get an idea of what style you want for your own wedding.'

Isla grinned at that thought. A few days before she would have thought her dreams of having Elliot and marrying Leo were impossible but now she was living the dream.

Leo raced towards the go-kart. As he got closer he heard Elliot let out a wail and a tiny part of him sighed in relief because if he could scream then he wasn't dead. He fell to his knees when he reached the kart, ignoring the pain that stabbed up his side.

'Are you OK, buddy?' Leo said, cradling his body and head and carefully bringing the kart upright, before a sickening thought hit him. If Elliot had broken his back or neck, he shouldn't have been moved at all. Christ, he knew this, he had been a firefighter for six months many years before. He had trained in first aid and when dealing with a car accident that was one of the first things to consider. But when faced with someone he loved involved in an accident, all his training and calm went out the window.

He tried to remember what he had been taught, but from the way that Elliot was screaming it didn't seem like he was having any trouble breathing and he didn't seem to be holding his head in any way that would suggest a breakage in his spine or neck. He scooted round to face him and nearly cried when he saw his little face was bruised and cut. There was blood all round his mouth but as he wiped some of it away, he could see that Elliot had bit or cut his lip.

'OK Elliot, where does it hurt?'

Elliot's screaming went up an octave as he pointed vaguely to all over his body. From the way he was holding his left arm, Leo suspected that might be broken.

Blood was still pouring from his lip so Leo ripped a bit of his t-shirt away and started gently dabbing at the cut as he reached round and unbuckled the seatbelt.

'OK, don't move for a second—' Leo started to say but as soon as the seatbelt was free Elliot stood up and flung his arms around Leo's neck, sobbing uncontrollably.

Leo held him tight but he let out another small sigh of relief. If he could move like that, then there was nothing too wrong with him.

Abandoning the go-kart, he quickly carried him up the drive and straight into the kitchen. Luke looked up from his dog basket, immediately circling around them, whimpering, sensing something was wrong. Leo sat Elliot on the unit top and grabbed a bowl of water and some kitchen towel to clear up some of the cuts, but the one on his lip did look like it might need stitches or at least some butterfly tape to hold it together. Elliot was still holding his arm strangely and screaming so he grabbed his keys, bundled Elliot into his car and took off to the hospital.

Using his hands-free, he dialled Isla's number but it went straight through to answerphone.

Shit.

As the car bumped over a rough patch of road, Elliot's screams intensified even more.

Shit. Shit. Shit.

CHAPTER 23

Sitting in a cubicle, waiting to be seen by a doctor or nurse, Elliot had at least stopped crying now, although he was still sniffling and casting hurt puppy-dog eyes at Leo as if he'd done it deliberately.

'I'm sorry buddy, I didn't mean to hurt you,' Leo said, apologising to him for what felt like the hundredth time.

In the gap through the curtain he could see the nurse who had checked him in talking to another through the glass screen of their office, pointing at Elliot's cubicle and swapping looks of disgust. Did they really think he'd done this to his godson deliberately?

He stared at the nurse doing most of the talking and realised he recognised her. She had her hair up now and the last time he'd seen her her hair had been spread out over her pillow. Eva. He'd slept with her once many years before and then never called her again. That was the kind of lowlife he had been back then. Most women knew what they were getting when they slept with him: one night, maybe two, nothing serious, no strings or complications. But despite the fact he never gave the women he slept with any false promises and made it clear it was always going to be something casual, he'd known he'd broken a few hearts along the way. Eva, he remembered, was one of them. She had called him several times and even turned up at his house offering to cook him dinner. He was polite but firm, he simply wasn't interested in any kind of relationship. He was the first to admit that he perhaps hadn't treated women in the best way in the past, avoiding their calls, sneaking out of their bedrooms early in the morning, not committing to any kind of relationship. But he would never hit them and for Eva or anyone else to think he could do this to Elliot was sickening.

A doctor came in then, all smiles as she addressed Elliot, obviously trying to keep him calm.

'Hello Elliot, I'm Doctor Hunter. I see you've taken a little tumble. I'm going to have a look at you and then we might send you down for some x-rays.'

Elliot nodded, solemnly.

She looked into his eyes first of all, shining a torch into them which made Elliot blink, and then she gently started feeling around his head and neck.

'Who is this with you today?' Doctor Hunter asked.

'This is Leo,' Elliot said.

'And is Leo your daddy?'

'Yes. But not my real daddy.'

'I'm his... stepdad,' Leo said. 'Sort of.'

'What's a stepdad?' Elliot asked.

'It's when a man that's not your dad marries your mummy, then he becomes your stepdad,' Doctor Hunter explained, as she felt gently around the front of his neck and shoulders. 'Is Leo married to your mummy?'

Elliot shook his head. 'No, he's going to marry Isla.'

'Who's Isla?'

'My aunty,' Elliot said.

Doctor Hunter frowned in confusion.

'Isla is his legal guardian,' Leo said. 'She's adopting him. We're engaged.'

'Ah, I presume that's why you're known to social services. Elliot's name did flag up on the system when you came in.'

'Yes, we're working with social services to get Elliot formally adopted since his parents are... no longer around,' Leo said.

Elliot winced as she touched an obviously sore part on his shoulder.

'You have been in the wars. How did it happen?' Doctor Hunter asked.

'Leo did it,' Elliot said, sullenly.

Christ, talk about hanging him out to dry.

'It was an accident, wasn't it buddy?' Leo said.

'I'd like to hear it from Elliot if you don't mind.' The doctor flashed him a smile but her eyes said she'd seen too many cases like this before and she wasn't going to take these injuries lightly. She turned back to Elliot 'Want to tell me what happened?'

'He pushed me,' Elliot said, his little sore lip jutting out in a pout. 'We were playing with the go-kart and Leo was pushing me really fast and then he fell and let go and made the go-kart roll over.'

He saw her shoulders drop a little as she relaxed. 'Well, that does sound very scary.'

'It hurt a lot.'

'I imagine it did. And you've been here before, about eighteen months ago. Can you remember? The notes said you... walked into a cupboard.'

She eyed Leo as if she didn't totally believe that version of events. Leo had a flashback to Elliot's fourth birthday party, chasing him with a water pistol. As Elliot had run inside the house, his wet feet had skidded on the kitchen floor and he'd headbutted a cupboard door. The lump on his head had swollen to the size of a potato within seconds. Leo had felt awful but Matthew had still been alive then and he'd brought him into hospital to have him checked over. Matthew had totally laughed it off afterwards as just one of those things and kids will be kids.

Elliot nodded. 'I was running away from Leo.'

This was just getting worse and worse.

'And why were you running away from Leo?'

'Because I didn't want him to catch me,' Elliot said.

She ran her fingers down his arm. 'And does Leo chase you a lot?'

Elliot nodded. 'Sometimes at bedtime, he chases me into bed and then he lies in bed with me and I like that.'

The doctor looked at Leo with a raised eyebrow. Christ, he'd always lain next to Elliot in his bed while he read him a bedtime story. He'd never thought anything of it before.

'What do you like about lying in bed with Leo?'

Holy shit, this was sounding all kinds of wrong now.

'Because…' Elliot was obviously struggling to find the words. 'It makes me feel all nice inside, like I'm happy and excited at the same time.'

Leo swallowed down the huge lump in his throat at the lovely way Elliot had described how he made him feel. He only hoped the doctor wouldn't twist that into something else too.

'OK, I think we'll take you down to be x-rayed. I suspect you might have broken your wrist. Do you want Leo to come with you?'

Elliot nodded.

Leo stood up.

'And one of the nurses has put a call out to your social worker, is it Karie Matthews?'

Leo nodded, his heart sinking. He liked Karie but what was she going to make of this?

'Is that really necessary?' Leo said and realised that made it sound like he had something to hide.

'It's just a formality,' Doctor Hunter said. 'If you have an assigned social worker, they need to be kept informed. Elliot, are you OK to walk to the x-ray department? It's just down the corridor.'

'Leo can carry me,' Elliot said and Leo smiled slightly at that sense of entitlement, like a king ordering one of his subjects.

Leo obliged and picked him up carefully. Pain sliced through his side again, which he tried to ignore. Elliot leaned his head on his shoulder. Clearly he had been forgiven. They followed Doctor Hunter down the corridor a little way.

'Is Elliot allergic to anything, any medication?' she asked.

'I... don't think so,' Leo said. He had no idea whether Elliot was or not. He wracked his brains for anything that Matthew or Isla might have mentioned but came up blank. He really should know stuff like this.

'OK,' she said, slowly, obviously not impressed that he didn't know for sure. 'We really need to get in touch with Isla then.'

Leo decided not to mention that he'd already phoned her twenty times. He knew that didn't look good either. 'I'll give her a call.'

⁕⁕⁕

Elliot had just finished having his arm set in plaster when Isla arrived, her face ashen with worry.

Leo tried to look at Elliot through her eyes. He knew he looked awful.

'Oh god, my beautiful boy, are you OK?' Isla said, hurrying to the bedside and giving Elliot a gentle hug.

'I'm OK, it doesn't really hurt too much any more,' Elliot said, bravely.

Leo was relieved that Isla had arrived now and not earlier when Elliot was still bleeding and crying.

'They've given him some paracetamol,' Leo explained. 'He has a broken wrist and a hairline fracture on his collarbone.'

'Leo has a broken rib,' Elliot said.

The x-ray nurse had taken one look at Leo when he'd stiffly placed Elliot down on the bed to be x-rayed and insisted on x-raying Leo too. Though there was nothing that could be done for a cracked rib.

Isla looked at him. 'Ah no, both my boys in the wars. I'll have to take good care of you both tonight.'

He watched her as she fussed around Elliot. Was she angry? Did she hold him responsible?

'Are you OK?' she asked Leo, after a while.

'Yes, I'm sorry,' Leo said.

She frowned. 'Why are you sorry?'

'It should never have happened. I was supposed to be looking after him.'

'It was just an accident, don't beat yourself up about it.'

Leo shook his head.

'My tummy is rumbling,' Elliot said. 'Can we go home soon?'

'Soon, buddy. Shall I go and get you something to eat?' Leo said.

Elliot nodded.

'Do you want anything?' Leo asked Isla.

'No, I had cake with Tori and Melody,' Isla said.

'Did Tori look pretty in her wedding dress?' Elliot said as Leo left.

He walked to the end of the row of cubicles to try to find his way out of the ward and to the shop.

'Did you see that man in cubicle three?' he heard a nurse say from the last cubicle. He hesitated because he and Elliot were in cubicle three; he wondered what derogatory thing they were going to say about him now. He peered through the crack in the curtain and could see a young nurse with Eva changing the bed. 'He is hot!' the young nurse said, fanning herself. He smiled slightly and turned to walk away.

'Leo Jackson,' Eva said, derisively. 'Have you seen what he's done to that poor boy? If bullies like that do it for you, Maisie, then something is very wrong.'

His heart sank.

'Doctor Hunter said it was a go-kart accident,' Maisie said.

Eva grunted. 'You don't know Leo Jackson like I do. I'm not sure what Isla is doing with someone like him. I don't know her very well but she seems to have her head screwed on right and then she lets a man like that into her home, leaves him alone with Elliot. This is not the first time Leo has put someone in hospital and I'm sure it won't be the last.'

'What do you mean?'

'He broke my brother's nose,' Eva said.

'Deliberately?'

'Yes, punched him straight in the face.'

He sighed. He had got in a lot of scraps when he'd been younger. Nothing serious and in fact Oliver O'Mara, Eva's brother, had started a fight with him because Leo had unknowingly kissed Oliver's girlfriend. He'd been quite good friends with Oliver in the years after school and college before he had moved away so Leo didn't think Oliver held any grudges against him. And that hadn't stopped Eva jumping into bed with Leo many years after that event so he didn't think Eva was that bothered by it either.

'Everyone in Sandcastle Bay and the surrounding villages knows he's a bad sort. He's been in trouble with the police more times than I can count,' Eva went on with her lies. He'd been arrested twice, all before his eighteenth birthday, hardly a long track record of criminal debauchery. 'He has a terrible reputation with women.'

'For hitting them?' Maisie said, shocked.

'Well, I've not heard that, but… most women only ever sleep with him once, what does that tell you?'

'That he doesn't like commitment.'

'Or they're too scared to go back.'

Leo rolled his eyes and was just about to walk away when Eva continued in her tirade.

'Elliot is already on the social services register,' Eva said. 'So obviously there are child protection issues.'

'Isla is trying to adopt him, as you are well aware,' Maisie said. 'He is under social services simply because his dad died and his mum wasn't around.'

'Well, I thought I better call them just in case. I think they should know,' Eva grumbled.

'That could damage Isla's chances for adoption,' Maisie said. 'Why would you do that?'

'She's already ruined her chances of adopting that boy by getting together with Leo Jackson. Why do you think the adoption has taken so long? Why do you think social services have been dragging their feet over this? The judge will take one look at Leo Jackson and his terrible reputation and probably take Elliot into care rather than grant the adoption. Seriously, would you leave your child alone with him? What was Isla thinking? The only way Isla is ever going to officially adopt Elliot is if she shows Leo the door and gets as far away from him as possible. Trust me, my friend is a judge in family law cases just like this, she's seen too many horror stories to just grant an adoption without any due care and consideration. They will consider all the factors and Leo Jackson is going to be a big negative.'

Leo moved away from the cubicle, blood turning to ice in his veins.

Was Eva really right? Could he possibly ruin Isla's chances of adopting Elliot? He knew what the people of Sandcastle Bay thought of him and none of it was good. He had carved a bad reputation in his teenage years and none of them had forgotten it. It would break Isla's heart if she couldn't adopt Elliot and there was no way he could let that happen.

CHAPTER 24

Isla came back downstairs after putting Elliot to bed for an afternoon nap. He was exhausted after his ordeal that morning. She stood in the kitchen doorway and watched Leo sitting at the table, staring into space, his cup of coffee untouched in his hand.

He had been almost silent on the drive home, barely saying a word. He had been distant since they had arrived back at his house. Something was wrong and she didn't know what.

Karie had arrived at the hospital not long after Isla had got there with a toy for Elliot to cheer him up after his tumble. She was all laughs and friendliness, and was almost bemused by why she'd been called out for what was quite clearly an accident. She hadn't been bothered by the incident, so Isla wasn't sure why Leo was.

Isla sat down with him at the table and his eyes flicked up to hers, hurt and pain haunting his face.

'What's wrong?' Isla said, gently, taking his hand.

He shook his head and withdrew his hand.

'I… can't do this.'

'Do what?'

'Be a dad to Elliot, be a husband to you. I can't. I thought I could, but I'm not good for you.'

'Don't be ridiculous. It was a silly accident.'

'Everyone in that hospital thought that I had beaten him up.'

She frowned. Had they really thought that? Was that why they had called Karie?

'Everyone in the village knows I'm rotten, the bad apple, and they're right, everything they say is true.'

'They must be very small-minded if they judge you on the person you were twenty years ago and not the wonderful man you are now. They don't know you like I do.'

'I am scum, self-absorbed. Matthew is dead because of me.'

She stared at him. 'How can you think that? You weren't driving the car that killed him.'

'But I was there in the pub with Alan, I watched him get drunker than I'd ever seen him get before. I did nothing to stop him drinking, I never asked if he was OK, I watched him walk out the pub with no thought to how he might be getting home. If I'd stopped him, if I'd talked to him, Matthew would still be here. I'm selfish and I don't deserve to have you and his son in my life as a reward for those thoughtless actions.'

Isla tried to process all this. She thought about how different her life would have been if only Leo had spoken to Alan that fateful night and she couldn't find one single bit of anger towards Leo. None of this was his fault. But this guilt had lain on his shoulders for the last year and a half and her heart broke that he felt this way.

'There are a hundred different things that led to Matthew being killed that night, tiny little unremarkable decisions and choices. You are not responsible for his death. You need to let that go.' She reached for his hand again but he moved it away.

Despair and anger rose up in her. As awful as it was to live with this guilt, he was pushing her away because of it. Her happy future with her perfect little family was slipping between her fingers and it was this guilt that was tearing them apart. And then another thought occurred to her.

'Is that why you became so invested in Elliot's life and mine? Out of guilt?'

'Of course it was,' Leo snapped.

Isla felt like she'd just been slapped. 'So what was all this?' she pointed between the two of them. 'Just one big guilt trip? You proposed to me every week for a year out of guilt. Did you sleep with me out of guilt as well?'

'You're being ridiculous.'

'And there was me thinking you were here because you loved us.'

'I do, Christ, of course I do. I've been in love with you for four years and I fell in love with Elliot very quickly, after spending all that time with him, but yes, initially there was guilt involved in my visits. Guilt that Elliot no longer had a father, that you no longer had a brother because of me.'

'It wasn't your fault. You can't let this destroy your life. Do you think Matthew would want that? Elliot needs you—'

'He doesn't need me. He's lying upstairs with a broken wrist because of me.'

'That was an accident,' Isla said, exasperated.

'They asked me if he was allergic to any medicine and I didn't know. They asked me what blood type he was just in case he needed to have surgery on his arm and I didn't know that either. What kind of dad would I be to him?'

'I didn't know any of that stuff when I came here to look after Elliot, in fact I'm still not sure what blood type he is. Do you think I know what I'm doing half the time? Do you think any parent does? I never know whether I'm too strict or too soft. When he asks me questions like what's a condom or how are babies made, I haven't got a clue how to answer him. Most of parenthood is making it up as we go along and hoping that we don't psychologically scar them or accidentally kill them before their eighteenth birthday,' Isla said.

'I nearly killed him today.'

'It was an accident,' she said, feeling like she should get it tattooed on the back of his hand so she wouldn't have to repeat it again.

'And what if I had killed him? Would you be quite so forgiving then? "Never mind dear, it was just an accident."'

Isla tried to think about how she would honestly react if Elliot had tragically died that day. Her chest hurt just thinking about it. But would she blame Leo for it? The calm and rational part of her brain assured her she wouldn't, that he couldn't be responsible for a terrible accident, but she knew there was nothing calm and rational about grief.

'You would hate me,' Leo said, quietly.

'So, what is happening here? You're breaking up with me? You gave being a dad your best shot and realised that it's not for you and now you're walking away. That's not what being a parent is about. That's not what being a husband is about. You gave me this ring and promised to be here for me for better or worse.'

'What I'm doing is better for you.'

'Shouldn't I be the judge of that?'

He stood up and kissed her on the head. 'I'm sorry.'

With that, he walked out the door.

She stared after him in shock, tears welling in her eyes. What the hell had just happened?

※◦≪

The sun had set leaving burnt orange, copper and golden trails across the sky when Elliot walked into the kitchen.

She hadn't moved from the table since Leo had left, alternating between crying uncontrollably and numb shock. Right now she was just numb, which she was glad about; she didn't want Elliot to see her cry. Though she knew more tears would come later.

'How are you feeling, beautiful boy?' she asked, her voice croaky from all the crying.

'I'm OK,' Elliot said. 'A bit sore. Where's Leo?'

The tears threatened again. How the hell was she going to explain this to him? It would break him. Anger swamped her. Damn Leo for this. He had no right to do this. And in actual fact, if he was no longer going to be a part of his godson's life, then he could damn well come back and explain that to Elliot himself

'He had to go to work, he has a firework display tonight.'

Elliot nodded, accepting that completely, and Isla vowed that would be the last time she would lie to cover Leo's ass.

'He'll be back for the Halloween parade tomorrow, though, right?' Elliot said.

Isla hesitated. 'I'm not sure, he's very busy. You know this time of year he has lots of firework displays.'

His little face crumpled. 'But he promised he would come to the parade with me.'

'Then... I'm sure he will do his very best to be here.'

Now she was standing up for him and he didn't deserve that either.

'Why don't we watch a movie tonight?' Isla said, hoping to distract Elliot. 'We can watch it together in Leo's bed, eat popcorn, whatever movie you want.'

'*Frozen!*' Elliot said, his disappointment forgotten.

'*Frozen* it is,' Isla said. 'And we can have pizza for dinner.'

'And can we eat that in Leo's bed too?' Elliot said.

'Sure, why not,' Isla said, not caring if they got crumbs, pizza sauce and cheese all over his sheets.

Isla closed the bedtime story she had just finished reading to Elliot and leaned over and kissed him on the head.

'Goodnight, beautiful boy,' Isla said.

'Goodnight, I love you,' Elliot said. 'Oh wait, I need to say goodnight to Leo.'

He quickly grabbed the walkie-talkie from the side of his bed.

'Honey, he'll be busy working, he might not have his walkie-talkie on,' Isla said, hating that she was lying again.

Elliot pressed the button to alert Leo that he was calling him. 'This is Batman to Robin, come in Robin.'

There was silence from the other end. Isla didn't know whether Leo was ignoring Elliot or simply wasn't anywhere near his walkie-talkie. She hoped it was the latter.

Elliot tried again. 'This is Batman to Robin, come in Robin.' Silence.

Then the airwaves crackled to life. 'This is Robin, what do you need, Batman?'

Her heart leapt up into her mouth. She wanted to shout and scream at him but she couldn't do that in front of Elliot.

'Just wanted to say goodnight and I love you,' Elliot said, simply.

'I love you too,' Leo said, his voice croaky and hoarse.

Elliot smiled. 'This is Batman, over and out.'

He placed the walkie-talkie on the drawers next to the bed and snuggled down.

Isla stared at the walkie-talkie for a moment. 'Elliot, I'm just going to borrow this for a few minutes. I need a quick word with Leo.'

'OK, Isla, goodnight.'

'Night, beautiful.' She placed a kiss on his head and gave Luke a pat on the head.

She picked up the walkie-talkie and carried it downstairs where Elliot couldn't hear her. She stared at it, wondering what she was going to say. Then she rang the alert button.

'This is Isla to Asshole, come in Asshole.'

Silence. Well she didn't really expect him to answer that.

'I know you can hear me and you're going to listen to what I have to say. Tomorrow is the Halloween parade and you are going to be there. Elliot has been looking forward to this parade for weeks and you are not going to let him down, do you understand? You promised him you would be there and you promised me that, no matter what happened between us, you would always be there for him. So you are god damn going to be there, not for me, but for him.'

Isla bit back a sob, tears streaming down her face. 'You coming back for the parade is not us getting back together, because we are too far past that now, but this is keeping a promise to a little boy who doesn't deserve to be treated this badly, who has done nothing wrong, whose only crime was falling in love with you and thinking he could trust you. You are going to be at this parade, you are going to wear your bloody Robin costume and you are going to prove to him that you're not an asshole. And then afterwards, you are going to sit him down and explain to him why you won't be in his life any more. I lied for you tonight, I covered for you when he asked where you are and I'm not doing that again. If you're going to let him down and break his heart then you can do that to his face.' She hated that Leo could hear that she was crying so she quickly let go of the talk button.

The airwaves stayed silent. He had no response to any of that.

She pressed the talk button again.

'I hate you right now, Leo Jackson. I hate you for making me believe in you and then letting me down so badly. I hate you for giving me all these wonderful promises about our future and then snatching them away. I hate you for what you've done for Elliot. And I hate you for making me fall in love with you. I can't just turn that off even if you can and I hate you for that.'

Silence.

She tossed the walkie-talkie on the table and, wiping the tears from her face, she went off to bed.

CHAPTER 25

Leo stared at the ceiling of Jamie's lounge from his position on the sofa. He had wandered around aimlessly the afternoon before, not entirely sure where to go, or what to do. When night fell he'd found himself outside Jamie's house, although it was evident his little brother wasn't in, probably spending the night at Melody's. So, using his spare key, he had let himself in and spent the night on the sofa, although sleep had completely eluded him.

He had made the biggest mistake of his life. Walking out on Isla and Elliot was walking away from the best thing that had ever happened to him. Listening to how upset Isla had been the night before had broken his heart.

He had reacted badly to Elliot's accident. In the cold light of day, he knew that. He'd felt so guilty that it had happened under his care, that he was the cause of it. But even worse had been everyone's reactions to it at the hospital. He remembered his friend Steve questioning his motives when he'd wanted to talk to Sadie at the hotel, wondering if he was going to hurt her. If even his old friends thought so little of him, it was no surprise that the doctors and nurses who didn't know him, or knew him when he was a kid, thought he was capable of hurting Elliot. But what really worried him was what Eva had said about the judge in charge of the adoption case refusing Isla custody if they knew that Leo was involved. If Betty and Frances could still think so badly of him after all these years then it could be that the judge, if they knew Leo, might have those feelings too. And it was that threat that had ultimately made him walk away. There was no way he could stand between Isla and Elliot's adoption.

In reality, he knew this was unlikely. If him being involved with Isla and Elliot was an issue, Karie would have raised it before now. And remarkably, for someone with such a bad reputation, Karie actually seemed to like him.

He sat up and sighed. Isla was right, he was an asshole.

The front door opened and a few seconds later Jamie appeared in the door to the lounge. Jamie started a little when he saw his brother.

'Well, this is an unwelcome surprise,' Jamie said, dryly. He took in Leo's dishevelled appearance and frowned. 'Did you stay here last night?'

Leo nodded.

'Hang on, Melody came home from her dress fitting with Isla and Tori yesterday afternoon and was full of the joys of how happy you and Isla were, that you'd got engaged, and that Sadie had agreed to the adoption. Everything seemed to be coming together for you guys. What the hell happened?'

Jamie clearly didn't know about the accident. Leo had finally managed to get hold of Isla after she had left Melody and Tori and was on her way back home, so they would have had no idea about Elliot's accident or probably the events after.

'Yes, it was,' Leo said. 'Everything was perfect. Then I cocked everything up.'

Jamie sat down on the chair opposite the sofa. 'She threw you out?'

'Worse. Less than twenty-four hours after I'd proposed and told her I loved her and would look after her and Elliot forever, I walked out on her.'

Jamie stared at him. 'Then you're a bigger dick than I thought you were.'

'Tell me about it,' Leo sighed.

'What happened?'

Leo told him about the accident and what had happened at the hospital, everything that Eva had said and how he'd let it fester inside of him, and then how he'd broken up with Isla when he'd got back home.

Jamie had nothing to say, no pearls of wisdom. But what was there to say? He had ruined everything.

'Honestly, do you think they'd be better off without me?' Leo asked.

'It depends. Are they going to have to deal with this kind of shit on a regular basis, you walking out every time things get tough? Because if they are, then I'd say yes, they are better off without you. Elliot needs someone he can rely on, who will always be there, and if you can't be that person, then it's better for you to be out of his life completely rather than dipping in and out whenever the mood suits you.'

Leo let his head fall in his hands. It was harsh, but Jamie was right. There was more at stake here than his and Isla's relationship, there was a little boy to think about too.

'I was trying to do the right thing for him, for both of them,' Leo said.

'I know, which is why, in normal circumstances, you guys are all great for each other. You have changed that little boy's life, for the better. You were there for Isla in the toughest moments of her life, but they saved you too. When Matthew died, I thought I had lost you as well. You were at your lowest, taking all that guilt on your shoulders, and they brought joy into your life again, gave you something worth living for. You all need each other, you're intrinsically linked now and you can't just walk away from something like that.'

'What about all that stuff about the judge denying Isla custody of Elliot because of her involvement with me? I could stick my fingers up to anyone who thinks that I'm a rotten apple, or anyone who thinks I hurt Elliot. I know the truth and so does Isla, so I don't care about anyone else. But I can't stand in the way of her adopting Elliot. That would break her heart.'

'You know that's utter bullshit. Those are the words of someone who holds a grudge against you, not someone who speaks with any authority or knowledge of your case. It will be Karie who will have the most sway in the case before the judge. The judge will listen to her assessment, they will see how happy Elliot is with you and that's what they will base their decision on. Not the person you were twenty years ago or that you slept with more women than you had hot dinners – the judge won't care about stuff like that.'

Leo swore. Jamie was right. What the hell had he done?

'Isla is never going to forgive me. You should have heard her last night, I destroyed her.'

'It will take some time,' Jamie said, honestly. 'Showing up at that Halloween parade this evening is a start. Then talk to her, tell her about your fears for the adoption case, be honest about why you walked away.'

'And if that doesn't work?'

'You two were meant to be together, she knows that.'

Leo sighed. He had a hell of a lot of making up to do and it was going to start with a Robin costume.

※※※

Isla waited nervously at the start of the parade as friends and families milled about exclaiming over each other's costumes. The parade was not due to start for another ten minutes but every minute seemed to drag by. Leo had to be there, he just had to. She couldn't lie to Elliot again.

'He'll be here,' Melody said, quietly, as she hovered nearby, dressed as Wonder Woman. Isla had already seen Jamie dressed as a WWI pilot outfit, clearly he was supposed to be Steve Trevor, Wonder Woman's sidekick.

'He's not going to let you or Elliot down,' Tori said, dressed as Merida, complete with bow and arrow.

'He already has,' Isla muttered.

In reality she needed him here for more than just Elliot. She had to know that what they had was real, that his promises the night she had accepted his proposal actually meant something. She didn't know if they had any kind of future together, but if he showed up today then it proved that what they had was at least as important to him as it was to her.

'You look great.' Emily came over with Marigold dressed in what was definitely a pink Spiderman costume or, rather, Spiderwoman. Emily had gone for a very simple Hermione Granger: long black cloak, bushy hair, carrying a wand and a stack of books. It must be hard to find any suitable costumes when you're eight months pregnant.

Marigold assessed Isla's costume. 'What are you supposed to be?' she asked, bluntly.

'She-Ra,' Isla said. 'It's a character from a TV programme when I was young.'

'That dress is very short,' Marigold said.

Isla knew that it was. It hadn't been her intention to dress like she was about to star in the porno version of the cartoon, but when she'd put it on, she felt like she was channelling some of She-Ra's power. She was brave and strong and she would be just fine without Leo. It helped that, complete with her long gold boots, she looked damned sexy; it didn't hurt to show Leo what he would be missing.

If he showed up.

Obviously, Marigold had already lost interest as she took Elliot's hand. 'Come and look at this costume, it's hilarious.'

They ran off to look at a man dressed in a big furry green monster costume.

'Hello,' Leo's voice came from behind her.

She whirled round to face him and for a moment he simply stared at her. Not at her costume or her big bouffant hair, just at her, hurt and regret warring in his eyes.

God, she had no words to say to him. She wanted to shake him and hurt him like he had hurt her but she also wanted to kiss him and hold him close and never let him go. But he was here for Elliot and that was all that mattered for now.

His eyes raked down over her body and they widened slightly. 'You look... amazing,' Leo said.

She took in his costume. She couldn't say the same about him. In his tiny green shorts, red waistcoat, gold cape, and green pointy elf-like shoes, he looked quite ridiculous, and her heart softened a tiny bit because of it. He had dressed himself up as an idiot simply to make Elliot happy.

'Thank you for coming.'

He pushed his hand through his hair awkwardly. 'Look, I'm sorry about last night—'

'Leo!' Elliot came running over and launched himself at Leo. Leo scooped him up and hugged him tight.

'Hey buddy, how you doing?' Leo looked down at what he was wearing in confusion. 'Where's your costume?'

'I'm wearing it,' Elliot giggled. 'Can you guess who I am?'

Isla smiled slightly as she watched Leo take in his clothes again. She had thought initially that Elliot could just wear Leo's clothes but the man was so big that even his shirt dragged on the floor. Instead, she had taken Elliot shopping and he had chosen a pale blue shirt similar to one that Leo wore a lot, and had even rolled his sleeves up to his elbows just like his godfather always did. He wore it over a pair of jeans with a small leather jacket from a charity shop that looked like one Leo owned.

'Are you Bruce Wayne?' Leo said.

'I'm you,' Elliot said, no longer able to keep it in.

Leo stared at him in shock.

'Yes, when I explained to Elliot what a hero was – someone who is always there when you need them, someone brave and strong and fearless – for some reason, I don't know why, Elliot thought of you. He thinks you're his hero,' Isla said.

Leo swallowed and when he spoke his voice was hoarse. 'Thanks buddy, this is amazing.'

'I'll have to get him to set the bar a little higher next year,' Isla said, coldly, knowing that would go straight over Elliot's head.

Leo looked at her and she turned away. She couldn't look at the two of them together, it hurt too much. As the crowd jostled around them ready for the start of the parade, she allowed other people to get between them. She knew Elliot would be safe with Leo and if this really was going to be the last time they would see him, then she wanted Elliot to be able to make the most of it.

She stepped away and joined Melody and Jamie as they all started walking down the main road towards the beach, everyone carrying their pumpkin lanterns.

Jamie looked at her with surprise. 'Have you two spoken?'

Isla shook her head. 'What's left to say? He doesn't want to be part of my family any more.'

'That's not true. He overreacted last night, he wants to apologise.'

Her fragile heart filled with hope for a few seconds and then quickly deflated again.

'I can't...' Isla started. 'It's too late for that.'

Melody squeezed her hand. 'He's not Daniel.'

'I know,' Isla said.

'Don't you think he deserves a second chance?'

'It boils down to the same thing, they both promised me forever and they both walked away from me. Only difference is that Leo actually put a ring on my finger first. I was so wary of getting involved with someone after Daniel let me down so spectacularly. I knew that whoever I went out with would have to be someone I trusted completely, not just for me but for Elliot. I trusted Leo and he threw it back in my face.'

'Look, I know he was a dick last night,' Jamie said. '*He* knows he was a dick. But don't you think you should listen to him so he can at least try to apologise for it? You owe him that.'

Why was she suddenly the bad guy in this? 'He walked out on me, I don't owe him anything.'

'I don't know about that,' Jamie said. 'How about the fact that over the last year he has taken on a load more staff at The Big Bang just so he could take more time off work and be there for you and Elliot?'

'What?' Isla said. She didn't know he'd done that.

'How about the fact that he has become a dad to that little boy? Leo has taken him into his life and loved him, he didn't have to do any of that. And what about him going to see Sadie and begging her to sign the adoption form, to leave Elliot out of all this mess that she had created, which she did?'

'He... went to see Sadie?'

'Yes, he didn't want you to know as you'd asked him not to, but he knew he had to give it a shot. Or how about the fact that the main reason Leo broke up with you last night was because he overheard some cow who he'd dated once say that the judge in charge of your adoption case would never give Elliot to you if they knew Leo was involved and he got scared that he could ruin all of that for you? He was prepared to walk away from the only woman he has ever loved to ensure that you could continue to adopt Elliot.' Jamie paused and continued, more gently. 'I'd say you owe him quite a lot actually.'

Isla stared at him, tears filling her eyes, emotion clogging her throat. 'I... I didn't know any of that.'

Christ, that was why Leo had walked away: because he thought that Elliot meant more to her than he did, when in reality she needed them both in her life. He really had thought that she was better off without him and had been trying to do everything he possibly could to make sure the adoption went ahead, including sacrificing his own happiness for her.

He was the most incredible, amazing, kind, generous man she had ever met. Why couldn't he see that?

He'd been to see Sadie. He was the reason why Sadie had suddenly had a change of heart. Oh god, Jamie was right, he had given her so much.

She looked around, trying to see him through the crowd, but she couldn't locate him.

'I need to find him,' Isla muttered and Melody and Jamie started trying to scan the crowds too. 'Jesus, he shouldn't be this hard to find, he's got a gold cape and tiny green shorts on.'

She stopped and waited for the villagers to file past her. He had been behind her at the beginning of the parade so it was likely he was still there. Several Supermen strolled past, a Luke Skywalker, a Captain America, a Thor, a Captain Kirk. Jabba the Hutt wobbled into her as he waddled past with an apology but there was no sign of Robin anywhere. The end of the parade tailed past her and frantically she moved back through the crowd, heading for the beach. Where the bloody hell was he?

She reached Sunshine Beach and scanned the crowds. Hundreds of people from other villages and towns had turned up for the event and the beach was packed as everyone waited for the fireworks. She spotted Melody holding Elliot, talking and laughing with him. She raced over to them. 'Where's Leo?'

'Looking for you,' Melody said, hopelessly.

Isla groaned with frustration. Why couldn't the bloody man just stay still for once?

'He went that way,' Jamie pointed and she moved through the crowds in that direction as the mayor took to the podium and started talking about how wonderful they all looked.

She saw a flash of a gold cape in front of her and she quickly moved that way but when she got there it was gone.

The mayor started counting down to the fireworks and the crowd joined in. As they reached zero, fireworks exploded in the night sky above them, silver, gold, blues and red, but Isla was barely aware of any of it.

The crowd shifted slightly in front of her and she saw Leo desperately looking around for her. She stopped in her tracks and then his eyes snapped to hers. For a moment they just stared at each other and then they moved together. He put his hands on her shoulders, holding her so she couldn't get away from him again. Fireworks exploded above them, filling the cold darkness with warmth and light.

'Look, last night, I was an idiot—'

She interrupted what he was going to say by placing her fingers on his lips. She suddenly didn't need to hear it.

'Jamie told me,' she swallowed down the emotion clogging her throat. 'He told me everything. And yes, if you think for one second that the judge could throw out the adoption because of you, then you are an idiot. You are the most incredible man I have ever met and one day you will see what I see. Until then I'm going to keep reminding you.'

'I'm so sorry,' he said against her fingertips.

'I am too. We are in this together. When things get tough, we'll be there for each other. No matter what we face, we face it together.'

He nodded. 'I just wanted to protect you and Elliot and I reacted in the way that I thought was best but it turned out to be the worst. I swear, there'll be no more running away. I love you both so much and I'm going to spend every damn day of my life trying to prove to you how much.'

She smiled. 'You can start by kissing me.'

As the fireworks reached a crescendo above them, he bent his head and did just that.

EPILOGUE

Christmas Eve

Isla watched the snow falling outside, the tiny flakes glittering in the inky darkness as they floated and twirled in the early evening sky. It hadn't really started to settle yet, but a lot more was due overnight. For the first time, as far back as Isla could remember, they really were going to experience a white Christmas. Elliot was beyond excited. They planned to build snowmen tomorrow on Christmas Day and go sledging. Leo had spent the last few days building Elliot the best sledge Isla had ever seen.

Isla leaned back on Leo's lap and rested her head on his shoulder. He kissed her on top of her head and ran his finger over her engagement ring. She smiled – soon she would have another ring on that finger.

She looked over at her wonderful family, who were chatting or playing happily with Elliot and Marigold. It had been a fantastic day with the people she loved the most.

Life couldn't be more perfect right now. In the last few months she had found a complete peace that she'd never known she needed.

The adoption hearing had been over very quickly, the judge delighted to make the adoption official, and Leo had stood by her side throughout.

Isla had been horrified to see Sadie sitting at the back of the courtroom. Sadie had actually taken their original offer of twenty-five thousand the day before, so Isla had presumed she'd left the country already. To see her there was a surprise to say the least. On seeing Isla clock her at the back, Sadie had stood up, given her a warm smile – the first she'd ever shown her – and a nod as if to say she was happy for them. Then she turned and left, never to be seen again. Rumour had it that she was going to New Zealand; it had made Isla a little happier to think she probably wasn't returning to Jim.

What was lovely was that many of the villagers unexpectedly turned up at the hearing to celebrate the moment with them too. Afterwards, many of them passed their congratulations on to Leo as well as her, which helped to reassure him that many people wanted this for him as much as he did. Most of them had seen how Leo had been with her and Elliot over the last year and a half. Obviously, not everyone in the village thought he was a rotten apple after all and their support clearly meant the world to Leo.

Isla had sold Hot Chocolate Cottage and, complete with Elliot, Luke and twelve tons of toys and books, she had moved in with Leo. He had been overjoyed. She had used some of the proceeds from the house sale to pay back all of the money she owed and now they were celebrating their first Christmas together as a family, here at Maple Cottage.

The timer on the oven suddenly went off, disturbing her from her thoughts, and there was a collective cheer from everyone in the lounge. She smiled and looked over at her family. Everyone was there to celebrate the festivities. It had been Elliot's sugges-tion that there should be a mince-pie-making competition and everyone had got into it with great gusto.

There was a mad dash into the kitchen and Elliot took Isla's hand and dragged her in there too. She smiled as Tori waddled in, her gorgeous bump protruding out of her Christmas pudding jumper. At over six months pregnant now, she had a wonderful serene glow about her. It helped that Aidan was so doting towards her. He followed her into the kitchen now, a gentle hand round her shoulders, wearing a matching Christmas pudding jumper too. Their wedding had gone off without a hitch at the end of

November. Well, almost without a hitch as the last hour of the evening had been interrupted slightly with Emily being rushed off to hospital to give birth to her beautiful daughter, Belle, who had been born at exactly midnight. Belle was asleep now, but it didn't stop Stanley, Emily and even Marigold from checking on her. Leo's mum Ruby had also flown in from Scotland to celebrate Christmas with her children and already she had spent many hours cuddling her new granddaughter.

Isla grabbed a pair of mistletoe-strewn oven gloves and removed the tray of misshapen mince pies from the oven. The sweet and spicy smells of the mincemeat filled the air. She placed the pies down on the kitchen top and everyone gathered round and *ooohed* and *ahhed* over the different pies.

Stefano and Agatha had insisted on making their pastry from scratch, as well as the filling. Stefano had said that he had been in the restaurant business all his life and his poor papa would turn in his grave if he knew that Stefano was using ready-made pastry. No one else had any issues with the roll-out stuff and were quite happy to just concentrate on making their own mincemeat from scratch. Agatha nudged Stefano now as she laughed at their lumpy-looking pie. That was probably the biggest surprise of the last few months, that those two had finally got together. After a few dates that didn't exactly run to plan, during which they didn't see eye to eye at all, Stefano seemed to fall under her spell. In fact, many people in the village thought she might literally have cast a spell, as they were poles apart, but he was clearly smitten and Agatha for once wasn't gossiping about this relationship. Although that didn't stop the villagers from talking about it.

'So how should we judge which pie is best?' Melody asked as Isla got a knife and started cutting a small quarter from each.

'I think I should be the judge,' Agatha said. Her new relationship had done nothing to soften her self-importance.

'I think Elliot should be the judge,' Isla's mum, Carolyn, said. 'It was his idea, after all.'

'How will I choose?' Elliot said, giving the pie he had made with Leo and Isla an affectionate poke.

'You just choose the one that tastes the best,' Isla said.

'It has to be a blindfold test,' Aidan said. 'So Leo's pie doesn't get an unfair advantage.'

Isla smirked. Elliot's adoration for Leo had not been dampened at all in the last few months since they'd moved in.

'Are you accusing my son of being biased towards me?' Leo said, in mock outrage.

'What does biased mean?' Marigold asked.

'It means that Elliot might choose Leo's pie as the winner because he loves him very much,' Isla said, simplifying the explanation a little.

'I do think our pie is the best,' Elliot said.

Leo laughed. 'Blindfold test it is then. We have to taste it first, buddy.' He grabbed a Santa hat he had been wearing earlier and gave it to Elliot to put on. 'Pull this over your eyes.'

Elliot did as he was told, giggling as he did so.

'First up is team A,' Isla said, giving him a tiny sliver. This was Carolyn and Trevor's pie. Isla still couldn't get used to the fact that her mum had a boyfriend now after so many years spent alone after her dad had left. And Trevor was so serious too, but it seemed that they were having a mellowing effect on each other. Her mum seemed happy.

Elliot pulled a face as he chewed. 'It's very sticky.'

Trevor laughed as Carolyn gasped in horror at the slur on her pie. Elliot giggled at their reaction.

'This is team B,' Isla said, giving him Leo's mum's piece of pie.

Elliot nodded thoughtfully as he chewed. 'Very sweet,' he said, eventually.

He went through each slice of pie, giving his verdict on each one.

'So… who's the winner?' Tori asked as Elliot removed his hat.

'Team C,' Elliot said decisively. 'Because I think that's mine.'

Everyone laughed.

'Actually, team C was Melody and Jamie's pie,' Isla said.

'We won?' Melody said in surprise. 'Really? We never win anything.' Jamie and Melody high-fived and Jamie gave her a hug.

Isla smiled at them. Melody and Jamie had moved in with each other a few weeks before. They had practically lived in each other's pockets since they'd started dating back in July, but now Jamie had made it official. He had made her an advent calendar with a surprise behind each door and the first door had held the key to his house. Melody had packed up her things and moved in within a matter of days. Although she was sad to leave her cottage on Sunshine Beach, it did make sense that, with five dogs between them and a crazy turkey, they moved to the slightly bigger house at the top of the hill. Isla also knew that behind door twenty-four there was an engagement ring, but Jamie was going to wait until midnight when they were alone to let her open that one. Isla couldn't be happier for them.

'Do we win a prize?' Jamie said.

'The knowledge that you're the best,' Leo said.

Isla grabbed the tin of Roses and offered them one each, which they took with a grin. Then everyone started trying each other's pies for a few minutes, with mixed results all round.

Leo looked at his watch. 'Right guys, we better go.'

Suddenly there was a flurry of excited activity as everyone pulled on coats and woolly hats over their best clothes and goodbyes were quickly said as their families left them alone.

Leo lifted Elliot up onto his hip. 'Right buddy, let's go and get ready.'

He carried him up the stairs and Isla watched them go, her heart swelling with love for them.

She followed them and went into the one and only spare room, now that Elliot had commandeered her old room as his toy room.

She closed the door behind her and slipped into her silver dress. It was a halter-neck gown that swept the floor and sparkled with sequins all over. She slipped on her ruby sparkly heels, which reminded her of the ones Dorothy wore in *The Wizard of Oz*. She grabbed the silver velvet maxi coat she'd found in a charity shop, which was perfect for the occasion, but she didn't put it on yet.

She left the room to find Leo waiting for her. His face when he saw the dress was something she would never forget. He had a complete look of love in his eyes.

'You look… magnificent,' he whispered.

Leo was wearing a smart black suit with a red tie to match her shoes. He filled the suit in all the right places.

'You're looking pretty incredible yourself.'

He grinned and placed a sweet kiss on her cheek.

Elliot came rushing out of his bedroom fiddling with his red tie. He had chosen to wear a suit tonight because Leo was wearing one.

'Here buddy, let me do it for you,' Leo said, squatting down to give him a hand. Elliot watched carefully as Leo tied the perfect knot and then gently slid it up to his throat.

'Thanks Leo,' Elliot said.

He didn't always use his name, he alternated between *Leo* and *Daddy*, and sometimes *Daddy Leo* as he experimented with the new title. Leo didn't push him either way. *Mummy* had seemed to come a bit easier for him, probably because Isla was the only mum he'd ever known. But, like Leo, she didn't mind either way.

Elliot looked up at her and his face broke into a huge smile. 'You look beautiful.'

'Thank you, and you look very smart too.'

A horn sounded outside the front.

'Taxi's here,' Leo said.

He moved round behind Isla and helped her on with her coat, his fingers grazing the back of her neck in the gentlest yet sexiest of touches, and then they went downstairs. Leo scooped up Luke, who was already wearing his collar and tie, and they stepped outside.

Waiting outside was not the taxi she was expecting but a beautiful white Silver Ghost Rolls-Royce, complete with a bow and ribbon on the front of the car.

She looked at Leo in confusion as Elliot ran forward to admire the car.

'I know you wanted a low-key small wedding but you had to arrive in a proper wedding car,' Leo shrugged.

She smiled and kissed him on the cheek. 'This is perfect, thank you.'

The chauffeur tipped his hat for them as he held the door open, which made Elliot giggle, and then they all got in.

'I'm excited,' Elliot said, sitting between them with Luke on his lap. 'And nervous.'

The chauffeur negotiated through the narrow lanes, the snow dusting the trees and sparkling as they drifted past the glowing fairy lights.

'Why are you nervous?' Isla asked.

'Because… what if I forget what to say?'

Leo smirked. 'You only have two words buddy, you know what they are.'

Elliot nodded. 'Everyone will be watching.'

'Everyone that loves you very much,' Isla said.

They had deliberately decided to keep the ceremony small; the only people who were going to be there were their families who had been at the house that afternoon.

They had hired a small room up at the Golden Bridge for the event. Leo insisted that they were going to have their special night up there as they had missed out on it last time, but other than a few bottles of champagne, and hot chocolates with maple syrup, they had decided to hold their celebrations at home prior to the big event with the people they loved the most. It had been the most unconventional but loveliest wedding day, playing silly board games, watching Christmas movies. They'd had a big celebration meal earlier in the day, which Elliot had decided should be pizza from Stefano's restaurant. Everyone had sat around on sofas and chairs, helping themselves to the different slices. It had been relaxed and happy and just perfect.

As they arrived at the Golden Bridge, Isla's heart started racing with excitement. They were really going to do this, in a few minutes she would be Leo's wife. She looked over at him to see what he was feeling and couldn't help smiling at the fact that he had the biggest grin on his face.

The chauffeur held the door open for them. Elliot shook his hand on the way out, much to the chauffeur's bemusement.

Once inside, Isla smiled at the huge Christmas tree in the reception area, twinkling with tiny white lights and golden glittered orbs hanging from the branches. They were shown upstairs and Isla quickly hung her coat up on the hooks outside, before taking Elliot's hand and walking into the conservatory with Leo. Their family was waiting for them in a room strewn with flowers, candles and sparkling lights, but it was the view outside the window that caught her attention momentarily, the snow floating past the window over a moonlit-covered sea. The evening was magical.

Their family was sitting in a circle and the registrar was waiting for them in the middle. Nicholas was an elderly gentleman with rosy cheeks, half-moon gold glasses and a white beard. Elliot was convinced he was Santa Claus and she had to smile that, although Nicholas hadn't gone for a full-on Santa Claus costume, he *was* wearing a red suit. He high-fived Elliot as they walked up to him. They had already met Nicholas for the second time a few days before to go over the ceremony and what they were going to say, but they had deliberately chosen him because of how laid-back he was about the ceremony. Elliot had even given him a few things that he wanted Nicholas to say in the wedding and Nicholas had been more than happy to oblige.

The chatter died down and it was as if the room was holding its breath.

'Thank you all for coming today. It's a beautiful night and I can't think of a more loving couple to marry here this evening,' Nicholas said.

Leo took her hand, holding Elliot's hand too, so they formed their own little family circle. God, she loved this man so much.

'Let's get the legal stuff out the way first,' Nicholas said, casually, as if he was not just about to change their lives forever. 'Are you, Isla Rosewood, free, lawfully, to marry Leo Jackson?'

'I am,' Isla said.

He repeated the question to Leo and he echoed her answer.

'That's good.' Nicholas bounced on the spot. 'Always have to check about those pesky skeletons. Now, let's get on to the good bit. Do you, Leo Jackson, take Isla Rosewood to be your lawfully wedded wife?'

'I do,' Leo said, giving her hand a little squeeze.

'And do you, Isla Rosewood, take Leo Jackson to be your lawfully wedded husband?'

'I do,' Isla said, not taking her eyes off Leo for a second.

'And Elliot, do you take Leo to be your awfully wedded dad?' Nicholas asked, giving Elliot a little wink.

Their family sniggered.

She and Leo had spoken to the registrar without Elliot and had said how important it was to them to make him part of the ceremony too. Nicholas had been chilled out about it all and said that as long as the legal declarations and contractual words were said at the beginning, they could do whatever they wanted with the rest of the ceremony. Elliot had suggested this part and

Nicholas was more than happy to do it, even using Elliot's exact wording of *awfully* instead of *lawfully*.

Elliot was taking this very seriously. 'I do.'

'And Leo, do you take Elliot to be your awfully wedded son?'

Their family laughed again.

'I do,' Leo said, a smile lighting up his beautiful face.

Isla's heart swelled with love for her little family. It was a nonsensical, silly, meaningless part of the ceremony and of course there was nothing legally binding about it, but it meant the world to her and she knew that Elliot and Leo appreciated it too.

'Do we have the rings?' Nicholas asked.

Aidan stepped forward with Leo's ring and Jamie stepped forward with Isla's.

Leo took Isla's ring and slid it onto her finger. 'I give you this ring as a token of my love and friendship. I promise to love and respect you, to always be there to listen, comfort and support you. Whatever our lives may bring, we will face it together. I promise to share happiness and laughter, good times and bad, to be your best friend, forever.'

Isla swallowed down the ball of emotion in her throat as she took the ring for Leo. 'I promise to love you, now and always. You have filled my life with so much happiness. You are the joy I didn't know was missing from my life, you are the strength that I never thought I needed. You are everything to me, my rock, my harbour, my lighthouse, the sunshine and the moonlight. And I promise to spend the rest of my life trying to give you the same. Today I gain not only a husband and a best friend, but a father to my children. As a family, we will create a home filled with laughter, love and understanding and I can't wait to take this next step in our life with you.'

He smiled as she slid the ring onto his finger.

'Leo and Isla,' Nicholas said. 'You have expressed your love to each other through the promises you have made and the exchanging of rings. You are no longer simply partners or best friends but it gives me the utmost pleasure to now declare you husband and wife. So you may kiss the bride.'

Leo smiled and bent his head and kissed her, a sweet kiss that was filled with so much love and promise. Everyone clapped and cheered and Leo broke the kiss to swing Elliot into his arms and envelop him in a group hug. Isla held onto Leo, kissing Elliot on the head and for the briefest of moments, Leo rested his hand on her belly, an acknowledgement of his love for her, Elliot and their unborn child. No one else knew yet that she was pregnant. Not even Agatha and her omnipotence. They wanted to tell Elliot tomorrow on Christmas Day before they announced it to everyone else.

The next few minutes passed in a haze of people hugging them and giving their congratulations, signing certificates, having their photos taken, then Leo was passing Isla her coat and bundling her outside onto the balcony.

'What's going on?' Isla asked, shivering a little in the cool night air.

'What kind of husband and pyrotechnician would I be if I didn't have fireworks for my wife on our wedding day?'

An explosion of gold filled the night sky and Isla tore her gaze from her husband to gasp at her very own fireworks filling the skies above the sea with a riot of colour, glittering amongst the light snowflakes that were still dancing through the inky air. The colours were amazing like nothing she had ever seen before; lilac, silver, rose, cranberry, blueberry and buttercup blazed through the darkness, several love hearts filled the night sky, fountains of gold cascading down towards the waves. It was incredible and rendered all the more special by the fact that this was just for her. As the finale set the sky on fire, she leaned up and kissed Leo. Darkness fell over their little group and their families cheered and clapped the wonderful display.

Leo smiled against her lips. 'Let's go home.'

She nodded. There was nowhere else she would rather be right then. She glanced down at her ruby shoes. There really was no place like home.

The End

A LETTER FROM HOLLY

Thank you so much for reading *Coming Home to Maple Cottage*, I had so much fun creating this story and I hope you enjoyed reading it as much as I enjoyed writing it.

If you did enjoy it, and want to keep up-to-date with all my latest releases, just sign up at the following link. Your email address will never be shared and you can unsubscribe at any time.

www.bookouture.com/holly-martin

One of the best parts of writing comes from seeing the reaction from readers. Did it make you smile or laugh, did it make you cry, hopefully happy tears? Did you fall in love with Leo, Isla and little Elliot as much as I did? Did you like the beautiful Sandcastle Bay? If you enjoyed the story, I would absolutely love it if you could leave a short review. Getting feedback from readers is amazing and it also helps to persuade other readers to pick up one of my books for the first time.

If you loved the other characters in this story, Tori and Aidan's story can be found in *The Holiday Cottage by the Sea*. Jamie and Melody's story can be found in *The Cottage on Sunshine Beach*.

Thank you for reading.
Love, Holly x

 HollyMartinAuthor

@HollyMAuthor

hollymartinwriter.wordpress.com

ACKNOWLEDGEMENTS

To my family, my mom, my biggest fan, who reads every word I've written a hundred times over and loves it every single time, my dad, my brother Lee and my sister-in-law Julie, for your support, love, encouragement and endless excitement for my stories.

For my twinnie, the gorgeous Aven Ellis for just being my wonderful friend, for your endless support, for cheering me on, for reading my stories and telling me what works and what doesn't and for keeping me entertained with wonderful stories and pictures of hot men. I love you dearly.

To my lovely friends Julie, Natalie, Jac, Verity, Jodie, Gareth and Mandie, thanks for all the support.

For Sharon Sant for just being there always and your wonderful friendship.

To my wonderful agents Hayley Steed and Madeleine Milburn for just been amazing and fighting my corner and for your unending patience.

To all at Bookouture, thanks for everything over the last four years. Thanks especially to the brilliant Kim Nash and Noelle Holten for the tireless promoting, tweeting and general cheerleading. Thanks for always being there, Kim.

To the CASG, the best writing group in the world, you wonderful talented supportive bunch of authors, I feel very blessed to know you all, you guys are the very best.

To the wonderful Bookouture authors for all your encouragement and support.

To all the wonderful bloggers for your tweets, retweets, Facebook posts, tireless promotions, support, encouragement and endless enthusiasm. You guys are amazing and I couldn't do this journey without you.

To Karie Matthews, thanks for the use of your name in the story, hope you enjoyed your character.

To Justin Parker for all the brilliant information on fireworks, thank you so much for answering my endless questions.

Big thanks to Lindsay Hill, Andi Michael for your advice on wills, probate and tenants in common.

Thank you so much to JB Johnston, Hayley Marie, Steph Hunter, Chris Longmuir for all the help with the adoption process and social services.

Thanks to Victoria Cornwall and Kelly Rufus for medical help.

Thanks to Zoe Gascoigne for help with qualifications for window dressing.

To anyone who has read my book and taken the time to tell me you've enjoyed it or wrote a review, thank you so much.

Thank you, I love you all.

37273281R00155

Printed in Great Britain
by Amazon